Legionaries of th

Book one of the Soldiers of The Boar.

Copyright © Allan Harper 2022
Revised new paperback edition 2025.

Cover photo credit to https://unsplash.com/@mike_swigunski

Some misaligned indents have transferred from the original of Legionaries of The Boar. This is regretted and it is hoped does not detract from your enjoyment of the novel.

Principal characters.

Velio Pinneius. Tesserarius drill instructor Twentieth legion. 'The Boar.'

Marcus Hirtius. Tesserarius drill instructor. Velio's best friend.

Servius Albinius. Military tribune of the Twentieth legion. In command of building the turf wall for the emperor.

Cornelius Paterculus Vatinius. Political tribune, newly attached to the Twentieth legion.

Hanno Glaccus. A centurion of the Twentieth legion.

Quintus Lollius Urbicus. Governor of Britannia.

Titus Rebilis. An optio, second in command to a centurion.

Ferrdigon. Local chieftain of the Votadini tribe.

Eilaver. His wife.

Enomani. Ferrdigon's son.

Vusiavi. Ferrdigon's druid.

Asuvad. War chief of the Dumnonii tribe.

Duald. Warchief.

Heruscomani. War chief of the Veniconii tribe.

Aulercas. Son of Heruscomani.

Tribal names such as Dumnoni are Dumnonii when Roman characters refer to them.

Modern equivalent place names.

The Bodotria is the Firth of Forth, and the upper river.
The Clota is the Clyde.
The Tavae is the Tay.
Carumabo is the Roman fort at modern Cramond, Edinburgh.
The Hill of the Resting Lion is Arthur's Seat, Edinburgh.
Eburacum is the legionary fort at York, home successively of the Ninth and the Sixth legions.
Trimontium is the cavalry fort at Newsteads, Melrose.
Dunpeledur is the main Votadini stronghold on Traprain Law, East Lothian.
Pinnata Castra. A short-lived legionary fort situated on the upstream Tavae river.
Deva Victrix barracks. Home of the Twentieth legion. Sited at modern Chester.
The hidden valley. Lies in the west central highlands of modern Scotland.

Northern Britannia in the early winter of AD 140/141.

At the mouth of a small tributary on the southern side of the Bodotria river, the 4th Cohort of the Twentieth Legion of Rome has just completed the construction of a fortress to defend the small harbour of Carumabo.

Winter has come early and there is snow on the ground.

Chapter 1.

The legionary encampment outside the fort at Carumabo.

Paterculus reckoned there must be many miserable shit-holes in the world but Antoninus Pius, emperor of Rome, had decided to send him to north Britannia, at the beginning of winter. Send my 'Hail and Blessings' to the august emperor.

Some ancestor lost a battle, leaving the family's account with the emperors forever in debt. Surely that was it, because posting Cornelius Vatinus Paterculus to the arse end of no-where could only, rationally, be an act of spite or revenge. A curse on their apple crops for all eternity. Or perhaps not. He might need their blessings up here. If he could have got back on his horse, the very first day after reporting, he would have done.

He huddled a little closer to the three lamps burning in his tent, pulling his cloak tighter around him to seal out as many of the draughts as he could. There was little light to read by but his last letter from home was already memorised. The couriered mail had reached him before he left the legionary fort at Eburacum. Before he set out for his final posting "up north" as the legate commanding the Eburacum garrison had put it. That bastard was probably in on the joke as well.

He liked the cavalry country around Trimontium on the way up. He could have reconciled himself to that. The open fields and meadowlands were perfect horse country. But Carumabo? This, end of the line, river-mouth posting?

'Gods, have I offended you?'

And it was not the greatest letter he had ever received either. It was not exactly a lover's impassioned plea for his safety and his sexual chastity in the interim before they next met. No, it was hardly that. It was more about all the things that happened at home two months ago including the arrival of his sister's latest child; a girl called Claudia. Then there was the oh-so-predictable paternal advice on going north of Hadrian's stone defences. Then a lecture on the perils that long ago overwhelmed Varus and his three legions in Germania. And the shattering impact that had on the whole of Rome. Then, more advice on learning whatever he could to advance his career militarily and in politics. Then the closing section in its usual sequence. Prayers to the family gods for his safety. His mother's love. Then finally, the soldierly virtues of good lines of communication. In other words, 'don't forget to write.'

He looked up and tossed the scroll onto the small table with his good hand. The scroll hit the table and bounced down onto the floor. He looked at it and wondered if his day was likely to get any better. There was a cough outside the tent.

"Tribune are you there? It's Centurion Glaccus, sir."

"Come in centurion," he said.

Hanno Glaccus was thirty-seven years old and looked like a centurion even when he was sitting stark naked in the bathhouse. Paterculus decided the offer of a cup of wine would be presumptuous until he had established whether there was going to be any animosity from him. The age gap, let alone experience gap, was obvious, but the centurion was here to command the men. He was here to command centurions and men. He was supposed to be the senior man in this tent.

"How is the hand sir?" Glaccus began.

He allowed himself a self-deprecating smile and ventured a wristy sword swing with his bandaged forearm. The stitches nipped and he scowled.

"I'll survive Glaccus, but I think the drill instructor was a little over zealous with me today. I think perhaps he was trying to prove something?"

Glaccus' easy expression changed a fraction, but he said nothing. The tribune waited and let a silence grow. Glaccus cleared his throat, silences were not something he liked.

"The instructors are normally ordered to give what we call 'quick-kill' practice sir. It's not meant to be pretty sword play. Two, three, four at most. Blows so hard they take the strength from your enemy's arm, then the killing thrust that he's too weak to parry. Picture those blows as the hammer hitting the anvil. As I say it's not meant to be pretty or skilful, but the men can fight for longer when they see their opponents dying quickly. They don't get so weary or disheartened. So, one, two, three, four and your man goes down, the centurions rotate the front ranks on their whistle. You only have to kill one or two and then you get a rest.

It's simple but it helps make the men go forward."

"One, two, three, four and the man goes down, it's that simple?" he wondered.

"The tesserarius you were with has a little more flair which makes him a valuable asset. We need men like him. But it does leave him a little exposed," Glaccus explained.

Paterculus struggled to keep his expression neutral. This conversation was beginning to lose him.

"Exposed? How so?" he said.

"The tesserarius concerned is still finding his feet, as well as the fact that when he is giving instruction, his rank is entirely irrelevant, sir." Glaccus paused.

Paterculus felt his face reddening.

"Giving instruction, so he was at liberty to damn near cut off my hand?" he snapped.

He was trying not to get angry, but Glaccus was choosing the enlisted man's side. How dare he offend a tribune?

Glaccus continued quite unperturbed; he had found the upper hand, the tribune's face was an easy read.

"It looks a nasty cut sir. The fact is you can't have him flogged or anything else, annoying as the incident was, it would be bad for morale and."

Glaccus let it hang unfinished for effect, before opening his hand as if revealing the secret.

"And it was my mistake and not his, is that it, centurion?" he offered.

Glaccus nodded in assent, "Tesserarius Pinneius was only doing his job, sir."

He took a minor pleasure in the centurion's obvious diplomacy.

"Then mea culpa, my mistake," he said.

Glaccus nodded and glanced around him. A shorter silence followed.

"Apologies for the accommodation sir, we are not quite organised. The commander will be giving you rooms in his house until we move back to the fort at Velunia, it's only a short march northwest of here. Things are a little tight for two tribunes."

Glaccus looked a little uncomfortable. A cut wrist and a tent to sleep in. It was not the best of welcomes for a senior officer. Paterculus saw an opportunity to regain a little ground.

"Do the men complain about it Glaccus?"

"They had two or three cold weeks in the tents, but it's only some grumbling and this will not be the permanent garrison, so they can put up with it for a bit longer. Velunia has full sized accommodation and barracks. They'll soon be there." Glaccus replied.

"Then we must set an example even in this weather."

"That's it exactly sir."

"Thank you Glaccus, I will see you tonight, I believe the senior tribune has a welcome planned for me?"

Glaccus smiled and the scar on his forehead made an odd contrast to the features below.

"The commander's table is always worth attending. His cook is one of the best."

He rose.

"Thank you Glaccus, until tonight then. But you will keep an eye on the tesserarius for me? I don't want this happening again. I consider that self-control is an important virtue for every soldier."

Glaccus smiled a little less, "yes sir. I will keep an eye on him," saluted and left.

'Point made, Cornelius,' he said to himself.

Outside the guards exchanged a glance as the centurion departed.

"Hear that? What are we going to call this one then?"

"Dunno but I think it may start with C."

*

Velio 'Swords' Pinneius sat down in the tent he shared with the other arms instructors, close to the weapons store.

"Those new socks, Swords? Is it your birthday? Lads, the wine is on 'Swords' tonight."

Marcus Hirtius slapped his shoulder.

"Cost me my left bollock to get them," Velio grouched.

"Oh, sounds like you've been attempting to trade with Mr 'I can do a fair price on that for you.' Always a tricky nut that one."

"Trading? Huh, more like robbery," he grunted.

"What a smart boy, you've got to admire him. Who would have thought that instead of buying a few extra jars of olives to bring north with him, he bought as many pairs of socks as he could stuff in his pack."

Marcus scratched his stubbled chin in admiration, his eyes bright with good humour.

"Bet the sheep were glad to see the back of him," Velio said.

"And not just for the socks," Marcus reposted, "well think of it this way, this is not a place to have no socks. If you thought guarding Hadrian's bloody wall was chilly of a night, you wait till we get this bastard finished. You'll be glad of a fight to keep you warm."

"You think they'll put up much of a fight Marcus? To try and stop us I mean?" he asked.

Marcus scratched his chin a bit more. He had a chafe mark from his helmet strap. It always looked red, and it bothered him.

"'Course, stands to reason. We march up here and start building, they'll get the hump, get nosey, then next thing they'll be at us in the night. We have not always had it all our own way up here now, have we? No, I don't think this will be a quick job Velio. It took six years to build the wall down south. But I have a feeling this one might take longer. We are much closer to the last real strongholds up here. We could be here for years," he said with a theatrical flourish.

Velio saw something in his friend's eyes, but it was for only a fleeting moment before Marcus smiled.

"Well, I've got a lesson to give, I should be off."

Marcus reached for a pair of weighted wooden training swords and stepped towards the tent flap. He gave Velio a malicious grin as if to say 'this is what you're supposed to use.'

"Try not to cut this one open more than is absolutely necessary. It's bad for business and my reputation. Velio didn't get his fee for this last one," said a very senior voice from the back of the tent.

Velio and Marcus looked at each other for a moment and burst into laughter.

"A one-handed tribune, can you imagine?" I don't think he'd ever faced a wrong-hand sword."

Velio smiled and lifted his left hand to wave.

"And not one as fast as you, Swords," Marcus grinned.

"Push off, the pair of you and give me peace and go past the oven and collect some bread on your way back Marcus," growled the voice again.

Chapter 2.

The commanding officer's quarters Carumabo.

Paterculus' body servant fastened his master's favourite non military cloak around his shoulders. Paterculus thanked him with a smile, adjusted the pugio dagger on his belt and swept out of the tent, leaving his servant to tidy up. He walked unescorted through the fort, taking salutes as he went, pleased despite himself, that the men appeared to know who he was already. The instant deference was what he expected but even so, he was a new face that might have caused stares before getting salutes. Not a bit of it, the men could not salute fast enough.

He caught sight of a native horseman leaving by the Praetoria gate. The late afternoon light was already failing but he was certain he was no army scout. It felt completely illogical, but by the way he departed, the gate-guard was casual. Why should a native have such a casual relationship with a vexillation that had been building a frontier fort for the last eight weeks? Father often said instincts were precious things. And they were frequently correct.

He stood for a minute inspecting the banner outside the commander's quarters. A red square of silk on a cross piece emblazoned with an embroidered golden boar: running. The emblem of the Twentieth legion. He wondered what sights that piece of cloth had witnessed. He touched the cloth with his fingertips and then placed a kiss.

"May the gods preserve us all," he said.

From what he had read only the premier cohort of the legion, the First cohort had it painted on their shields, but the boar sign was everywhere he looked. There was no doubt which legion was encamped here.

"Sir, Tribune Cornelius Paterculus Vatinius is here," declaimed the servant with the etiquette of his full name.

Paterculus knew what frontier manners could be like, so it was remarkable to have his name announced in full. He touched his wounded wrist and wondered if it was going to be an omen. It appeared he was the last to arrive.

"Hail Cornelius Vatinus Paterculus," the commander smiled, "come and get warm. Have some wine. You and Hanno have met I believe."

He smiled at them all, "who was that?" he asked, gesturing over his shoulder.

"That was Ferrdigon. He's the local Votadini chief. He brought me a gift of a wolf. A fine male, the skin will make a good replacement for the signifier's current one. It's getting a bit shabby. I'm having it skinned as we speak. His stronghold is that queerly shaped hill to the southeast, the one that looks like a resting lion. It's the oddest-looking hill I've ever seen. The Votadini king sits south of here at a place they call Dunpeledur or some such. I find their language impenetrable," the commander said.

Straying for a moment, he smiled, returning to his gift.

"It really is a magnificent beast, superb fur, white flashes on shades of brown and just a hint of the black night. What a cape he would make for a general or an emperor."

He raised a finger to halt Paterculus whom he sensed was about to make a loyal intervention on behalf of the absent emperor.

"I'd steal that fur for my wife, just to make her smile at me again, but, alas, my sweaty signifier will have it and my wife will have to settle for something else a soldier can give her," the commander teased.

"It's too big. Such a fur would drown a woman's shoulders," Glaccus offered.

"Wouldn't that be a treat?" his commander replied.

Glaccus coughed in laughter. Paterculus decided their humour was eluding him. How best should a new tribune respond?

"Why would he do that? Ferrdigon, I mean?" he asked.

The commander gave him a long speculative appraisal. Wolf furs and conjugal jokes aside the lad had focus. But did he have the wit between his ears to back it up into something remotely useful as a frontier soldier?

"Tribune, the Votadini have been compliant for years, they probably took one look at our armour and decided to leave the fighting to others. It's just a goodwill gift."

"So, you trust them?" he probed.

The commander favoured him with a benevolent smile he found patronising.

"There are now generations of them who have lived and died since we came to these islands. Do I trust them? You can never be sure when an upstart chief in waiting will arise, but for the moment, the fact is I do trust the local ones. The ones in the west and north I don't, as it happens. They are brutal bastards, and Agricola did not entirely hammer them into the ground. A rare error of his time here because Agricola did much to pacify this country with his sword," the commander replied.

He waved the tribune to sit and pressed a silver cup of wine into his hand. Glaccus was already seated close to the fire. His eyes were quick to salute him and then retreat to the safety of the flames in the iron brazier. Paterculus decided to make clear he was not going to be taken for a fool. By anyone.

"I hear tell of a Ninth legion sword. Is it true?" he said.

"You are well informed, tribune," the commander commented, his smile not wavering one iota. Paterculus sensed a slight fidgeting from Glaccus.

"Sir, as a tribune I need to be."

He knew it sounded pompous and immature. If he could have pulled the words back and rephrased, he would have done. But it was too late and in truth he was not sorry.

"One has turned up after all these years, as a matter of fact. Well tribune have some wine, please this is my own personal stock, I think you will find it palatable," the commander purred.

"I would like to know who has the sword," he persisted, trying to keep his urge to demand all the facts tightly under control.

The commander held the rank of Tribune Augusticlavius, a very senior frontline officer. Whilst he was only a Laticlavius, a political appointment, and though he was the cadet tribune to the legate himself, he was very junior, by comparison. Though he theoretically outranked the augusticlavius, in practice he most definitely did not. Neither did he want him as an opponent. That would not end well for him.

"I hear one of the arms instructors has it. A patrol took it off a Caledon stealing a horse. They had an auction for it apparently," the commander quipped.

He seemed amused by the idea.

Glaccus intervened, "tribune, the Ninth legion swords were, in all probability, sacrificed to local gods in bogs and ponds and rivers. Probably rusted beyond repair. Our swords are not to Caledonii liking. Their value would be as gifts to their barbarian gods, not as weapons."

Paterculus allowed himself to be taught a little of the local history.

"How so?" he asked.

"They are too short. The Caledonii prefer a long swinging blade. Much more flashy. Our infantry swords are too short, though they would take a fancy to our cavalry blades I suspect."

Glaccus waved his hand around in a mimicry of Paterculus complaining about Velio Pinneius in his tent. He let it go. Now was not the time.

"If that is true then why are we interested in Ninth legion swords. Should we not extinguish the memory?" he said, following the official army line.

The commander leaned forward a fraction.

"Did I say I was interested? Glaccus, did I?"

"I believe not sir," Glaccus said, staring into the fire.

The commander took a moment to explain.

"As it happens, I am interested, because we do not fully understand where the strongest tribes are hiding. The hills over the river are just a fringe. Beyond them the land opens out to the north and east but to the north and west are bigger mountains. That is where Agricola felt the danger was always to be found. The appearance of these swords, if there are more of them, may indicate a growing confidence in the tribes. How is the wine, Cornelius?"

"It is good," he affirmed.

"I'm gratified," the commander said.

"So, the armour, all the legion's armour and portable ballistae is also lying out there. I mean they won't have offered that to their gods, will they?"

He was unable to let it go. He wanted the answers.

"Well perhaps they might have. The bogs are deep in these lands," said Glaccus.

"You joke with me Glaccus?"

"No tribune I do not," vouched the centurion.

He started looking for the decisive point to win his argument with the commander because it was already becoming a contest to have respect in this tent.

"And it's expensive. Agricola burned the bodies of his men after Mons Graupius and retrieved all the armour and brought it back to the fort on the Tavae. Didn't he?" he continued.

"That is correct," Glaccus replied, seeking approval to continue with a brief look to the commander.

More wine was topped into the cups. The servant retreated. He noted the commander's man was an exempted soldier. There was nothing reserved in his movements or his demeanour. He was, he realised, in a den of lions. His early gentle chiding from Glaccus that the tesserarius was only doing his job in nearly amputating his hand and could not be touched for it was now beginning to make sense. The commander seemed relaxed. And yet he sensed an intellectual weakness in the room. They were just soldiers. He was destined to be a future politician in Rome, he was certain of it.

'Politics is having sufficient power to send men where we want to send them. The men we send are powerful and powerless. It is Rome's secret shame. That we let thousands of men bleed for us.'

The words of Father's educated and cold patrician disregard. Father believed the shedding of blood by other men's sons was not bloodshed because it counted for nothing. Their lives and deaths were flour spilt from the grinding of the wheel of Rome. The duty of his ancestors had been to make sure the right people ate the bread. Men had died and would continue to die without understanding that their purpose was simply to provide families like his with money and power. He knew he could win.

"And what happened to that armour?" he pressed.

"It was reissued tribune as I think you probably know quite well," the commander said.

"Exactly," he replied.

"Armour is expensive and time consuming to make. It belongs to the legion and so it is reissued to new intakes and as replacements for damaged kit, which the men pay for," the commander explained.

"What precisely are you implying tribune?" asked Glaccus frowning a little.

"Only that the loss of a legion, its manpower and its eagle is a crime against the senate and people of Rome. Which has to be avenged. The loss of the armour is a distinction I make because it could be retrieved. And the remains of our men could be burned honourably. The eagle is almost certainly drowned. The legion's honour is lost, forever," he answered.

The commander cleared his throat, but it was Glaccus who spoke first.

"When the Hispana marched out, what few records survive show there were three hundred and twenty-seven of them left behind in various regimental infirmaries, at Eburacum and elsewhere, just the usual rates of illness and injuries. Nothing untoward. And two full centuries were detached on other duties. A total of four hundred and eighty-seven men were spared. The Hispana was the weak legion in the province. It only numbered three thousand men at best. Plus, we know it took two cohorts of auxiliary with it when it marched. It's more than thirty years ago. Before any of us sitting here had any interest in Britannia or much else for that matter."

Paterculus bit his tongue, but Glaccus had not finished.

"Somewhere their bones are lying under the mud. No one has ever found them. Were they all killed? Who knows? Were there survivors taken captive? Again no one knows. I don't imagine many legates fancied authorising the search. Are some of them still out there, slaves to native chieftains? It's not impossible, though the chances must be slim any could still be alive."

Glaccus paused, marshalling his thoughts. He began again.

"Two centuries were saved because they were on detached postings and three hundred and twenty seven saved because they were wounded or incapacitated. Altogether, they would make an understrength cohort at best. Or would you have divided them up as the basis of ten new cohorts? What would have been the point? The Ninth legion was to all intents gone. Its senior commanders, all gone. The men were reassigned to the other legions. The legion records quietly burnt I suspect. That is why the Sixth Legion were brought over to replace them.

Their loricas are their coffins. Are you suggesting we strip the armour off their bones? What auguries would sanction such acts? The men would not do it, I tell you sir, they would see it as a blasphemy. As for their honour, with the greatest respect tribune I don't think any of us here is in a position to comment on their honour."

Glaccus finished and grimaced in distaste.

The commander was silent, impressed by Glaccus' stinging passion and irrefutable logic. The new tribune did not appear to like hearing the facts. The thought that Roman legionaries might have been living for years as hostages a few short marches to the north while the garrison of Britannia let their history and traditions wither and fade perturbed him. The idea had never crossed his mind until Glaccus put it there. Intuition made him doubt any man would have lasted a matter of hours after whatever nightmare overtook the legion. But it was an uncomfortable reality that it might be true. He pushed the idea away. The new tribune steepled his fingers unabashed. The bandage on his wrists was showing a faint redness. Glaccus frowned at the weeping wound.

"Retrieving the armour, or as much of it as we can, would send a message to the barbarians," Paterculus offered the thought like a bait.

He avoided the idea that men might be worth rescuing. He had not come to rescue men.

"What message would it send tribune?" queried Glaccus, intrigued in spite of himself.

The new tribune was making waves and he had only just got here. What the commander was thinking he dared not guess.

"That we are more powerful than them in death as well as life," he replied.

Glaccus thought he was going to laugh but he held it in.

"Tribune with respect, you have had a long day. Hot food, good wine and a full night's sleep will work wonders for you," the commander spoke with the tone of absolute authority.

Paterculus heard the warning and decided not to back off.

"Commander, I am sure you are right. But the wall will take years to build and until it is finished we are open to attack. The unburied dead and all the accoutrements of the three thousand men of the Ninth legion lie out there somewhere reminding the Caledons we are not invincible. I believe we should do something about that," he said.

"By retrieving rusty armour and a few helmets?" the commander replied.

"Yes, if you want to put it as bluntly as that, then yes I do," Paterculus said.

Glaccus wished he was invisible but took a draw on his wine instead. The commander breathed out and smiled at the zealous tribune.

"We cannot consider what you say until the wall is built. That is our primary duty, and it will take a couple of years to achieve, even building it in turf and timber. Until it is completed there can be no thought of anything else. Gentlemen, we must be as one on this. I insist on your loyalty. No good can come of fomenting false hopes that we could in some way wipe out the stain on the empire's honour. The Ninth has gone and we cannot get them back. After thirty years all we have is one gladius in the knapsack of a tesserarius. I suggest we let this dog lie. Let's eat. I am hungry and our brave Tungrians arrive tomorrow. Lookout all."

He smiled a commander's smile. Glaccus swallowed his wine and accepted a refill. The commander continued to smile, and Paterculus tried hard not to let the flush warming his face bother him.

Chapter 3.

Early Spring AD 141.

The easternmost fort of the new wall was Velunia, and it was an easy march over easy ground, over new bridges and through safe forests. The fickle winter was softening its grip and the snow was melting. The ground was now wet and muddy under the boots. Velio marched and watched and grinned. Up ahead the officers' helmets bobbed and shone in the sunlight, the horsehair plumes bright and distinctive, swaying to the movement of the walking horses. The signifer positively swaggering, showing off at the head of the column in his new wolfskin. The commander appeared to be relaxed, to his left the new tribune was keeping the reins of his mount in his good left hand and protecting the healing wound in his right. Behind them Hanno Glaccus trotted along, dealing with the scouts' reports. Velunia was not far, and the Votadani were peaceful. Velio chewed on dry bread as he marched, enduring the trumpets' marching tune. Marcus however seemed to be enjoying it. The Tungrian First cohort had eventually turned up at Carumabo to take over. The smoke from the Votadini fires on the "resting lion hill' causing them to detour for a few miles: auxiliary caution.

Paterculus was pondering what need there was for scouting today. He said nothing, keeping his thoughts to himself. His views on finding and recovering whatever matériel there was to be found of the Ninth legion had ruffled a few feathers, not going down at all well and he had decided to take more care with his words in future. The prestige in Rome would be enormous for him and the family if it could be done after all these years, but he would have to be careful; that much was clear.

The commander was anything but relaxed as he rode his horse. As much as he had tried to quash the tribune's foolish notions of recovering the lost impedimenta of the Ninth, the idea kept worming around in his head. Both the threat that it posed as a diversion to the urgent task of the wall and the vague, intangible whisper that it might be worth considering sending out a small quick-moving patrol to test the theory. The idea of soldiers kept imprisoned by the tribes was a nightmare. What were the odds of that though? It did not seem credible. He frowned. The tribune had brought him an unwanted problem. He barked at the horn-blowers whom he usually favoured and had silence for a mile or two.

Velio finished his bread and was grateful for the peace and quiet after the sudden crushed cessation of the bugles; an awful noise, who could think it tuneful?

"Marcus what do you wish for?" he asked.

Marcus glanced over and thought Swords was not his normal confident self. This did not seem the appropriate moment to take the piss out of him.

"Well, that I live long enough to wake up tomorrow," he answered.

"Eh?" Velio replied.

"See that forest, Swords, in there are barbarians waiting to gut you. If you get out of there and have anything to cook and eat before nightfall you will be lucky. To wake up knowing you will see another tomorrow would be like having a whole wineskin to yourself. When you see a forest in front of the banners, coming towards you, it's good to be on foot. A running man is quieter than a horse. The Caledonii go after the men on horses. We foot soldiers, they can hunt at leisure. But we can hide more easily than a horseman. So, when I see another forest in front of the signifier I think, 'Mars and Jupiter just get me to tomorrow morning, and all will be well.' Food tonight would be a bonus, wine would be Elysium," he said, patting Velio on the shoulder.

They marched through the forest and began the approach to low-lying Velunia. Even at a distance it looked as if it was already completed. Cavalry patrols were flashing around in their usual self-important way, horse-hair plumes waving from the troopers' helmets. Velio glanced at Marcus and grinned.

"At last, no more sleeping in tents for a while, I bleedin' well hate tents," Marcus said.

They found the barracks for the vexillation to be warm and dry. That night they went to find the wineskin that would calm Velio's nerves.

*

Up on the windy heights of the hill the Romans called 'The Resting Lion', Ferrdigon was sitting in his wooden chair under his sooty roof timbers watching the gift of wine from Velio's commanding officer doing the rounds. The chair was a high backed, carved thing of beauty. He was a man of slight build, forty-five years old with long grey hair and a beard and moustaches of mismatched black and red. There were times when he felt he was nearing the end of his life. There might not be so many berry seasons left to enjoy as he wanted. Enomani was waiting for his time; patient and respectful. But he had not lost his grip. Like his fathers before him, the game with the Romans was about acquiescence and he understood its rules. He knew all about the Tungrians moving up from the fort at the three hills. They would be his new neighbours. He would trade with them. They would be easier to deal with than the legions because they were once tribal warriors themselves. They would understand what it was like to be in the position of the Votadini. The Votadini were once a free people.

Sixty years before, an entire legion had passed within sight of where he was sitting, heading north to build a fort on the banks of the Tavae. It was the glory-time of their warrior Agricola. He went on to win a great battle against the Caledons that impacted the Votadini not one whit. Yet within three summers Agricola's legions retreated south. The pomp and trumpetry of the northern advance destroyed by the tail between the legs retreat so soon after. What had they seen up there that frightened them enough to head back south after inflicting such a slaughter on the Caledons? He wondered. His great grandfather had taken it as irrefutable proof they were beatable. The Caledonii had been beaten, or at the very least dispersed, but Rome had still chosen to retreat and not consolidate its power at the exact point when there was no power north of the Tavae strong enough to oppose them. Was it a weakness, or fear, or mongrel judgement? Great grandfather's priest had seen it as a sign being given. And ever since the Votadini had been well placed to benefit from the legions' one-eyed readiness to fight the enemies they recognised and ignore the tribes they did not see.

There were thirty or more, men, women and youths in the hall. Kinsmen, warriors or just plain favourites of his, gathered to eat and drink with him, share his fire and sing the songs that bound them.

"They build a wall, another wall like the great one in the south," he said and waited for a response from the room.

"One to hem us in and make us pay more taxes."

The usual complaint about paying tribute did not surprise him.

"One to keep us where they want us."

A new suspicion, that he shared.

"Rome makes us rich. Our crops are ours and our surplus fairly paid for so we will not oppose the wall," he suggested.

"There are reports of thousands of Roman soldiers from here to banks of the Clota. We risk a war if we oppose them."

The voice of elder counsel. He knew who it was, and it generated a lot of nodding and agreement.

"But we don't want them to build another wall," a young male voice complained.

"No."

Yet more agreement.

"So, we will send word of our displeasure to our northern neighbours, the Venicones and the Dumnonii," he mused.

"And let them fight the wall," growled a warrior.

"Yes, let them weaken the Romans. Perhaps they will drive them off."

He frowned at the wishful thinking.

"And will they turn on us afterwards for not fighting with them?" he observed.

"Ah that is the trick," said a wise sounding voice, "we will supply the information to them and let them do the fighting, until it is safe for us to join with them. We incur neither the wrath of the Romans nor our neighbours, before, during or after the wall is stopped, or destroyed."

"We are clear on one thing. We cannot permit another wall," he said, deciding to test the mood.

He had a feeling his policy of appeasing the Romans was being undermined by factions in this same room.

He went on, "I know killing Romans sounds like the answer, but the question is how do we kill them? Killing Romans may only bring more Romans to avenge them. Do we fight a battle here on our own hillside or down there in the flatland? Do we try to pin them against the shore? Or lay traps in the woods? How, where, and when would we kill them? Once we have those answers then I will consider fighting them and joining the tribes of the north."

He gestured for the wine jug, pouring the contents of his cup to the floor so they could all see.

"Bring me another," he said, "I curse them but I paid for this, so I drink their harvest,"

He paused and drank the fresh cup.

He looked around, "it will take them years to build this wall. We can afford to be patient."

There: he had released the hawk into the air. What would it bring back to him?

"I have no more patience. We must not accept the wall. We must fight every stone they raise. Take a life for every stone," growled his personal champion.

He smiled, "I did not say we would not oppose the wall. I merely suggested we should not do all the dying."

He looked around to gather consensus. His wife was scowling. His priest was scowling, in support. His champion was nodding his big shaggy head, looking around for anyone that seemed reluctant.

'Shit,' he thought, 'this is not what I wanted to hear. They no longer want peace with the 'sons of the wolf'. They want to fight them. May our fathers be with us.'

He sat back in his chair wondering if overplaying the difficulties had simply whetted their mood.

Chapter 4.

The area of the planned wall.

To a Roman soldier it looked like an empty landscape, bleak and unforgiving, merciless even; bereft of kindness. That was a deception because it was anything but empty. The rolls and dips and hollows concealed numerous small villages and single homesteads. Generations of farmers had removed the best timber. It was wet ground with relatively few safe trails. And all the while the north and westerly rain bore chilling winds over the mosses and peat bogs.

Within thirty years of the invasion Governor Bolanus and his successors began pushing Rome's line of occupation northwards, towards the hills and mountains of the Caledonii. They named the two rivers that wound inland towards each other, creating a narrow choke point, Bodotria and Clota. This was augmented by a useful escarpment. There was a natural barrier here to be exploited, an almost perfect defensive line if they wanted it. A little weak in the west perhaps where the Clota wound inland. The north close bounded with hills. The middle section holding the best of the craggy escarpment. In the east it was more open and favourable for deployment. But marshes, and rivers made it wet and difficult ground. Local timbers rotted in the wet faster than expected. Good oak was ferried up the east coast.

Agricola, in his turn, installed more watchtowers and signalling stations. After victory at Mons Graupius, he retreated south, deeming his war won and conceding all the lands that had been paid for in blood. For two generations Rome appeared to be disinterested in the north, wearied by a land that fought them as much as the tribes. But now, some sixty years later, Roman horsemen were back inspecting the escarpment they had once dominated.

The Dumnoni scouted southwards keeping a close eye on the invaders. The enemy horsemen came first, working their way in from both coasts along the lip of the crest, red cloaks billowing in the breeze. Then within a single turning of the moon, squads of legionaries clearing the few trees on the hill tops. The Dumnonii watched, as their ancestors had done, the rituals of Roman building.

Ropes and sticks set in the ground, the peering and gesturing, the shuffling and movement of sticks. Like a game perhaps? Then the next phase. The rebuilding of the old camps as well as building new ones, clearing out old ditches at frightening speed. Thousands of Roman soldiers marching in from the east.

They saw the beginnings of the long trench across the high points, hilltop to hilltop, so shallow at first that it could be jumped over. But in places it got deeper and wider. Behind it, less than a spear throw, a layer of stone started to appear, then, the cutting and stacking of turf. The southern Votadini, softened by contact with the legions watched and joked. But Dumnonii priests came and looked. They sat, did not eat or drink, but watched the work. They arose and made counsel. The Votadini joking stopped.

*

The Governor of Britannia, Quintus Lollius Urbicus could travel incognito when he wanted. He discarded the coloured toga of office and chose only one secretary to attend him, the one who was not in fact the best scribe, but a man with other gritty talents; donned the leather armour of a commander and picked his favourite saddle and his sturdiest mount. He travelled without fanfare from Deva Victrix in the west to Eburacum on the east. His province was as fractious as Germania. The south was succumbing and softening to the delights of olives, wine and security from inter-tribal warfare, but the north kept him awake and kneeling at his altars of Jupiter and Mars. From there, right up until the moment he arrived at the solid oak gateway of Velunia's western entrance, he was busy verifying for himself all the intelligence reports.

A picked 'ala' of cavalry came with him, nearly five hundred good men. As he rode, his equestrian abilities became obvious. Urbicus moved from being a named figurehead of questionable courage to a hard riding soldier who experienced days and nights in a wet saddle and carried his sword at his hip. They nick-named him 'iron-arse.' By the time he crossed into the real heartlands of the unconquered province he knew he had their allegiance. And, they enjoyed the covert nature of the hunting and fireless nights, sometimes within touching distance of a tribal settlement.

Urbicus came to see how well his nominated man was coping with his detached duty from the Twentieth. He was not looking for failure. He was hungry and thirsty for an update on progress. Having already inspected western sections of the new foundlings of the turf wall, he already had first-hand answers to the questions he intended to ask; which is the only way to hold a profitable interrogation. Servius Albinius was lucky. It was that same evening the Dumnonii commenced hostilities.

Velio and Marcus were sitting in an unfinished, as yet unnamed and unloved fort on the line of the wall, twenty miles west of Velunia. It felt like nowhere, worse than Gaul, worse than Germania, surrounded by mist and rain. The sentries for the night watch had just been set in front of the fort's northern gate which in turn overlooked the escarpment and the plain below. East and west the ditch line was in various stages of completion.

Their calls sounded out every few minutes as they settled into position. The mist made shapes move in the gloom and fomented creeping enemies out of dripping bushes. Their nervousness was palpable but they settled down to cursing the purpose of guarding a ditch when their backs were covered by sentries inside the construction camp. Two sets of sentries seemed pointless.

Later, Marcus took Velio across to visit a contubernium of his pals, the cohort's blacksmiths. Somewhere among the tent-lines voices were singing a filthy song accompanied by the sweet tone of a shepherd's pipe. As he tramped alongside Marcus he smiled at the rape of music by the song of soldiers. Marcus tapped the goat skin tent wall which drummed under the tension and stepped through the flap into a den of wickedness that only men living without the presence of women can achieve. They were all there. With Marcus and Velio's arrival, ten of them crammed into a tent designed for eight, passing wine flasks to keep out the cold.

In the blacksmiths' tent news of a Ninth legion sword, returning from the past, aroused some curiosity. There was a mixture of responses sweeping through the camp, ranging from outright indifference, to what Velio walked into; open interest from men who knew a bit about weapons. The eight shuffled to make space for Marcus and Velio. Quick introductions and then a pause. He unrolled it from the cloth. There was a moment of silent looking, as if it was a baby. It got picked up and passed around. There were a few tuts and shrugs; all part of the initiation.

"Standard pattern infantry blade. Legionary's issue, no officer's inscription that I can see, no dedication or decoration of any kind, just the Hispana marking and it needs a good clean. Can't see what all the fuss is about," was the opening salvo.

Velio ignored it.

"What d'you want a Ninth legion sword for?"

"Not exactly lucky, is it Swords?"

"Needs more sharpening I think Tesserarius Pinneius Sir, Swords, Sir, I mean sir."

The smiths as a legion trade were infamous for their general disregard for everybody under the rank of emperor, a trait they did not care to hide much. Commanders might huff or grimace disapproval of such degrees of disobedience, but it was taken in good part. And their slender insurance policy against a flogging was the quality of their work in a steel world.

"It'll have to be Swords Sir, from now on, you wait."

"Very funny," he said.

Then it came at him from all sides, thicker and faster than Germans in a forest.

"It's nearly there, just needs a final edge so it can take the hairs off your arm. Then it'll be ready for a bit of fun."

"How long has it been out there?"

"Well, since the Ninth got screwed. How else?"

"So, how long?"

"About thirty years."

"No."

"Can't have been lying around in the shit all that time. Look at the condition. It's hardly lost its shine."

"Some Caledon has had this tucked away somewhere dry."

"Like up his arse?"

"If you say so."

"You're not going to fight with this, Swords, are you?"

A delicious mixture of feigned incredulity and hamming about.

He smiled, Marcus had known them a lot longer than he had, so he had not quite worked out which of them was the principal comedian and who were the straight men. There was clearly a bit of competition for that honour. And he had no doubts he was going to get it wrong.

"Yes, I like the feel of it. Better balance than my legion one," he said.

"Oh, so you sayin' the Ninth made better blades than we do in the Twentieth?" the tent leader identified himself and went on the attack.

He had found his opponent, the rest were there for the fun and the wineskins. He relaxed, stole a glance towards Marcus who had other things on his mind.

"Give me the wine before you drink it all, you miserable bastards," Marcus yelled at the back of the tent.

"No really, is that what you mean Swords? I need to know."

The soldier was forty or more years old, pure infantry of ridiculous, muscled, proportions; a creased face where a mule might have kicked him on more than one occasion, heavy eyebrows and straight white teeth. A face like that with undamaged teeth was the clearest warning that this soldier was a lot sharper and faster than he appeared. Or he was very lucky. And that was not to be discounted either.

Velio raised his hand, "no, what I mean is that sword," he pointed for emphasis, "feels better to me, than the one I have already."

"Sounds to me like you are saying our blades are shit."

"Not every sword, just comparing those two," he interrupted and wished he could reword that a little bit.

"Wine anyone?" Marcus said passing the skin over to Velio's opponent.

The blacksmith took a long pull and winked to his mates.

"Oh, so not every one means then that most of them are. Is that the way of it? This is getting worse. Does the tribune know you say these things?"

"He's pulling your pisser, Swords," said one of them at the back, safe and out of reach.

The main man wagged a finger in admonishment.

"It's only fair to warn you that some of the blades Gaius makes are, in fact, shit just in case you decide to ask him to make one for you," offered a voice pretending to moderate but stirring in plain sight.

"So, you're Gaius,' he clicked the name.

"You gets what you pays for," Gaius replied slapping the back of his hand into the palm of the other.

Velio looked harder. None of his features quite fitted in with its neighbours. Whatever grace he might have had as a young lad was lost in the ruins of his later life. Except for those white, straight, wolf's teeth.

"Can't see what the fuss is about, it's just a bleedin' sword," from the back of the pack.

"Now there speaks a true blacksmith of the Boar legion," Gaius grinned.

The game was over or perhaps it was just changing; Velio sensed he had either come through it or his erstwhile rank was preventing all out piss-taking.

"Now put that away young Velio. Are we playin' dice or not? How much do you lot want to lose? Marcus, your credit is good. but Swords is definitely in need of a big win," Gaius quipped.

"A big win for 'words, I don't think so. Not even with his dice," another teased.

Velio took back his gladius, tucking it away.

Gaius grinned and slapped the ground with a meaty paw.

"We'll get you fixed up with a decent one, much better than that old Hispana, Tesserarius Pinneius sir, Swords sir, I mean. A nice shiny one," he whispered, waving his hand at the bundle, "and you'll be ready for them nasty Caledons. Don't you worry, you'll see. We'll get you fixed up. You'll see, your Uncle Gaius will look after you."

"Piss off," he suggested in reply.

Gaius looked at him, his face not quite expressionless. The suggestion of a smile, betraying what might have passed from a father to a son who pleased him.

"More wine, let the Baccanalia begin," Gaius clicked his fingers and called to invisible slaves.

"Baccanalia," they chorused.

The alarm sounded outside. The heavy clanging of hammer on iron ring.

"Hostiles, hostiles," called a sentry, his voice rising to a shout as he repeated the alarm.

He sounded near at hand. The call was taken up along the walls. Inside the tent the ten men looked at each other.

"Swords and shields boys," Velio grunted, and they sprang to it. Gaius too.

Back at their tent the rest of tesserarius instructors were assembled and waiting with shields and helmets, still buckling up their armour. Velio wrapped his headcloth three times around his head before pulling the helmet on. Their centurion strode past in his full armour, crested helmet under his arm, weighty vine-wood swagger stick in the other hand. He halted for a moment and gave them a commanding glare. Velio wondered whether Caledonii stupid enough to get into the camp would be swatted with the swagger stick or would the centurion deign to draw his gladius. He fought hard to bite down the picture in his head.

"We stay in camp, understand? No one goes outside. The sentries are being recalled. Get with the century and keep them in line. No heroics until I know what we've got on our hands here. Marcus, Velio, with me. Come as you are, there's little time."

The trumpets and buccinas were blowing "Stand to the Eagle," bringing the cohort tumbling out of its tents. They grabbed their shields and helmets and followed. Their tents were in the sinistra quarter of the tented back-lines. The north facing gate was closing with the last of the sentries piling back inside. The centurion went to the timbered gate house and climbed up to the observation tower, two steps at a time, Marcus and Velio following at his heels. Along the ramparts on either side the palisades were filling with legionaries. The buccinas were still blowing but the men were moving with a low murmur. On the platform the two duty guards pointed to the lip of ground beyond the new diggings where the ground fell away to the plain below. The lip seemed to be a moving line but whether it was the mist shifting or men creeping forwards was hard to say. The centurion however had no doubts.

"Dumnonii," the centurion intoned.

His helmet was still in the crook of his arm.

"Will they attack sir?" Marcus asked.

"Getting close enough for a javelin sir," advised the nearest sentry.

An arrow thudded into the gatepost above them. The aim too high. The centurion put on his helmet.

"Light the warning beacon. Is there sign of any beacons to the east or west?"

"Too foggy to see sir," the sentry replied.

"I'm not sending messengers out in this. We will stand to the wall and send them packing. You two, get word to the centurions and optios to meet me here then return to the century. Make sure you find everyone."

"As you command," Velio and Marcus said.

"We will commence firing the scorpios. Alert all century crews. I want arcing fire immediately on each side of the fort. We may already be surrounded," the centurion continued.

Velio looked to Marcus.

"I'll go around the artillery, you find the other centurions and the optios," he said.

Marcus didn't have to go far to find the other five centurions of the cohort. They were already making their way forwards to the north gate. In the few short minutes since 'Stand to the Eagle' had sounded the camp had transformed into a seething mass of activity and then almost as quickly into a quiet, focussed weapon.

The artillery men were already anticipating the orders. The cohort's six scorpios sitting in the centre of the fortress were arranged in a loose arc facing out towards the nascent trench.

"Arcing fire now, centurion's orders," Velio shouted.

The "thunking" noises from the tortioned scorpios sending destruction out into the night was reassuringly loud. The optios moved along the rows of their men, encouraging and calming. The centurions taking post on each gate tower closest to right hand end of their century so that they could survey the position outside the wall and shout commands to the legionaries. Torches burned every ten paces making the men closest to them the most vulnerable to enemy arrows and spears. It was an uncomfortable position, but the torches added to the defensive strength. The Boar shook its mane and pawed the earth. Velio stood at his post in the Fourth century beside the optio and peered out.

"Shields up," he shouted, seeing a few men resting their shields on the ground, "your knees are the safest bits of you tonight so get those shields up where they do some good."

The optio looked over and nodded.

"Blacker than Hades out there," Velio said.

"That it is, and nearly as friendly," the optio replied.

The main attack came at the four gates. Arrows flighting downward from out of the fog. There was nothing for the cohort archers to aim at and the commanding centurion withheld the usual order to return fire. Within twenty minutes the arrows eased off and ceased. No attack had been made on the camp itself. And then, almost by common consent, the legionaries knew it was over. It became quiet. The tribesmen had faded back into the night. They stood and waited, moisture dripping off helmets and shields, torches crackling and smoking, shadows from the flames of fire arrows embedded in the palisade and the towers: tents burning. The smell of wet earth and sweat. The sounds of five hundred men breathing out in relief. Muffled obscenities and low laughter.

"How many d'you think it was?"

"How should I know?"

"Didn't fancy it much did they?"

"Didn't fancy it up their arse you mean."

"That'd show who were the men and who were the boys eh?"

Velio heard a quiet sniggering from the direction of the centurion's platform. The foe diminished and shrank into a joke. He shivered, missing his cloak now that the adrenalin of fighting was ebbing away.

The optio gave a faint smile, "just testing out our sentries I think."

Their centurion had decided something similar.

"Get any wounded men to the medicus. Bring me numbers. Stand down centuries One and Three. All men to remain in armour," he ordered.

"Relay that," called the other centurions.

"Centuries Two, Four and Five will cover the wall. Century Six will put out all external fires at the gates before standing down," their centurion called out.

"Bad luck lads, you get to guard the walls tonight," Velio cackled to the men around him.

He made his way to the steps down from the rampart to a dry tent beckoning and an even dryer cloak. He was immune from the drudgery of standing guard. Real fighting was different.

"Thanks for all your help, tesserarius," chirped someone.

"Just you keep them shields up," he growled, "because if the Caledonii don't have you, I will."

But that was just the start of it. The Dumnonii attacked the central forts along the line, the most isolated, for the next four nights. Governor Quintus Lollius Urbicus had not expected the repeat attacks. He thought it a little presumptuous of the local tribes to keep provoking him. After the third consecutive night he knew he had a problem. His personal ala of legionary cavalry wore better armour than any of the auxiliary cavalry. Should he take them out on a retaliatory strike over the marshes with some infantry support or, concentrate on the wall? Dilution of effort would delay the good progress being made here. He called for Servius Albinius and made him a gift of the problem.

Later that day Servius Albinius, Urbicus, Paterculus and Glaccus sat together in the commander's house. The food remnants were cleared away without mention of the pressing nature of their gathering. They relaxed, wine cups in hand. The military clerk spread out a map of the escarpment, the disposition of the army forts and the low grounds to the north leading to the mountains. Servius had been playing with the problem in his head since Urbicus handed it to him, so he had the advantage of surprise on most of them.

He looked at Paterculus, "how is the wrist now, has it healed?" he asked.

Paterculus smiled, "much better thank you sir, I mean Servius."

The off duty switching to first name terms was still catching him out.

"Good, that is what I wanted to hear. I have been considering your interest in the unknown location of the dead Ninth."

Urbicus' eyebrows climbed up his forehead in surprise, but he said nothing, giving Paterculus a measured look that could have easily been career ending or, enhancing.

'Mithras, what has he got in store now?'

Glaccus marvelled at Servius' ability to plot.

"And the recovery of as much of their equipment as might be worth saving. Cornelius, there may be more merit in your idea than I first thought," he went on.

Paterculus felt his spirits rising, sipping his wine more than he intended and holding his glass cup out to Servius' servant for more.

"What has this to do with this Dumnonii insolence?" Urbicus asked.

Servius smiled at them all, took more wine and made sure they were all topped up. Urbicus took only a half glass. He exchanged a meaningful look with Urbicus. The governor eased back in his chair and listened.

"Governor," he began, refusing to use the familiar, "you asked me to deal with the raids on the building work. And our good friend Cornelius made a reasonable request to me that we should make some attempt to establish the fate of the Ninth and recover what we can. I have been considering both and it may be the two are linked."

"How so? The Ninth are long gone," Urbicus pointed out.

"Agreed but the memory of the victory might be stirring the tribes up now that they can see what we are building here," said Paterculus.

Servius smiled in support.

"An old victory left unavenged breeds confidence and also disrespect in equal parts," he said.

Hanno Glaccus frowned, unconvinced. What was Servius up to? Servius pointed on the map to the lands north of the new line, to the area where years ago Agricola had set up his advance defensive lines before launching his final push to subdue the northernmost tribes. Two lines of forts and watchtowers had once blocked the Caledonii attack routes out of the mountains. The historian-writer Tacitus had named the decisive encounter 'Mons Graupius' but Tacitus had been a man of political bent and had never been viewed as a reliable vendor of military accuracy. Fifty and more years later the tribes described as smashed were giving every indication of mocking the lesson Agricola imposed upon them.

"You will go to Pinnata Castra, to the old fort of our legion on the bend of the Tavae. You will make that your base to scout the hills. The fort was thoroughly levelled so there is no good reason the Caledonii will pay it any attention. Also pray to the gods you are not spotted because I cannot help you if you are attacked or cut off. And if you do find any remains of the Ninth, note the spot well and bring me evidence but nothing more. I cannot send Hanno with you, but you will have twenty of my best men. Hanno, you will pick men who are good with a sword. Stealth will be your best protection tribune, that and the blessings of the gods," he paused.

"We can discuss a suitable optio to act as Cornelius' second. And I'll give him Pinneius and one other instructor. The men will be more confident with those two along," he added.

"How would you get over the marshland without being spotted?" Urbicus asked.

Servius smiled.

"I'm going to authorise a patrol of two maniples. Highly visible, three hundred and twenty men, Hanno will lead that part, with auxiliary cavalry support. The patrol will be too big for the Dumnonii to attack at short notice, though I think it should move quickly all the same Hanno. Don't sit around and invite trouble. The patrol will skirt along the southern edge of the mountains and at a suitable spot, you Cornelius, will detach quietly with your men. Hanno, you will continue to wave the standards along the frontier and return. It will seem as though we are simply showing our swords as a response to the last few nights activity. And in part that is exactly what we are doing. The other part is you are deflecting attention away from the tribune's patrol."

Urbicus scratched his chin, concerned the young tribune was about to go on a one-way mission to Hades. Paterculus was sitting up straight like a hunting dog. Hanno Glaccus looked at his commander.

Servius continued, "but let me be frank. I do not believe that there is anything to be found of the Ninth. And if there is, it will be another thing entirely to go and retrieve it. But I have thought about the points Cornelius has made to me and I can see his logic. Leaving them unavenged may be like feeding rats with food from our own table."

"Servius, with respect, we have no idea how far, or in which direction, the Ninth actually marched," Hanno Glaccus said.

"Cornelius should start at Pinnata Castra. That fort was intended to be the centre pin for all the forts guarding the glens to the northwest. When Agricola beat the Caledonii at Mons Graupius, where did they run? To the northwest, into the Grey Mountains. That is where you must look Cornelius. But if you cannot find the legion in ten days, I want you to return."

"And how will he get back across the moorland?" Urbicus probed.

Glaccus smiled as he guessed the answer.

"I will take a patrol back to the same place, and we will gallop back together to hot baths and hot food," he replied.

Servius nodded as he tapped the map with the point of a pen. Urbicus smiled too.

"Ten days is not long but Cornelius, we share your grief over the fate of the legion. If we can avenge it in some small way, then of course we will. But the emperor's wall comes first. You must understand that. You must also understand that unless we can show that the Ninth died well, we must leave their memory to fade. Their loss was a heavy blow to the prestige of the province. Despatches had to be sent. Blame had to be apportioned. That blame was put onto the dead men of the Ninth themselves. They didn't complain," the governor stated.

The room went quiet. Servius beckoned his clerk to bring more wine. This time Urbicus took a fuller cup. His expression was troubled, but he gave Servius time to speak.

"So, do you still want to go?" he asked Paterculus.

"Yes," Paterculus assented, "and if I can't find them, I can find the strength of the enemy."

Servius looked at him, appraising the thinking.

"Now, that knowledge is even more important. Bring me that information and I will give you men to recover the Hispana. But remember the Ninth aren't going anywhere. We must consolidate first," he said.

Urbicus coughed at Servius' outright promise of men. They exchanged looks.

"If there is more left of them than can fit in three waggons, I'll stand night watch for a month. We could spare some cavalry and waggons if Cornelius finds them," Servius said.

'Fat chance,' thought Glaccus, *'but it'll keep him out of the way for a while.'*

Paterculus stood up. The room was warm, and the wine was rich and thick in the mouth.

"Twenty good men and ten days," he said.

"Ten days and twenty good men," Urbicus breathed, "I will allow it. Hanno, I count on you to get them over the marshlands. Servius, you will hold a full cohort and cavalry ala in reserve to support their return if required. And gentlemen, the reasons we discuss here, stay in this room. Rome must never know that we are still rolling these dice."

He paused for a moment choosing his words.

"Even if you find them and they can be judged to have died well and it is possible to retrieve anything of them, the best I will allow is prayers and a cremation of everything to send them honourably to the afterlife. Rome will not know and no one in this room will speak of it."

He paused again, frowning, expressing the thought that had been his immediate reaction from the start of the discussion.

"Bringing them back might not be good for morale."

"How would we stop the men from speaking of it? The veterans could not be silenced," Glaccus chimed.

"I did not say where or how such rites would be permitted," Urbicus said, "and you will retrieve nothing without my order. Am I clear Cornelius? We only require confirmation."

"Perfectly Governor," Paterculus assented.

"Servius?"

"Perfectly," he replied.

Urbicus waited for Servius to dismiss his subordinates and took wine from the tribune's clerk, waiting until Servius had his own cup filled. The clerk bowed and left. He leaned forward to conspire. He had not the slightest doubt that there were ears attuned on the other side of the wall.

"Perhaps you can enlighten me now Servius? Why are you sending him to steal olives from a vineyard?"

The tribune smiled at the governor's graphic turn of phrase.

"Because he is an insufferable little rat and it will do him no harm at all to get cold, wet and hungry for a few days and nights out there in the wilds. He is so damned certain the Ninth are out there and must be brought back that he does little else that is useful. Quite why you gave him to me fails me."

"He needs to learn the art of command," the governor murmured.

"Well exactly sir," he said.

"And you are the best teacher to hand."

Servius raised his hand in mock despair.

"Please Quintus, no flattery. Well, the lad will learn the art of command out there very quickly, or I'll have to promote the optio to centurion. He is almost ready now. Provided he brings them back safely I may have no option but to make him up," he said.

"Is he trustworthy? Is he good enough?" the governor asked.

"He is the most scratchy little bastard we have. I think he will do fine."

"The tribune needs someone with talent, he does not need a parade sergeant," Urbicus commented.

"I think he'll find the optio far more cunning and deft than he looks. I think he is far too bright for the tribune. I just hope he remembers his rank and lets the tribune make all the stupid mistakes so that he can correct them. And Pinneius is a good lad, a sensible soldier. I have no doubt the optio and Pinneius will get them all back. The optio will command, Pinneius will obey, and the men will hear his voice and think all is well, while our tribune rides his horse and goes to find his lost legion," Servius replied.

Urbicus snorted in derision.

"Cornelius will ride out to the north and somehow find the remains of a legion that's been lost for thirty years? He'll touch the exact spot with a needle? If Caesar himself was alive and here in this fort, he could not accomplish such a thing."

He drank and wiped his lips, "but the tribune might bear a little more humility on his return than when he leaves, I think, eh, is that it Servius?"

"Something like that would be a blessing. He could hardly carry any more confidence in his own ability."

"He is a lad that loves himself," agreed the governor.

"And for little reason."

"His politics offend?" asked Urbicus, intrigued.

"Quite so, governor."

"This optio though? Are you sure a sending a centurion would not be wiser?"

Servius smiled, "a centurion will make decisions and act. An optio will make the same sort of decisions and ask permission before he acts. That is the difference. That way our little tribune will be flattered and believe he controls his men."

"And if he, what is the expression they use here?"

"'Get's chopped', Quintus?"

"Indeed, if he somehow gets chopped. What then?"

The governor looked him straight in the eyes over the rim of his wine cup.

"No, I mean if the optio gets himself chopped?" he added after a moment.

"No, you did not. The death of an optio would not ruffle an old fox's bathwater," Servius reposted.

Quintus smiled.

"So, because it will come as a shock to you personally that someone so full of potential has been lost to the empire a long letter of personal sorrow will be sent to his mater et pater," he continued.

The governor shook his head a little. His bald pate shone in the lamp light.

"Servius, I'm not sure I approve. Twenty men is cutting it to the bone. Make sure he is given the best horses. That is an order," he intoned.

"Of course, Quintus," Servius raised his cup to acknowledge it.

Urbicus paused once more, regarding the man he had selected to lead the huge vexillation of men building the emperor's wall. Three legions were hard at it. Mainly the men of the Second. Logically, on the basis of numbers, he should have given overall command to their legate but sickness, or fate, had intervened to send him to the infirmary, where the reports were not at all promising. And frankly there was no one else to spare. Jupiter and Urbicus had given the Boar's senior tribune a chance to shine. Dealing with the inevitable rumblings about favouritism from the tent-lines was just another challenge brought by higher command. No one under him would ever fail to laugh at one of his little jokes ever again. And so far, as he could tell, all Servius' difficulties had been simple ones. Now, the ghosts of the Ninth had been wakened and were rising up to make a fool of his future; the opportunity to command his own legion.

"Do well, make me write a letter of recommendation to the emperor and it could be yours."

He knew Servius wanted a legion. He would not have trusted him if he argued the opposite.

"You're not really intending to send three waggons and a cavalry escort to fetch back any remains, are you?" he asked.

Servius smiled, "a pinch of salt is needed in every stew. Otherwise, it will not be swallowed. That's all."

He relaxed; Servius' wine was really very commendable.

Chapter 5.

Hill of the Resting Lion.

Four nights after probing at the wall's defences, Asuvad the Dumnoni warlord called on the Votadini. Normally he would have kept his distance as, like all Dumnoni, he considered the Votadini had gone soft. Around him a feast was in full chaotic flow; singing, ale, thrumming harps and servant girls. Amorous hands with empty ale horns. Casualties of course but the surrenders were good natured. It was as good a feast as he could remember. His bladder made him leave the hall and he was glad to breathe in the cold hilltop air. It was dark and the lights in the heavens were bright and clear. He pissed in the pit behind the wattle gate and readjusted his breeches. The hall door opened behind him, more feasting sounds floated out. Three couples took the opportunity to sneak away. Through the walls of a nearby hut he heard the low gasping of lovers. He listened for a moment and then curiosity piqued, and he leaned on the door. In the guttering yellow light of rush-lamps a couple were on a low trestle.

It was the face and raven hair of Ferrdigon's wife, Eilaver. She had her nails buried deep in the hard muscles of their druid's back. Asuvad watched the enthusiastic bulling of the chieftain's wife. Her hair was full and shining, his back a rippling display of power. They had not been going at it long enough to build up a sweat.

He coughed out of malicious delight. The man's hips froze in deep thrust. Her face was transformed from hot, lusty encouragement into horror. Thousands of words and possibilities died unsaid. Only the fire in the hut crackled. He raised his palm towards them and began a retreat. Over in the feasting hall Ferrdigon, chief of this little kingdom, was getting drunk with his Dumnonii guests. He sighed for his plans.

"Ruins," he murmured, "blood and ruins."

Chapter 6.

Bergessia, the Fourth cohort's fort on the wall.

The senior arms instructor called Velio and Marcus into his small tent. He got straight to it.

"Centurion Glaccus has specifically requested you two. Get yourselves over to Velunia today and report to him. Full fighting kit but no shields."

"Why no shields?" asked Marcus.

"Guess."

"Full fighting kit needs a shield," he persisted.

"Indeed, just not always an infantry one," replied the senior man.

"We're going cavalry," said Velio.

"Well done. Well at least you won't have to walk Velio."

"Where are we going, do you know?"

I"It's a cavalry escort duty for your favourite tribune. But Centurion Glaccus is sending an infantry optio and he wants you two to support the optio as required. I suggest you keep your head down and keep the optio between you and the tribune as much as possible. Stay out of trouble. Got it?"

Marcus raised his eyebrows at the strange mix of the escort.

The senior instructor shook his head, "don't ask, just do."

Velio saluted left the tent with a single thought, heading straight to the outer rampart of the fort to the smithying area. He found Gaius hammering iron nails, a huge pile of various sizes was lying on the grass at his side. Thousands would be needed along the front. He knew the production of nails was a daily drudgery for every blacksmith in the legion. He had his back to Velio and only realised he was there when Velio walked around in front of the anvil. Gaius had a healthy sweat going and he wiped his wet forehead with the back of his wet forearm before putting his hammer down. This time, in the daylight, beyond the safe confines of his tent, where more or less anything except mutiny was permitted, he was more respectful, nodding, "tesserarius."

Velio nodded back, "Gaius I need you to put an edge on this sword for me. I have to go on patrol."

"The Ninth blade sir?" Gaius smiled.

"Indeed."

He drew it from the scabbard and handed it over.

"Rough sharpening or razor?" Gaius asked, quick to the matter in hand.

A rough ground edge would be less sharp than a smooth-grind but it would inflict hideous lacerated wounds; wounds that would make a medicus suck his teeth. It would hold its relative sharpness in battle and do wicked damage to bone. A smooth finish would lose its edge quicker but would be devastating, delivering frightful piercing and slashing wounds. A blade thrust beyond an enemy's neck and drawn back would open the carotid artery and put a man on his knees in seconds; it was a favoured and well-practiced stroke, thrust past the head and kill on the pull back.

Some men, given a choice, preferred the batter of the rough-cut edge to see the damage they inflicted and some, the venom of the smooth. Gaius hefted it and made the four defensive parries, upper right and left, lower right and left; stepping back into the alert posture. He was no mean hand with a sword.

"It does have a balance I'll grant you, but I think we can improve it just a whisker. A bit of love and sweat must have gone into this one," he ventured.

Velio knew he had chosen the right man.

"I want to be able to shave with it," he replied.

"Can you leave it with me for an hour or two, sir?"

He nodded and went out to inspect the finished headquarters building and the almost complete commander's quarters. Then he wandered along wallum ditch, killing time. He watched the cavalry mounts grazing in the gap between the wallum and the front wall of the fort, admiring their beautiful glossy coats and intelligent faces; they cropped the rough grass, flicking their tails, giving as good an indication that all was peaceful as could be imagined. He finished up watching three engineer officers arguing about the stone founds for the turf wall. Everywhere the ordinary men, the 'mules', were sweating and working; whistling, always a good sign. The noise was constant, axe and saw on wood, hammers pounding chisels into stone, picks on earth, shouts and curses, occasional laughter; the progress was quick. The founds for the infantry barrack blocks were already marked out and the trenches begun. Within a few short weeks the fort would be finished, and the designated section of wall complete and ready for its dedication slab. Another small victory for the Twentieth and after that it was extend everything further west to meet the Sixth coming eastwards. And all along the support road waggons were trundling by the dozen, laden with timber, clay, wattle and roof tiles for principia and commanders' houses.

When he went back for his sword it looked like a different weapon. The blade now had an even, gleaming edge. Somehow the pits in the steel had been ground out improving the overall shine of the blade.

Gaius coughed, "I've put a new grip on it for you. The old bone was cracked and rotted, it would never last and a new pommel of course, can't do the handle without changing the pommel. It was rotted to buggery underneath."

Velio gazed at the indented bone handgrip which had been ground down to six octagonals so the smoothened grooves sat naturally and comfortably in the fingers. Gaius must have a stash of them. He could not have done that part from scratch in the time available. The oak pommel was lighter in colour than the hand guard but was a fairly close match. How Gaius had achieved this in two hours was a mystery.

"It doesn't look like the same sword Gaius."

The smith pointed to the Ninth legion marking, "it's the same sword, tesserarius."

He made a few practice strokes. The grip made quite a difference. Gaius coughed again.

"I've made the pommel heavier to improve the balance, do you feel it?" Gaius asked.

It felt the exactly the same, but he decided not to argue with what was evidently a favour.

"Thank you, Gaius, it's perfect," he said digging into his pouch and handing a whole sesterci to him.

After a brief moment he handed him a second. More than he had intended but it was worth that much.

"Can't have you going off to fight them Caledonii with that old handgrip on it, can we? 'We must look smart in front of the enemy,' Gaius mimicked the rising cadences of the centurion's favourite parade ground bark.

Velio sheathed the blade and tried not to like the man.

"Remember sir, any time you want a new sword, you come and see me. Forget what I said before."

"Thank you, Gaius."

"Sir?" Gaius said.

"Yes," he answered.

"We've fought in these islands for near a hundred years. The ones who wanted peace with us have taken it. These bastards up here in these hills, they don't want peace. Remember that and you won't be deceived."

"Thank you, Gaius, I will.

*

They rode through the north gate into the sobering, thoughts-of-mortality provoking, green light of dawn. The cornicens started blowing "Farewell brother."

Glaccus recognised it as soon as the opening notes began. It was a nice touch he thought, to accord the new tribune with the traditional veterans' salute. At first they made good progress. The land was firm and the tracks well established. The column followed the southern banks of the Bodotria heading upstream, watching as it narrowed from sea estuary to major river; watching the far banks and hills come closer and closer until it was a meandering river winding through flat and marshy land. The soldiers waved to the Votadinii children they saw, and most of the children waved back. The next day at the first crossing point available Paterculus peeled his small command off from the main column, waiting before it had disappeared from sight before taking them over the bridge towards the disputed lands. The horses' hooves echoed on the wooden boards in a slow calm rhythm. Marcus glanced across to Velio as they brought up the rear. The sixteen cavalry troopers ahead of them were signing away unlucky spirits and gazing with mock casualness in the direction of the vanished maniples of Glaccus. Even the most hard nosed among them sent a silent prayer. The optio kneed his horse next to Paterculus.

"Do we take the road sir or do we stay low?" he asked.

Paterculus had been thinking hard about it.

"Staying on the road makes us visible but we travel faster," he said, stating the obvious, "so, we stay on the road until the light starts to go, make as much time as possible, then we will slip off and make our way to Pinnata Castra, unseen," he said, as if it were a simple infallible act.

The optio looked across at him recalling Glaccus' personal instruction.

'Provide support to the tribune, make sure the men follow his orders, don't let him make any bad ones, make sure they all get back alive. You are also the only man with any knowledge of the ground. He relies on you. This could be your promotion to centurion.'

"We'll leave the road as soon as the light goes sir," he agreed, "I know a couple of places that will do."

They were going outside of any help, going beyond the Votadini country and north into the grey zone where the Dumnonii and Veniconii lands abutted; an area of tribal strife in its own right.

For two days they crossed innumerable streams, skirted around forests, slept and ate little. Always seeking a sheltered line of advance, it was hard going. The land was as spiteful as the driving winds. If it had been an ordinary patrol within controlled territory, it would have been a tedious affair. But the land grew emptier the further north they probed. Velio knew it was an illusion. Every mile made them more exposed. They rested as ordered at Pinnata Castra and dried off around small fires, protected by the trench defences of the old fort, trying not to think what their comrades might be doing at this exact moment back in the relative safety of the wall. Without doubt they had been spotted. Perhaps they were too few to stir much antagonism, though he was not convinced that was the reason. That night the tribune told them the double headed nature of their patrol. From a pack horse he produced a wine skin and handed it to the men. After he finished speaking, he left them and sat talking to the optio. There was no need to hear the mens' views of their infantry officers.

"What do you make of this?"

"Pointless, that's what."

"Likely to get us hung up from trees."

"There's a happy thought."

The next day Paterculus made a decision and headed west into the high ground; the hard ground. His time was nearing the halfway mark. It was time to roll the dice a bit harder. On the fifth day he crossed an empty dank moor. He could see mountains beyond, and pressed forward. It took three hours to draw up to the foot of the mountains. He halted the command at the lip of a long twisting glen that dropped away and down into the distance, towards the sea he presumed. Velio watched the men checking their weapons, patting the pommels of their long spatha swords, seeking reassurance in this strange place. He glanced at Marcus who shook his head urging silence. This was not the time for loose comment. Ahead of them the optio took a long slow look around. There were thick stands of pine trees on both sides of the lower slopes of the glen. They were tall and still in the calm silence. They rose up presenting Paterculus with the age old problem for any commander of small forces.

What was in those trees? What were they concealing? Were they concealing anything? Was it safe to advance further?

"Middle of nowhere," murmured his second in command.

"Far enough away to be a bolthole," he replied.

The optio saw him gazing at the problem presented by the tree lines. He motioned the men to stay quiet. The glen seemed to stare back at them.

"It's easy to see Caledonii everywhere up here," said the optio. The next question surprised him.

"What do you think?" Paterculus flicked a glance at the trees.

The tribune was asking for advice. Glaccus' instructions came straight to him, *'he will need you, so be ready.'*

He scanned the woods on both sides and breathed out.

"I say we can try it sir," he said at last, "any slight movement and we pull back. We have the height advantage here."

"Good," Paterculus agreed.

"What would the Ninth have been doing up here though?" he asked, "I mean sir, is it likely they would have come this way over that moor, with the waggons and equipment I mean?"

Paterculus did not answer. What few maps that were available from the navy suggested deep cuttings inland from the sea on this side of the country. Off to the right-hand side of the glen were steep cliffs. High up on the left were a series of smaller entrances that could only be other smaller valleys feeding into the main one. Each one was a stiff looking climb up from the floor of the main glen. They had an ominous presence as they loured down upon the small patrol. Whatever was up there oversaw everything and everyone below. Perfect defensive positions. Yards from where he stood two black mountain streams united into a brutal torrent that plunged down a short rock face, spewing foam and smashing its way into the glen. In the distance he saw it winding off until a bend in the valley cloaked it. He turned to the optio.

"Is it likely they came this way with the waggons and equipment, no, I don't think so. At least not voluntarily, if you follow me. Send scouts to those valleys up there. I want to know what's in them before we go further into this," he said.

"Sir," the optio replied.

He pointed to Velio and Marcus and gestured to the glen furthest into the valley.

"You two, take that one."

Velio and Marcus looked at each other.

"That one? There'll be nothing up there but goats and deer," Marcus replied.

"Well, get up there and find out if they're friendly," the optio pushed back.

"You'd never get a legion up there, what's the point sir?" Marcus persisted.

Velio saw real rebellion for the first time in Marcus' face. The optio moved closer and lowered his voice so that neither the tribune nor the troopers around them could hear.

"I want you two to get up there and find out. I don't want some trooper more worried about his horse going up there. We're looking for signs of the legion. Go, have a quick look, and come back. Don't argue. Got it?"

Velio pulled Marcus' arm, "he's got it sir," he said.

"Right, then get to it," the optio looked at both of them, tapping the rank discs on their armour.

The threat did not need explaining. Surrendering their mounts, they set off.

Velio glanced at his friend, "what are you thinking? I thought you were going to refuse an order. Are you mad?"

"He's given the horse-boys the easy ones and us the hardest one. Bastard," Marcus hissed.

He began scaling down the side of the waterfall. Before them was thigh high, tough, heathery ground. Behind them they could hear other nominated scouting parties followed their lead while the rest were dismounting to rest the horses. Skirting their way past the trees they found the nascent river blocking their path. The mouth of the hanging valley was gaping high above them but there was a discernible path up through dense bushes and small trees. They looked at each other before wading across the icy river. For forty minutes they stumbled up past boulders, rockfalls, trees and bushes. Their only comfort a stream rushing past with enough noise to mask their climb. A hundred Caledonii warriors might be within spear's throw and they would have no means of knowing until it was too late. They pressed on, praying to Mars, Fortuna, Jupiter and all.

*

Velio stood at the top of the rise, breathing hard. Marcus was a few yards behind him. Stepping forward he could see he was in the narrow funnel of a narrow corrie that opened out in front of him. It had no exit. A steep and forbidding head-wall faced him several hundred yards away. On all sides the place was steep and rocky with purpling heather growing in impossible cracks. Yet the canyon floor was lush and green in parts. He stepped further in and felt something against his boot. Not a stone. Not a plant. Something else. Ravens started rising up in the high blue air above the valley walls and they broke the silence of a wilderness he felt was closing in. He had never hated the sound of ravens so much in his life. Reaching down with his hand he searched for the object by his feet, fingers seeking through the damp grass while he kept his other hand on his sword hilt and scanned the glen for threats. It was very quiet. The ravens had gone. There was not even the startled jump of a deer. The glen was empty and silent.

He touched it, ran his fingertips along it, understood what it was, and then picked it up and looked down at it. Once, it had been a centurion's helmet. A thing of polished pride and red feathered splendour; reward for a lifetime of service to the Empire, and a generous measure of courage and ability. Velio looked for a moment and held it out sideways for Marcus to see. A cold nervous shiver made him wriggle his shoulders under his armour. They were a long way from the wall.

"If that is what I think it is, then I think we are in big trouble," Marcus opined.

He took it in his hands and tossed it a few inches in the air like a ball and caught it in his cupped hands. Tossing it back to Velio he looked at him and said nothing more.

"What do you think?" said Velio.

"Could just be one lost soldier, poor sod," his voice was a different tenor from any sound Velio recognised.

"Just one, d'you think?"

"May be."

Velio bit his lip looking around for anything that might help. The nearest troops were down through the steep ravine. Across a river and commanded by an arse of a tribune.

Pointing into the valley he said, "let's go in a bit further. One helmet means nothing."

"What do you want? Piles of bones? Swords, look around you. The grass looks green to me. Well manured, if you get my drift," Marcus' eyebrows rose in alarm.

"Marcus, it could be some unlucky soldier from the earlier campaigns or a whole patrol. There are probably dozens of helmets lost in every battle or campaign. This is just a helmet. There's no head or anything. It could be some barbarian trophy from Agricola's time for all we know. Look at it. It's rusted to bits. Just a bit further. Let's be sure. Look, that bastard optio sent us to get proof, well let's ram it down his throat," he snarled.

Marcus shrugged and pulled his gladius from the scabbard.

"Windy, Marcus?"

"Don't speak to me unless you find the head that belongs to that," he replied, pointing at the helmet.

Velio grinned back. But Marcus was right about the grass. For such a high rocky valley the grass was quite lush. They split up and explored opposite edges of the valley, stumbling on the rocky scree and keeping away from the open centre ground. They met at the far end.

"Nothing?"

"Nothing."

"Well, that's it. Back out the way we came in and we'll call it one lost helmet. It could have come from anywhere. No weapons, no bones, sod all else. The optio can make of that whatever he likes. Agreed?" he summed up.

Marcus nodded and struck out towards the entrance at a steady pace determined to get out of here as soon as he could: Velio followed. The valley floor was a strange mix of rock and thick grass. He stopped at a thick patch, dug his sword back into its scabbard and started pulling away at the grass on impulse, ripping it from the ground in tussocks that surrendered with little fight. The white ribcages of several men lay revealed at his fingertips. He swallowed and pulled more grass aside. Bones, big bones. Arms, legs; a rusting strip of loin guard armour. This was a distinct hump in the ground. He had not noticed the contour as he followed Marcus out, but now when he looked at it more, he realised it was a small, but raised, mound of grass.

"Marcus," he said, trying to keep calm, "come and look at this."

Marcus already had the jitters. The more he looked the more it became clear the middle ground of the small corrie was the only grassed part of it, like low green waves in a sea of brown and pinkish stone. Marcus took several steps back towards him. He beckoned him to come closer. Marcus came further.

"Well?" he said.

"Sons of Dis Pater, Velio," Marcus spat.

He scanned the scene, his face changing, "so that settles it. The only question now is how many are in here?"

"Well, it's not the Ninth. Can't be. Far too small an area."

"A patrol? Cavalry scouts?"

"Most like."

"Up that path?" Marcus wondered.

"Perhaps they came here willingly," he replied, "defensive position, narrow entrance."

"A fight to the finish you mean? Up here, doesn't make any sense. Wasn't much of a defensive position!" Marcus snorted.

"It could have been and you're right, it doesn't make much sense."

A sound came echoing off the valley walls, making them freeze.

"Was that a voice?" he asked.

"I can't see anyone," Marcus paused, assessing whether his ears were playing tricks.

High overheard, somewhere out of sight, the ravens that had greeted their arrival started their foul cawing once more. Marcus lifted his head to listen and looked back on the pale bare bones Velio had uncovered. That was enough.

"Run Swords. Run for your life, forget what we have found. For mother's sake let's get home," cried Marcus.

So they ran.

*

Paterculus turned in the saddle to face the optio.

"Where is our sly young Ulysses? Why have he and Achilles not returned?"

The optio had enough insight to see the tribune had a grudge. The story of the scar on his arm had got around. Swords had been reluctant to talk about it, but little by little the lads had wheedled it out of him. In the deep green of the glen there was movement. He saw it first.

"Could be trouble sir. Helmets on," he ordered without waiting for permission to give the order.

There was not a word from the men as they readied themselves. Paterculus gazed down on a group of tribesmen men rushing towards his tiny command, grateful the ascent up toward the position he had taken was long and rough. If they attacked the patrol they would be winded by the charge. Pinneius and the other scouts had not reported back. Without any archer support, he had at best guess five more minutes before he would have to mount and take the men back out of the glen. Dying here was not an option. Even four archers might have been enough to hold them off.

"Blow the recall," he ordered, "and pray they hear it,"

The optio shouted the command as soon as he heard it. The military bugle split the air and echoed off the cliffs.

"Defensive line, he shouted.

"No, there are too many," Paterculus countermanded, "give the order to mount. Who are they? What tribe?"

"Veniconii, bad bastards, the whole blue painted lot."

Paterculus swivelled his tall frame in his saddle and looked hard at the thin faced soldier who had answered him.

"Are you sure, we need the intelligence."

"Veniconii sir, I'm certain," the man replied.

"Your men had best be quick optio, they mean business I fear."

Paterculus swung around to monitor the situation unfolding before him, calculating the triangular distances between his men and the enemy and the scouting parties.

"Optio, we're not going to try and make a stand here. And we're not going down into the glen to pull them out. As soon as they get themselves out, we ride. Once we get to the moor, we should be clear. Have the men show themselves in a line. We may be able to make them think twice. Keep that bugle going. We must get them to think there are more of us than they can see."

"Immediately sir," the optio agreed.

Up in the high valley Velio and Marcus tumbled down the side of the stream. Bushes and trees scraped them. Rocks bruised them. But fear of invisible barbarians at their back propelled them down to the valley below. Once they got over the river they stopped and looked back. There was no one behind them. A funk? A fear of the head and the heart. They drank some water and grinned.

The bugle call changed everything. They stared at each other. From out of nowhere an arrow took Marcus in the throat. He grunted and fell face first into the river. His armour pulled him under the surface. Velio rushed to grab him and rolled him over onto his back. Marcus looked up at him blinking like a hooked fish. His eyes flashed in pain and surprise. His lips moved as he tried to speak but blood was pulsing out of his wound. The arrow point had nearly gone all the way through his neck. His fingers gripped Velio's arm in a desperate vice.

"Hold on Marcus," Velio cried.

But Marcus' brown eyes faded, his hand fell away, and he was gone.

Velio swallowed, "Marcus No. Not this way brother. No. Please, Mars and Jupiter, No. Aw no, Marcus."

It was useless. Marcus was gone, in front of his eyes. He let him go and the clutching current took his friend. Velio looked on in horror then grabbing the helmet that had cost Marcus his life ran to the sound of the bugle. Ahead he saw four cavalrymen making their way back to the horses. They were several hundred yards in front. And then he saw the danger; they were closing in to block his escape. He floundered in the tussocky thick grass and heather. It was like trying to sprint on deep sand.

"Mars and Jupiter, thou Best and Greatest, help me and I will give you heathen blood in a bucket, hear me gods, I swear to you," he shouted.

He pulled his gladius and ploughed on, heart pumping, lungs screaming for him to stop. There were perhaps forty of the barbarians strung out in a ragged arc. He was not far from the short rock face of the incoming river.

"Move tesserarius!" he could hear the optio shouting.

Then the calls of the auxiliary. He was close, very close. He could hear the water gushing down the rock.

"Swords, look out," came a call.

He turned around in spite of all his better instincts. To stop and fight here was the end. He could see why the tribune had not brought the patrol further into the glen. It was a fiend's trap. The four other scouts were ascending the water drop. He was the last man, the defender of the gate. There were three Veniconii warriors, younger and fitter than the rest, hungrier for fame and praise poems. They were almost upon him. He doubted they were more than fifteen or sixteen years old but the hatred on their faces was palpable.

Each one was taller and leaner than he was. Lives of perpetual struggle in a hard land were reflected in the blue painted intricacies on their faces and arms. They wore thick woollen trousers, leather jerkins, wide belts and were armed with wicker shields, short spears, long swords and helmets. Their faces were undecorated by much hair; they were the sons of wealthy men or perhaps a chieftain. In the thrill of the hunt they preferred using their spears to stick him like a wolf or a bear.

He squared up, got a steady stance on the uneven ground. The first one came on too quick, much too quick. Velio cut him down on the second stroke. The boy fell, surprised at the pain. His eyes met Velio's and registered the unknown, the indefinite, and perhaps a forlorn desire to start his attack afresh. The second one he could not remember. Face, fight nor conquest; his mind thereafter held nothing of him. The third he caught with a sideways head blow of the old centurion's helmet to knock him off balance. It was rusted but still solid enough to deliver a shock. After that it was simple. He slaughtered in a blurred frenzy of strokes.

They fell, sliding off his sword, victims to the blade of the Ninth. The old helmet in one hand and the gladius in the other. It was a strange thing to fight the last battle of a lost legion. But of everything in that evil day, beyond the death of his best friend Marcus Hirtius, he never forgot the yell of incarnate rage from their oncoming relatives and brethren.

Turning, he sprinted to the rock face and fought his way up, ignoring the biting coldness of the water that gushed over him. The patrol cheering him as he got to the top. The tribune sat on his horse and looked at him. There was a moment that passed unsaid. Velio thrust the rusted helmet up to him. The tribune stiffened in his saddle, his eyes widening into something like the joy of victory.

"Absolutely not a word of this to anyone here or at the fort, do you understand tesserarius? If anyone asks, deny everything."

"Sir," he said turning around to see the oncoming torrent of warriors.

"Shit," he muttered.

"I don't think that quite does it justice, tesserarius," Paterculus replied with dry laconic calm.

It was the first charismatic thing anyone had heard him say.

"Where's Hirtius?" demanded the optio.

He shook his head, "he's not coming sir," he said.

The optio nodded to the cavalry decurion to lead the retiral.

"Move out at the gallop," he ordered and they turned and galloped for safety.

A mile or two on they slowed to rest the horses. Behind them the savages were still following but could only catch up if the patrol halted to rest or sleep. Paterculus frowned as he reworked the distances in his head and the odds of interception.

"Back to Pinnata Castra sir?" suggested the optio.

"Let's see if they still follow once we've crossed the moors," he decided, "if they keep coming, we'll have to push on through the hills again. But Pinnata Castra is a long ride from here."

He spurred them on in a fast trot. Velio took the rear guard with the two cavalrymen charged with leading the tribune and optio's spare mounts. After an hour the far edges of the wet moorland fell behind them and dryer ground beckoned. Velio and the two cavalrymen dropped back to keep the enemy in sight. Paterculus halted and waited for them to close up.

"Report," he said.

"They have halted," Velio said.

"Are you certain?"

Paterculus sounded like a dominus schoolmaster.

"I am certain," replied the eldest cavalryman with the merest hint of annoyance that the integrity of such a simple report could tested by anyone who had not witnessed what they had seen. Velio waited.

"Good. Optio, lead the men on to the passes we came by. I want more distance between us by nightfall."

Chapter 7.

Aulercas and Pasnactus, Veniconi warriors, picked up a strange horse trail west of the old road. Without a word they began following it. They caught up towards evening, alerted by two very small camp fires and settled down to observe from a grassy ridge two hundred yards away. Their quarry was keeping very quiet. No shouting, singing or drinking. They made no rampart and didn't bother with a ditch. Before the fires burned too low to see more the Veniconi caught the tell-tale glint of grey mail. The horses were tethered close at hand.

"They're trying to pass through unnoticed," Pasnactus said, "it's not like them."

"We should take them," Aulercas said.

"Both of us or just you?" grinned Pasnactus in the dark.

The next morning they woke before dawn and waited. The horsemen began heading west at a steady walking pace. Aulercas smiled and they followed at a judicious distance, waiting at times until the horses were out of sight before moving from cover and running to catch up. At times the horsemen halted and sent out scouts. Then regrouping they pushed further into the hills and passes. At midday the two of them rested and ate what they carried while they waited. The horsemen mounted up and moved again. They were heading towards the great moor and its marshes. Beyond that barrier were the unconquered tribes of the north.

"Now why are they riding that way? There are no forts. They move quietly. Has someone told them something? Are they looking for something?" Pasnactus breathed.

"They might veer off and head south again. Perhaps they are breaking in new horses," Aulercas said.

"Yes, that could be it. A few days riding to test them out," Pasnactus replied.

"Or is it more than that?" quizzed Aulercas.

Pasnactus shook his head dismissing the idea. Aulercas sat on the grass to think, stabbing his knife into the earth repeatedly. His brother-in-law sat beside him.

"What do you wish to do?" he asked, letting Aulercas decide.

Aulercas made a quick decision.

"Once we are certain where they are heading, we must get around them and raise the word. We can trap them and kill them if we get help. There are good horses to be had."

Pasnactus smiled, "then all we have to do is get around them."

"We follow until the sun dies then we pass in the shadows," Aulercas decided.

That night they circled around the Roman campfires and jogged on to the villages of the western Veniconi, cousins and second cousins of Pasnactus' own family. Duald was their chief.

They arrived exhausted and wet in a bright moon light, through a veil of trees, at timbered gates. In the light of a burning torch Aulercas could see an ancient Roman helmet with the rags of an animal skin pinned to a post. He wondered for a moment if the head was still inside. It was too dark to be sure. A ring of men surrounded them before Pasnactus was recognised. They were ushered inside Duald's hall. He came down from the heights of his sleeping platform, beaming his welcome. Aulercas fretted through the courtesies, imagining the horsemen coming. It all ended with a firm "tomorrow," from Duald who retired back to his bed. Pasnactus and Aulercas bedded down by the fire to dry off.

In the morning the noise of the blacksmith's hammer beating out his greeting to the new day woke them. Duald's servants, his wife and daughters sat waiting for them to waken. There was laughter as the two men woke to an audience. After all, Aulercas was not yet spoken for. Duald, their host, came striding to over them, clapping them to his chest in his great bear's hug. He pinched Aulercas cheek, grinned at him and asked the question his eldest daughter wanted to ask; had he slept well?

"So we go to war," he said without waiting further, "your father sends you to get the hard hill men to come south and gut a few 'wolf soldiers' with you? I keep one at my door for company," he laughed, "he carried a standard in my grandfather's time. He wore the wolfskin on his shoulders. You can still see the remains of it. Now he greets my visitors and frightens children."

They smiled. Duald had told them this many times before, leaving Aulercas wondering not for the first time why their generals and leaders did not wear the fur into battle. It was confusing.

They sat down together and were eating when the blacksmith ceased pounding outside and came in. He had a shining sword in his arms. He knelt and presented it to his master.

"It is blessed by the blood of a buck, so it will be fleet and fastmoving in your hand, light and nimble in the killing of your enemies," he said.

"You washed it in fresh blood?"

"The deer died this rise of the sun. I took its heart for the power. The body cannot be touched further. It must not be eaten."

"We go now to hunt men," Duald said taking the blade in his hands, "and when we return victorious, I will sing a lament for my old sword, the one my father left me and his father to him. The sword I will not use again."

"This sword is special, I believe the buck died well for you. All its strength and energy is in the blade. You will not be beaten as long as you carry it," the blacksmith vowed.

Aulercas glanced at Pasnactus whose eyes were tight shut in a dreamy expression of prayer. His lips were moving as he spoke words in his head.

"Eating is over, there will be no more eating this morning. Whatever is in your bellies is what you have to fight on. We go now. Aulercas, Pasnactus lead us to your enemies."

The chief gestured to the smith, "bring your sword and you can enjoy the hunt with me."

He raised the new sword and shouted out, "look what he has made for me. Is it not beautiful?"

Within twenty minutes they were moving on horse and on foot for the last place Aulercas had seen the Roman patrol. He rode at Duald's side while Pasnactus rode further back amid his cousins. Behind him strode fifty or more warriors. They headed for Duald's traditional ambush point.

Chapter 8.

When Pasnactus saw the Romans, they were on foot, walking their horses around a bend in the valley; the best one by far to mount an ambush on men escaping off the open moors back into the high country. Waiting for a moment, he let the full number of them come into sight. Not many, certainly not as many as Duald's men. They looked tired but alert. He suspected they were eager to find a safe spot to halt. The question was would they halt and sleep, or halt, eat and keep moving on? Darkness was coming soon. He stood up from behind the cover of the grey mossy rock, turning back to Duald's concealed position and crying out for permission. Duald rose in reply and answered his cry. The Veniconii of Duald's household stormed out of the rocky hillsides and rose up from the low folds in the ground.

As a campaign soldier, the optio was beginning to think about the luxury of a small cooking fire and hot food. The tribune was walking ahead with his face lowered in thought. He suspected it had been the tribune's first independent command and the young man was beginning to tire. He was thinking that he should offer an ear to keep the younger man's spirits up when Veniconii sprang up from out of nowhere. The silent glen erupted as the attack came at them. One look told him they were outnumbered. He stopped, horrified at his own laxness, the way he had led them into this trap. He should have expected this.

"Mount up and ride," he cried taking the decision away from the tribune.

No time for politeness now. Arrows came fleeting into the column like low flying birds, grey in the cooling air. Troopers and horses were being hit. Animals rearing. The crash of armour hitting stony soil. Others were mounting and moving. Shields were going up.

"Don't stand here. Ride," he ordered.

He turned to the tribune, "sir are you hit?"

Paterculus stared up at him in astonishment and then something in his eyes changed. The spirits of his republican forefathers, the shades of men who had fought and commanded for Scipio took over.

"Lead on optio, find us a way through this. We must not be stopped or turned. Pinnata Castra lies to the east. I will bring on the rest. Find a way for us. Optio, do not stop to look. Take the men and ride for a safe place. I'll meet you there when I can."

The optio put his arm out and shook the tribune's arm.

"Sir," he acknowledged, "Pinneius, bring up the rear," he barked, "ride men, we do not stand here. Follow me."

He glanced back at the tribune, "I am leaving Pinneius with you, you won't find a better man."

*

Aulercas joined the attack, howling his war cry as the Romans took to their horses. Their wounded companions were being abandoned without compunction. Men were rising into saddles while men on the ground shouted to be saved, horses bucking and snorting. What had been an ordered walk of mounts into the valley was now every man for himself. Duald had caught them off guard.

He felt nothing for them. The stories were true. For all their metal armour, the banners and the trumpets, the 'sons of the wolf' were cowards at heart. Brave in their massed ranks and behind their entrenchments but cowards when caught out in the open in small numbers. And in this little winding glen twenty of them were going to die to please Duald, and his own father.

He charged into the complex mass of men. Men pulling at men trying to mount frightened horses. Arrows flying, too little space for wild sword sweeps but dirks and short blades flashing. Shields smacked into faces obliterating features, sending teeth to the ground. Grunts and gasps of pain, inward sucks of air.

Pasnactus was beheading a soldier he had dragged onto the ground, helmet and all, he stood up and waved it in triumph. It was a short-lived triumph. A Roman horseman lopped Pasnactus' head off his shoulders and charged away. He halted in horror.

Pasnactus fell in two pieces. His head hit the ground before his body toppled over. Pasnactus' face lay away from him so he could not see if his brother in law's eyes were open. He stood transfixed while the skirmish carried on around him. Hearing it as if he had fallen underwater and the sounds had become distorted. It only went quiet when Duald's men ran out of Romans to kill, the survivors' horses' hooves drumming on the grass as they went barrelling out of danger. Echoing off the close sided walls of the glen, the hooves beating a rhythm that faded. Then the Romans were gone and the glen was silent. He could hear elated voices as bodies were stripped of the prized grey chain armour. Swords were traded while their owners were still warm on the ground. It sounded as if only a few of Duald's warriors had fallen, the arrows had done their work. Then they started taking Roman heads as trophies.

Aulercas wanted to savour his first real clash with the 'sons of the wolf.' His eyes never left the two pieces of Pasnactus. His sister's husband should have been part of the celebrations. The man who made Pasnactus a corpse had stolen that joy. In all the utter confusion a sound that might have been a name or a war cry bounced around in his head "Pinnaaayus."

The one who had killed Pasnactus.

*

It began raining a thin drizzle that would not cease. Paterculus let the optio choose the night halt to regather and count the losses. No one who failed to get into his saddle had survived. The patrol was reduced to himself, the optio, the tesserarius and nine others with four spare horses that followed the herd to escape. Those four animals were carrying rations for dead men and some spare weapons. Three of the men were carrying light wounds; only three, a blessing of sorts. Those arrows had done the damage.

Whilst the auxiliaries secured the animals, the optio sat with Paterculus. Fires were impossible in this weather, and it was growing colder. They were cold and uncomfortable, but they were alive. Velio lay in his cloak under a dripping tree and waited for morning.

Dawn came in reluctant steps through the dull sheets of rain. The horses stood, heads hanging low, looking every bit as miserable as the men felt. Titus Rebilis stood up and rubbed his arms for warmth, gazing around the group. Not for the first time he felt the chill of wet armour. If he didn't get it dried off it would start to yield to the ever-present gods of rust. What a miserable fucking country this was, cursed by the gods and scorned by the sun. If this carried on, they would need the navy to rescue them. The tribune was already awake and tending his horse. He beckoned him to come over.

"Titus, we must get moving. I think we have only three days to get to Pinnata Castra and down to the river crossing where Glaccus will meet us."

Titus nodded, "tribune," he acknowledged the order.

"Pinneius fought well yesterday, didn't he?" Paterculus said as the optio turned away.

Titus was surprised at the sudden change of heart. Perhaps a single brush with the enemy had put comradeship in perspective. Or perhaps he was not himself this morning.

"And he found a helmet sir. Perhaps he has proved you right? Are right," he corrected himself, "just a pity about Marcus Hirtius. He was a good man."

"Who?" Paterculus asked.

"The other tesserarius instructor, the one who went with Pinneius up to that valley."

"Oh, yes. Well, I've lost more than Marcus Hirtius haven't I?" Paterculus admitted.

Titus shrugged, "it can't be helped."

"Those tribesmen. Do you think they planned the trap?" Paterculus said.

Titus frowned and eased the chafing of his helmet chinstrap with a finger and looked around the camp for a moment. Their conversation had woken the last of the sleeping men. The trees they were hiding in streamed with water. The branches dripping like small rivers. The men stamped and swore, wringing out their sodden heavy cloaks. Without fires for warmth, it was a miserable place, but no one was complaining. Underneath it all he could feel the mens' unrepentant aggression. No one liked being chased out of a fight.

"I don't know sir. It was unlucky that we took that path off the moors and rode smack into the second lot. How could they know it would be that path?" he replied.

"Coincidence then that they were armed and ready?" Paterculus replied.

Titus looked at him, "they were too far apart to coordinate their attacks," he reasoned.

"A signal between them then?" Paterculus said, thinking ahead to the report he was going to have to make.

He nodded, "that would be my guess, tribune. That, and the fact this is their land. They know it better than us. From that glen and across the moor, our road might have been the obvious one to lay a snare."

Titus paused and chose his next words with care.

"Leaving those men behind sir. It was necessary. It's never a nice thing to do but obeying the emperor's commands means we sometimes have to serve the greater need."

Paterculus nodded and smiled. He was looking very pale. It was the sort of thing he should be saying to console the optio, not the other way round. Somehow things had become undone and the shades of the Ninth legion were probably laughing at him.

"Let's get moving before we drown here," he said.

Heading home was faster now that they had news to carry. The tribune held them at Pinnata Castra for a few hours to shelter from the rain. Safe only in the thought that the Caledonii would find the rain as difficult on foot as they were finding on horseback. The ground smelled sweet and earthy. Rich with the intoxicating zing of pine. The river curled around the low plateau of the old fort and grew noisier as it filled with waters from the mountains. The plain was beginning to flood, cutting off their escape routes to the south.

Paterculus took stock of his men. The surviving auxiliary cavalry were a tough bunch from the low country in northeast Gaul. Most, if not all of them, were under thirty years of age. They were fit and strong, but the water level was making them edgy. They sat watching the waters rising. Getting the horses across the river was now an impossibility. It had probably been impossible several hours before they had arrived. The current was too swift. To get south to the Bodotria crossing, the tribune would have to lead them down the western bank and look for a favourable spot.

Velio sat and listened while they talked it through. They were ready to move and by a unspoken consensus sent glances to him. He knew they wanted him to talk to the optio and get the order to saddle up. He did not much care for the rising water himself. He had Marcus' last moments in his head. Part of him wanted to stand right here and fight Caledonii until this river choked with their blood. Then, once he had killed them all, he would consider withdrawal to the Bodotria crossing. The other part, the professional part, knew he had to help the optio get them all back without any more losses. He chewed his damp ration bread and nodded back at the nine troopers nominally under his command. Titus approached and sat down beside him.

"Water's rising sir, we should move soon sir, or we'll be caught here with nowhere to go. We can't defend this," he stated and waved his hand at the old fort ditch.

"This side of the Tavae is not the road we came on. It'll be a fine game dodging our way south," Titus replied with a short smile, "I'll speak to the tribune."

"Well, the men are getting impatient and while they follow orders, I think on this occasion they have a point," he pushed.

Titus got up, "staying here serves no purpose. If we thought we were travelling unnoticed, yesterday taught us otherwise."

He found the tribune to be of the same mind. Paterculus appeared to know what his optio was about to suggest,

"Get them mounted Titus, we're moving out," he ordered.

It was a slog south through a wet landscape. The horses had a hard time of it picking their way up and down an endless number of long slopes that barred their retreat, skirting the worst of the forested ground for sake of a clean line of sight. On the morning of the tenth day, on time and to plan, a fact that made Titus shake his head and snort after what had occurred, the Bodotria was in front of them. Paterculus hedged his tired command eastwards hoping to find the bridge where they had parted from Glaccus and his maniple. It took most of the day but at last he found it again. He dismounted to wait.

Glaccus did not come, and he had left no sign. Slow evening came creeping like ink from the west.

"We camp here and head back tomorrow," he ordered.

"Perhaps we should move closer tonight while there is still some light sir?" Titus suggested.

"I want us to keep to the plan. Centurion Glaccus will cover our return," he answered.

"It's too late now sir, the tribes will know we had a fight. Where we went," Titus continued.

Paterculus folded his arms and breathed down onto his armour. Titus could not see what secret there was to be kept now. They had been spotted and as a covert patrol it had been a failure. The chances of it ever succeeding unnoticed were now, in hindsight, laughable.

"Anything short of a major battle will be of no interest to the northern tribes. The Veniconii? They may have a small victory to sing of, but no other tribe will care. They'll go rushing off to boast about killing a handful of us. Get fires lit, send out a couple of men to the river while there is still some light. Bound to be shellfish in it, if not something better. Some hot food is what we need optio. If centurion Glaccus does not reach us by noon tomorrow we will take our chances and head back alone. There's not much more the Veniconii can do to us down here."

*

The banners of Glaccus hove into view in the next morning. Delayed by the rain and atrocious ground conditions he too had halted to take shelter. Velio noticed the misery was not confined to their own small patrol. He had never seen, or been part of, a more mud splattered set of soldiers and horses. Paterculus saw the standards coming and thanked his gods. Glaccus pulled his horse to a halt and looked at the remnants returning with the tribune.

"It did not go well then?" he said.

Paterculus shook his head, "there might be news worth hearing, but it's cost me some men. As you can see."

Glaccus saluted. Velio led the nine auxiliaries to the rear of the column past rows of curious looks while Titus and Paterculus rode up front with Glaccus. It was then when he was surrounded by the living that the loss of Marcus began to hurt.

Chapter 9.

Aulercas returned to his father with a heavy heart. He took the news of his daughter's husband's death with a disbelieving shake of his shaggy head. The next day they set out for the nearest Votadini stronghold with their unhappy news.

The 'sons of the wolf' have found the graves in the high valley. They will not rest now. The tribes must join up and arm.'

*

Ferrdigon's hospitality was, by reputation, ferocious and several happy days passed before they were joined by emissaries from the Dumnoni who had also been alerted to the Roman patrol's journey. The news was causing a hubbub in the great circle of warriors, counsellors, druids and chiefs assembled in the hall. The light was fading outside when he called them to order. It was hot. He always kept a good fire burning and the crush of Votadini and their guests made it airless and stifling.

"Aulercas, begin and tell us the news. Duald is not here," he called out.

Aulercas got a push to stand from his father. This was his first time addressing an assembly of other tribes. He was more used to speaking to his father's warriors. Ferrdigon smiled to encourage him and lifted his hand for silence.

He began relating Duald's ambush of the patrol and Pasnactus' death. His voice faltering until his father nudged his knee. He regathered as murmurs of condolence for the loss of Pasnactus rippled around the hall. When he was finished with nothing more to say he sat down. Then it really started.

Asuvad waited and listened. The wall between the rivers was reaching a critical point. The easy flat land in the east had been ditched and walled and it was the difficult rock ledges in the centre ground that were eating up the Romans' efforts. They had committed a lot of men. An attack now, from both north and south would be like a stab in the loins. Made with enough conviction it might just persuade them to pull back. A major defeat of an entire legion could tip the balance and make Rome retreat back to Gaul. Or at the very least back to their stone wall for good. A big defeat might bring the Brigantes back into revolt too. Was it possible this earthen wall could actually provide the means to end the occupation? An attack from the unguarded south would be the surprise. That was where the damage could be done. But if it failed, the Votadini would be left below the wall while the Veniconi and Dumnoni would be above it. The Votadini would either be slaughtered in reprisal or made slaves and their sons shipped off to serve in the legions of Gaul or Germania.

Ferrdigon was listening too. The talk was edging to the inevitable call for war. That war could mean glory for his warriors, or it could mean enslavement for his people. In old Gaul, Vercingetorix had led a great revolt. His story was well known. He had been the mightiest of chieftains but even he had been defeated and hauled off to Rome. As for his people; pity the tribes of Gaul.

He slumped dejected as the parleying continued. Late in the night he called the meeting to adjourn. Aulercas' father agreed and that was enough to settle it. Aulercas felt Asuvad's eyes on him. The Dumnoni nodded as he left and went with his own people to sleep in another hall. Ferrdigon hoped sleep would bring him wisdom from the ancestors, but he sent his druid off to the high summit to speak to them. The hall emptied leaving him alone by his fire with Aulercas and his father. He put his hand on the young man's shoulder.

"It sounds like your brother-in-law died well. Fighting Romans. We will try to avenge him and bring a little comfort to his widow. We will speak more tomorrow."

It was a lie he felt compelled to utter. The Veniconii and the Dumnonii brought these things on themselves.

He lay down beside his wife. She was turned away from him, her shoulders a mound in the blanket skins, rejecting any advances. She was angry no doubt because he had sent her lover to the hilltop to seek guidance. It would be cold up there, he hoped it would be cold. She did not know he had found out about Vusiavi and it amused him to watch her wrestle her words when he mentioned the priest's name, or brought him to the hall to talk. She thought he was an old fool. Vusiavi disappointed him. He had trusted him and given him status within the village. He had a fine horse from Ferrdigon's small stable. At least he had the consolation of knowing where his enemies slept; some of them.

Did the whole village know? Did he need to act and punish his own priest? He drifted off to sleep thinking about Aulercas' emotional recounting of Pasnactus' death.

Down below their sleeping platform, the hall-fire crackled in its embers and settled down for the night in its own way. The hall grew dark and quiet. Eilaver lay still for a while waiting for the drink to take him off to sleep. Around her neck on a leather thong, resting in a leather sheath between her breasts was an iron hair pin with a needle-sharp point. Easing herself around to face Ferrdigon, she blew into his face. He twitched and muttered and remained comatose. Easing the iron stiletto from its leather holster she cupped the small round haft in the palm of her hand, placing the point a fraction above his skin, over his heart, breathed out and pushed from her shoulder through her elbow. He stiffened. His body tightened around the needle. She felt the living tremors of his muscles shivering through the metal. His life flickered like lightning down the metal pin. His eyes wanted to open but they could not. He gasped once without a fuss or a struggle. She waited for him to breathe in. He did not breathe again. She pulled out the weapon and put the point of her forefinger against the tiny wound, preparing herself to hold it there all night; praying the exit wound would be so small it would pass inspection. There must be no blood; it must be as though the gods had taken him. Her son was now chief, and he wanted war as much as she did.

Chapter 10.

<u>Velunia fort on the wall, Servius Albinius' headquarters.</u>

Servius looked at the battered rusty ruin of what had once been a glorious centurion helmet. He got to the point.

"Jupiter's balls, where in the name of all that's holy did you find that?"

The sheer impossibility of it was incomprehensible to him. Then his cold logic took hold.

"But the real question is, have you found a soldier or a patrol? And what has it to do with your search for our missing legion?"

He turned to his clerk.

"Epeius, check all regimental records you can find for reports of patrols that never returned. Get help if you require it from the tribune's clerks of Sixth and the Second. Be discreet, I want it done properly."

He picked the helmet up, turning it in his hands, rubbing off rust with the balls of his thumbs, taking pieces of corroded metal with it, levelling it so he could stare into the cavity and wonder what the missing man's name might have been. Had he heard of him? Had he been famous or just another anonymous servant of the emperor? Time had not been kind to the helmet, but all things considered it was not in too bad condition, he supposed. Broken, dented, feather crest gone along with the fittings, leather rotted away, one cheek flap missing, neck guard hanging off with signs of taking a heavy blow, the crown pitted with rust. What story could it tell?

"Was this the only one you found?" he enquired.

Paterculus returned his straight appraising gaze, trying to be calm and soldier-like.

"Pinneius found it with Marcus Hirtius. I did not go up to the high valley myself," Paterculus replied.

"Pinneius? So, it's one man's word as to the circumstances, as Hirtius unfortunately got himself killed I am told."

Paterculus nodded.

Servius blew out his cheeks and took a squint at the ceiling for a moment, shaking his head.

"And you're sure Pinneius has told no one and none of the men got a look at this?" he said.

Paterculus nodded, "I only brought half of them back so it does narrow the risk."

Servius chose to ignore the crassness of that remark, the auxiliary cavalry were not to be squandered and wasted. He kept weighing the helmet in his hands and wondering whether the helmet had failed the man or vice versa.

"The auxiliaries won't care because they won't understand the significance of it."

Paterculus pleased himself with his own logic.

Servius paused and sipped the cup of water on his desk, savouring the cool sweetness of it.

"They have good water here," he remarked.

Paterculus waited, feeling like a schoolboy. Servius put his cup down.

"As long as only you and I know a helmet has been found there is not a problem. But I do not want the rumour machine sending iron bolts through the camp. Does Titus Rebilis know about the helmet? Of course, he does. He must," he said, answering his own question.

"The optio is sworn to silence. He saw Pinneius give me the helmet," Paterculus replied.

Servius drew a deep breath.

"Rebilis is a good man, I'm sure we can rely on him. But proof of what this represents is the thing we need most. It is a pity you did not see the spot for yourself," he said, laying it on with a trowel.

"Do you want me to go back?"

Paterculus heard his own voice rise a note as he tried to mask the surging horror of riding back to that valley where there could be no pretence of a discreet reconnaissance a second time around. Servius waved his hand.

"Don't worry, if I send men back it will have to be a bigger expedition not an exploratory patrol. You led a small one and brought most of the men back. A stronger one will have to go now. If the tribes get a sniff of an idea that we are going back it could get a little bloody. But until I am told by Epeius that there is no record of a missing patrol I am going to do nothing. But if he tells me that it is the case, then someone needs to go back and determine if this was a lone and unlucky officer."

"And if it is not any of those?" Paterculus probed.

Servius pursed his lips, "it simply cannot be the Ninth legion, Cornelius. Be serious. You found them, forgive me Cornelius, you found them in a single, ten day, reconnaissance. Of all the glens and valleys up here, you picked the right one. Why are the Ninth not lying below Hadrian's wall for that matter? There's absolutely no reason why they should have been anywhere like as far north as here. It just seems too impossible to be true, that's all. Tell me, how many valleys did you search on your patrol?"

Paterculus blanched.

"We traversed through many but when I got to the head of the one where we found this, well, it felt so remote that I sent scouts to check the higher ground. I might have passed through it like the others. I know this will sound stupid Servius, the place had a strange feel about it. Eerie, you understand? Then while the scouts were out, we saw hostiles coming towards us, I ordered the recall and Pinneius brought that back. He had to fight his way out."

He halted feeling embarrassed.

'What a complete failure of command. He thinks I'm an idiot.'

Servius raised an eyebrow at the little outburst and waited.

"If Epeius' answer requires action, you will send how many men?" Paterculus said, re-focussing on the promise.

"We only have the word of admittedly a good tesserarius to rely on. I might authorise a full ala of cavalry to get something done quickly," Servius stated.

"Five hundred men," Paterculus repeated.

It did not seem enough.

"Five hundred men," Servius repeated.

"Best to be cavalry to escort the waggons," Paterculus agreed, thinking of the promise to retrieve bodies for prayer and funerary rites.

"There'll be no waggons. Forget what I said in front of the governor. If we can get to them, whether or not "they" are the Ninth, or just some unlucky men, we will burn what bones we can scrape together and sacrifice to Mars."

"But if it is the Ninth you have to do more Servius," Paterculus burst out.

Servius looked him straight between the eyes. His voice took a steelier tone.

"If it is the Ninth and you can vouch for that fact before Lollius Urbicus himself we will retrieve whatever we can. Otherwise, it will be an expedition simply so that we can close an old account. We will be able to say men were trapped and butchered in a hilltop valley or some such. They and the emperor deserve that much," he said in a tone that was not to be countered.

"Tribune, we might have to fight our way in and fight our way back out," Paterculus countered.

"What did old Caesar tell his generals, 'the die has been cast'? So be it Cornelius, you have chosen to pick up the dice and play. We however are honour bound to pay the debts that arise, quite possibly for the sake of a single helmet found in the wrong place."

"Will you tell the governor?"

"He probably already knows, perhaps not all the details but sufficient I imagine," Servius replied.

He took a grim satisfaction at Paterculus' startled expression and refusing to explain, carried on

"You should have thrown the helmet away," he paused, "do you believe in the gods Cornelius?"

"Of course."

"I think now would be a good time to go and pray to the one you think likes you the most."

Paterculus flushed and got to his feet, "as the emperor commands," he said tight and angry.

"As the emperor commands," Servius Albinius replied, "and one other thing. Do not mention what we have discovered in any correspondence you send. Not a word of it."

Once Paterculus left, Servius opened his 'private orders' chest. The stored scrolls filled it to the brim. He pulled out a fistful and raked down to the bottom for his copies of the monthly reports to Quintus Lollius Urbicus. The late spring report was the one he was seeking. He untied the ribbon closure and unrolled the top of the scroll. Across the formal greetings he used on all his correspondence to the governor, Urbicus had overwritten a note, coded enough to confuse any unauthorised reading.

'Facere, quid necesse Servius.' *'Servius do what you must.'*
and returned the report.

On a document providing a monthly update and logistics for the rate of build across the Bodotria/Clota isthmus it read like unnecessary approval to a senior tribune, or a bland anodyne encouragement to 'get on with it Servius.'

Only he and Quintus Lollius Urbicus knew the real message underlying the code. He gazed at the words then rerolled the scroll, burying it back in the depths of his correspondence chest. He regarded the wall of his office, the wooden 'horse' with his breastplate and helmet, the fire burning in its copper pan, his table, the table of Epeius, the document chest, the window that he hoped would be fitted with a glass plate before winter came again; and sighed.

Later that evening Paterculus settled down to write his first honest letter home since he had arrived in Britannia. A good stylus, bequeathed to him by his maternal grandfather, a scroll of decent paper not the usual army stuff, ink and a full goblet of Falernian; an unexpected gift from Servius. He was convinced Servius did not really like him and yet here was a flask from the tribune's own personal stock. The man was a conundrum. He eased his shoulders and wondered where to begin. The night attacks on the wall perhaps and then his first real command beyond the line?

*

Velio returned to the fort on the mid-section of the wall and was surprised by how much it had developed. A legionary pointed the way to the Fourth cohort's new barracks. The senior arms instructor was no longer living in a tent. The cohort instructors had been roomed together in the Fourth century's block. Velio trudged mud past the small rooms for each eight-man squad. The third last room before the optio and the centurion's private quarters was the century tesserarius' room and he threw down his kit on the one of the two unoccupied beds, his and the one that should have been for Marcus. It already had the comforting smell of home. He sat down on the bed and looked at the senior instructor sitting on the bunk at the wall.

"Well, how did it go, young Swords?"

He was tired and getting irritable. His slender diplomatic skills waved farewell as they left the room.

"Marcus is dead," he replied, "that's how well it went."

"What did you tell Tribune Servius?" his senior asked.

"That place where the helmet was is a death trap. If we go in they can bottle us up and also fire down on us from above," he replied, happy to get the secret off his chest to someone he could trust.

"A perfect killing place then?" his mentor said with a soft smile.

"A place where you could herd deer and take your time picking out the one with the best antlers," he replied.

"Is he sending us back?" the senior instructor queried.

"Us, I don't know about us, but I'm afraid because I found a helmet I'm going to get ordered back," he said, staring at the floor.

There was a forlorn eloquence the instructor found odd for such a grizzled young tearaway.

"And Marcus, I sent him to take care of you, Velio. And you, lost him. How is it the man I sent to watch you gets killed and you survive? Did you do something I need to know about Velio? Did he have to bail you out?"

The instructor leaned forwards. The accumulated pale scars on his arms flexed as the biceps beneath them tightened.

"I'm sorry. It was an arrow. We had no chance, Marcus never saw it coming and, it took him through the throat. I couldn't save him," he said.

"I know lad," the instructor replied.

"How can you know?" he said and looked up.

He felt confused and desolate.

"Because he would be here in the infirmary if you could have saved him."

*

Servius' next interrogation was the optio chosen by Glaccus, Titus Rebilis. He stood at attention for almost a minute waiting for the tribune to look up from his paperwork. He understood why, so he stood at the attention and looked at the patterns in the clay on the wall at the tribune's back. Servius put down his pen and closed the draft report for the governor. Men and horses lost; equipment lost, hostiles alerted or aggravated or both. Imminent attack on the building work was therefor a fair bet. But what of the young tribune? How had he fared out there in the 'dirty wet,' beyond Hades Arse? A sorrier looking tribune he had not seen. The men had grown a little taciturn but Pinneius had them in hand, that was clear. The optio and Pinneius had done enough to see it through. A consolation prize then.

"How are your wounded Rebilis, will they live?"

"All three have been seen by the medicus, stitched up and released, absent from duties until he removes the sutures. A week as normal sir."

"Have they been fed?"

"Yes sir."

"Have you been fed Rebilis?"

"Not yet sir."

"Well, sit down man, don't go falling over in my quarters for want of food. Epeius, bring me a plate of food for this man."

"Instantly sir."

Titus smiled his gratitude.

"Instantly, hear that Rebilis? My Greek clerk will bring food instantly. Beware the Greeks when they bring you food instantly. The man's got an unusual name don't you think?"

Titus sat down and looked his supreme commander straight in the eyes, and dared to not be taken for a fool.

"Epeius was the name of the man who built the wooden horse that was used to take the city of Troy, sir."

"Yes, it was. Indeed, it was. You know your history Rebilis because you are a good soldier. Soldiers understand history because we realise the importance of learning from it. History is the long story of mistakes made and what price was paid in blood to correct those mistakes. So, what did we learn during the last ten days out there Rebilis?"

"Begging your pardon sir, I don't think we made many mistakes on the patrol."

"Not all of my auxiliary rode home, so what did we learn?" he purred once more.

Titus took a swift look at the floor to gather his thoughts,

"We learned the Veniconii were remarkably quick to respond to our patrol. Too quick for it to have been anything other than a continual trailing of our men. They are deadly at close quarters, as always, if they get the chance to spring a trap but otherwise, I do not think they are to be feared when legionaries face them in rank and under orders," he reported.

Epeius set a broad platter of cold meat, bread, cheese and olives before them on the table with a jug of wine. Servius gestured to Titus to help himself. He waited as the optio chewed a hunk of venison.

"So, if I send you back as part of a bigger detachment, no words outside this room for the moment on this you hear, if I send you back, you would be confident of what exactly?" Servius posed the thought.

"Give me more men and I will do what you ask," Titus replied through the food.

"Good I'm glad to hear that from you. But you may be working to a centurion next time. A centurion called Rebilis if I'm not mistaken."

Titus could feel his heart beating and then it seemed to erupt in his chest before he breathed to try and calm himself. He swallowed and washed it down with wine. Servius twisted around in his chair and reached down behind him and turning back, placed a vine rod on the table.

"Titus, I'm making you a centurion. I have a gap to fill in the centurion register, and I cannot think of a better optio in my command. Here is your vine stick."

He reached out and picked up the heavy, gnarly, wood staff.

Servius smiled and continued, "you will have to make do with this one until you can cut one that pleases you. You may have to wait for your next leave for that I'm afraid. But as a centurion you must ensure success. You are the emperor's man in my absence. At all times you serve the emperor, but you answer to me. Do you understand?"

"Completely."

"Don't be afraid of using the stick when you have to. The men respect strong leaders. Punish when you have to, and only as much as you have to. That might be punishing men more than you want to, do you understand the difference?"

"Yes sir, I hear you."

"Titus, I want you to go back and tidy all of this up. Everything I've heard makes me think we have a potential cesspit on our hands. It's most unlikely the Ninth are there but get rid of whatever is there. Do you follow? Get rid of this problem. Make it go away. And bring me word their name will not haunt this army anymore. I have a wall to build and a province to secure for the governor. I cannot hold six thousand men from three different legions here indefinitely so I must finish this without distractions."

"And Tribune Paterculus?"

"I have not decided if he will be going with you."

Servius raised his hand palm forward to quell the confusion he knew was coming.

"He has other duties that are equally as pressing. He found them, it, whatever," Servius waved his hand, "well, I understand that it was Pinneius who actually found the helmet, but he can't really vouch for more, can he? And frankly it's not the job of a tesserarius to make a tribune's decisions, but that is beside the point.

Now you must wipe the slate. And you don't need the tribune's help to do that. Your commission is effective from now. Epeius will put it in writing for the legion's records and copy you in. Tell the quartermaster you require a centurion crest. You can ask him to have the crest fitted to your existing helmet or you can insist on a new one. Personally, I would insist on a new one, but it is up to you entirely. I do have an old one here that has just landed on my desk, but I doubt it would bring you good fortune."

Titus smiled at Servius' little joke.

Servius carried on, "dismiss and find some wine. You've earned it. And Titus, remember, make my problem go away. Oh, bye the bye, how did Pinneius do?"

"He did well sir, killed three in the glen where we found them, killed another at the ambush. Helped me rally the men and get them back."

He nodded to show his approval as much to Servius as himself.

"Thank you, Titus, you see, there is some good news."

Chapter 11.

The Hill of the Resting Lion.

Asuvad looked down on Ferrdigon's white faced corpse

'I hope you are already feasting in the halls of your fathers,' he intoned.

Although he looked at peace, somehow Ferrdigon's beard and moustaches swallowed up his face so only the nose, closed eyes and forehead were left of him. He was lying with his arms by his sides, hands half clenched. The battle scars of his youth traced pale lines on his paler flesh. But the man himself was gone. The hall that was full yesterday was empty today and yet he was everywhere.

He was in his high-chair, his drinking cup, his rack of spears on the wall; helmet, armour, shield. But there was no voice and no sound of him, except in Asuvad's head. The great-hearted man had only wanted peace for his people. Asuvad did not agree with him that it was possible to have peace in a Roman world, but Ferrdigon had tried. And paid a price. What would the Romans make of it once they heard? He thought Eilaver was too calm in the circumstances, showing no grief, no tears; not even a few token ones for appearances. She was too calm, just a little too much composure. He remembered how he had stumbled in upon her and the druid. So perhaps she was not so bereft after all. Ferrdigon had not been a warlike man and that made him a weakling in the eyes of many Votadini. Yet he had held his position for years.

'Too much composure, too much composure Eilaver.'

His mind whirred. Was it a blade or a potion that did it for Ferrdigon? Both were the tools of dangerous men. Or a dangerous wife. This was not the proper way chieftains were changed.

He looked away from the wax faced corpse feeling guilty that he had come to bully Ferrdigon into gathering his courage. To tell him, face to face that if the Votadini would not join the fight, they would fall to the spears of the Dumnonii and the Veniconii once their Roman friends had been chased away. Did Eilaver or Enomani realise that threat was real?

'Poor Ferrdigon. It's probably for the best', he mused.

The man deserved a fleck of pity, because nothing was straightforward anymore. He might have yielded to persuasion. The tribe might have risen, joining the Dumnonii and Veniconii and even the Taexalii. That would have been their mutual safety. The legions always preferred picking off their opponents one at a time and consolidating what they left in their wake. Never leaving an enemy at their back. They certainly did not like enemies who united.

Ferrdigon's druid, was watching him. Vusiavi was muscular and tall. He took a long appraising look at him. He did not see the priest very often in daylight. Vusiavi might have passed for a warrior except for his permanent state of blue paintedness; symbols and shapes on his arms and forehead. He always wore his symbols. He was sure Vusiavi was like every other he had met, they all shared a sickness of the head. It must be the herbs and the praying. One day he would have to kill him if only so that he could sleep untroubled in this village.

Eilaver exchanged a glance. Vusiavi left without a word making him wonder if they read his mind. Vusiavi would be a man who would fight naked with shield and spear, inspiring others to shed their blood. There was a warrior boiling away inside the druid, who was just panting for blood. That was their druid nature; they always seemed to be panting for blood.

Enomani was standing by the bed with his chin on his chest and his eyes closed, shutting out the horror. Eilaver was trying to console him but he was not responding. The lad had loved his father.

He decided it was not a scene for him. Outside a quiet crowd had gathered. For a second he wondered if they blamed him. Vusiavi was striding up to the high peak of the hilltop. To the views of heaven. Bodotria to the distant hills, to the islands in the river and the flat coast and the signal rock on the horizon. He found Aulercas sitting with his father and their open and honest faces bore the same confusion at Ferrdigon's abrupt passing.

"This place smells of Votadini treachery. I'll not stay here," he told them. Aulercas' father nodded.

"I was thinking the same, Asuvad, they can hide up here on their hill and think they are safe but they aren't."

"The whole reason for being here has gone. It will wait until Ferrdigon has gone to his ancestors," he replied.

He gathered his possessions and his horse. Eilaver came out, looking whiter faced than before. The lad Enomani was more concerned at his departure than any one of Ferrdigon's court.

He looked around. The goddess of the long winters was, at last, releasing her grip on the land, grudgingly permitting warmth to come and live its short time. Cetshamain was due in a few days. They would try to forget the cruel old woman of winter. Enomani seemed a good lad. It would be a good time for him to step forward as heir. A time of renewal for everything. Bonfires would burn on all the hills and both sides of the gates. He would be a good chief for them if he got the chance.

Not certain he was doing the right thing he pressed on. He was not Enomani's champion. He was not a Votadini so it was not his problem, but somehow it felt like it should be. He kicked his horse forwards through the gates raising his hand in farewell. A grizzled warrior leaning on his spear raised his hand in reply. And with that small acknowledgement he left the Votadini to despatch their dead chieftain to the afterworld and choose Enomani to replace him.

Up on the summit Vusiavi watched Asuvad depart. Eilaver had done well by him. She had agreed his plan to murder Ferrdigon. Enomani was next for death. But he had kept that part from her. He looked down at the steep cliffs around the south and western sides of the hill. Enomani would fall slipping on wet rock, at night perhaps. No, in daylight would be better. There would be less chance of suspicion if the lad fell in the daytime. He would be found in the bushes on the lower slopes once his body ceased rolling. It would be bloodied and broken by the rocks, his face scratched by thorns and stone into an unrecognisable pulp. How heartbreaking. She would not know how he fell, of course. She would turn to him in her grief, and he would comfort her. After a while when she was calm, he would set about ruling through her with little words of advice, suggestions, withholding agreements to bad ideas; all under the mantle of love for her.

'Vusiavi, you will be a chief in all but name,' he told himself.

He could have the Votadini fighting the 'sons of the wolf 'until they had driven them south to the Brigantes. If he was clever enough it could be done in such a way that they would never know the precise moment when generations of Votadini found courage and manhood. But to succeed in that he would need all the Votadini, not just this small hill. Dunpeledur and the high chief was the key. What better time than Cetshamain gifts and the opportunity to confer with his fellow druids? There was much to do. So much plotting. He knew those druids well and the feast was arriving at the fortuitous time to disguise his plans.

He ordered Ferrdigon's pyre to be built on the slope opposite the fort, above the reed pool as befitting a chieftain of his people.

When Asuvad reached the Dumnonii fortress he dismounted stiff and sore at the foot of the hill and led his horse by the bridle up the slope and through the gates. Traversing past the Roman wall and the forts had taken him a lot longer than expected. The enemy was all around. It was only when he reached the marshlands north of it that he began to relax. It had been a trying ride. He was tired and hungry, and the day was dark and girdled in mist and thin persistent rain. His horse didn't seem to mind but he did, his woollen trousers had been chafing his legs and his cloak was as wet and heavy as his mood. Up ahead his wife, children and fireside were waiting for him. Enomani slipped from his thoughts.

Chapter 12.

Bergessia fort, midway along the wall.

On the sheltered reverse slope of the escarpment, behind the fort, Brutus Carruso came downhill at Velio, shield and gladius raised, swinging a dangerous mix of high and low blows. His face was a mask of hate. Velio's in contrast, felt serene and calm. He retreated under the fusilade, parrying, deflecting, alert and poised, taking care not to lose balance on the uneven ground. He felt his wrist find that liquid power, moving the blade, absorbing the blows. The senior instructor turned to the horseshoe of men around the two adversaries. The uphill tiers were enjoying the best view of Brutus at work.

Brutus Carruso was a journeyman donkey from the slums of some crappy town on the edge of Marsala which was an even crappier town of sailors, wharves, whores and wine shops. He was taller, heavier and older than Velio by about five or six years. His long lunging put his own torso out of reach of Velio; a game of bull against bullock. Only one winner? The Fourth century of the Fourth cohort listened to the senior instructor, whilst laying their bets at the same time. A win against the tesserarius instructor was looking more and more likely as Brutus got warmed up.

"Watch the difficulty of killing an opponent armed with a decent shield that he knows how to use. Not every barbarian out there is a mindless savage. They can fight with a shield as well as we can but ours just happen to be heavier and stronger. Come on Carruso, make an effort man. The tesserarius is making a fool out of you. You haven't landed a blow yet," the instructor bawled, "Mars must love you. He's keeping you alive for a reason that escapes me. Come on Carruso you useless dog, you island wharf-rat, make a kill for once in your useless career."

Carruso scowled in impotent rage while the galleries laughed and jeered. Velio grinned just to annoy Brutus a bit more, feinted high, bumped shields and nicked his opponent's upper arm drawing blood. It was a scratch really but the wooden blade had enough of an edge to open the skin. The tell-tale red dribble a clear point to Velio. Carruso redoubled his efforts. Velio dumped his shield in outright provocation standing back and waving his sword like a flyswatter, goading Brutus on. The men of century Four went silent. Brutus halted and licked his lips before flicking an inquisitive look at the senior instructor.

"Carruso, if you can't kill a man without a shield you are no use to me or the Fourth cohort," he shouted, "make a kill before I count to ten or you lose the bout and every bet that's been placed."

The century took up the count as Velio parried and probed, seeking the wound of Brutus' arm, like a wasp. The count finished.

"Put down the shield, it's obviously too confusing having to do two things at the one time. Try again with just the gladius."

The audience liked Carruso's angry flush. He threw the shield towards Velio's ankles and charged in for a body check with his blade rising up towards Velio's ribcage.

"Better," called the senior instructor.

Velio, swiped the blade aside with something akin to contempt and put the point of his gladius a fraction away from Carruso's throat. It was over. The instructor regarded his audience. A murmur of disappointment made the creases around his eyes deepen a fraction in amusement. Velio lowered the wooden training blade. Brutus Carruso's expression changed to sullen frustration.

"How do you do that?"

"Practise," the senior instructor replied without looking behind him.

"Marcus Hirtius is dead, so I have a place to fill. The Fourth cohort provides weapons instruction to every cohort except the First. That's because the pretty-boys of the First cohort think they know it all," he lectured.

He waited for his captive audience to laugh and quieten down.

"Until one of you can make Tesserarius Pinneius sweat a bit more than Brutus Carruso did, there will still be a vacancy. The practice is over for today. Tomorrow, we begin again. Any one of you who fancies a shot can come and talk to me or the tesserarius. Dismiss."

*

Hanno Glaccus kneed his horse forward down the tricky path on the escarpment, down to the low plain. Ahead of him the haunches of Paterculus' horse swayed as it picked its way, its tail in opposite motion to the particular hind leg moving. It took them a few minutes to descend. When he reached the bottom Paterculus swung round and looked up at the escarpment and the section of turf wall with its new wooden palisade. Glaccus drew alongside and together they inspected the defences. Paterculus backed the horse up a few yards, continuing to inspect the top of the crest.

"Some lilia pits along the base of the slope are needed to finish this off but I think you can commission the dedication slab now. Tell the mason. The Boar of the Twentieth will tell everyone who passes that we built this on time. I'll inform Tribune Albinius. He will be pleased he can tick off another section," he said.

Glaccus nodded. It seemed more likely the barbarians would take one look at this section and mark it down as not worth attacking. There were easier sections east and west. Funnelling potential attacks towards weak spots would make the defence of those same weak spots easier too. There were no real weak spots of course, but as long as the barbarians thought there were, that is where their attacks would fall. A few pits of sharpened stakes would provide just one more incentive to avoid this section.

Paterculus nodded in return and turned his horse west, looking up at the wall as they rode along. Its abruptness had split families and small villages from their neighbours. Most satisfactory for keeping the natives under the heel. They rode on for a couple of miles through lush grass, enjoying the warm summer sun until they arrived below the foot of Medio and its defences. The forward mound of the ditch obscured the gateway, but the top of the gateposts and its sentries were visible. Outside there was a sea of blue, yellow, white and red flowers with purpling grasses moving in the light wind, busy with insects; a peaceful contrast to the wall and its message. The birdsong was unremitting. How much greener than the dry tired colours of Rome. By this time of year, the fruit trees at home would be full of promise, olives would be ripening.

"One more year and this entire country should be completely sectioned off. All this will be finished," he commented.

"Sir," Glaccus assented.

"It can't come soon enough. It's so damn cold up here. What do you think they will think, when they see this? The Taexalii, the Veniconii and the rest of them?"

"I don't care," grunted Glaccus.

Paterculus raised an eyebrow and swivelled around. Glaccus thought again, deciding to tell the tribune what he wanted to hear.

"That they are beaten, I hope. I really hope they will think they are beaten and there is no longer any point in defying us. That submission to Rome is their only path to peace with the legions," he said.

"I hope they fight. I hope they smash their best warriors against our wall and water the fields with their blood. There will only be peace when they are all dead. And I can go home. You too, if you wish Glaccus," smiled Paterculus.

Glaccus held his tongue. The tribune carried on gesturing to the wall.

"If we can do this quickly, it will all have been worth it. The south will remain safe behind the wall of Hadrian, the north will be partitioned off by this one and the bit in the middle will be secure. Perfect. We will have tidied up Britannia."

Glaccus chose his words with care.

"Sir, what about the helmet found by Tesserarius Pinneius? Up there?" he nodded his head towards the hills.

"Tesserarius Pinneius, has yet to pay for giving me this."

Paterculus raised his hand. The scar was neat and dull across the lower part of his forearm. Glaccus could see it had only just missed the major blood lines in the wrist by a fraction. Even in a practice Pinneius' eye for the incapacitating cut was spot on. Had it been intended to be a gentle scrape of the skin to indicate the area Paterculus needed to practise more? A wooden sword could have done that service. The real thing had led to this vivid scar. Pinneius' senior instructor had no doubt ripped him to shreds for it.

"I know what you said Hanno about his 'protected status' as an instructor, but he insulted me. This scar is an insult to me. Every time I touch something it shows, reminding me.

"How did you acquire that Cornelius?' people will ask? And what will I say? That I got it, not slaughtering savages but in a practice," Paterculus complained.

Glaccus waited for him to finish.

"In my experience people seldom ask the where and how of a soldier's battle scars and it's better to have one than none at all. And a scar like that gained in training shows how hard you train sir.

'If he fights like that in training' they'll say, *'what is he like when the legion fights for real?'*"

Paterculus smirked at him, delighted, "you think so Hanno?"

Hanno Glaccus smiled a confidential assurance. Paterculus returned to his theme.

"Finding the Ninth is something I need to do for Rome, for the army, and for the emperor," he said.

"Pompous ass," Glaccus thought to himself.

"The tesserarius, I need to do for myself."

Glaccus licked his lips and swallowed, busying himself with an invisible tangle in his reins before patting his mount's mane. The tribune did not seem to notice his reluctance to speak. He was looking at the scar.

"Hanno, get me a man you trust. Pinneius must pay. If you say I cannot flog him, and Servius would not hear of demoting him, then I will have to use another path."

Hanno shrugged trying to be indifferent to Paterculus' venom. Orders were orders and Pinneius was not indispensable, but this was not justice. Servius would nail him up if he ever found out. He knew whatever he did now was going to bring him a bad outcome from one or other tribune.

"I will have a word and get you a man you might use," he said, playing for time.

*

Newly promoted centurion Titus Rebilius was admiring the shiny new helmet his batman had finished polishing up for him. It sat on his desk and gleamed back a distorted image of a very happy man.

"You've stolen the light from the harbour at Alexandria," sounded a cheerful voice.

Titus looked up. Hanno Glaccus extended his arm to shake.

"My sincerest congratulations Titus, I always hoped you would make it to the rank of centurion," he said.

"You'll take a cup of wine to help me celebrate Hanno?"

"Delighted to help you get pissed in your new rank," he replied with a grin.

Titus went and got the wine himself. His servant had gone to get some better provisions to restock his personal larder. Titus' better provisions were also his better provisions. Centurion pay bought better wine and olives. Setting down a fair-sized jug and two plain cups with simple 'XX Leg.' markings, Titus poured for them both.

"To victory, success and promotion," he suggested.

"To bloody wars that end quickly, wasting only other men's blood," Glaccus replied with his lopsided smile and drank.

They smiled like boys and put away a couple of cup's worth.

"What century have you been given?" Hanno Glaccus asked.

"The Third," Titus replied.

"Ah, I had heard that Pulla has breathed his last. Unfortunate for him but good for you," he said, "not the way you'd have wanted it, I'm sure Titus, but the Fates can be unkind," he let it trail off.

Sympathetic words did not always do justice for these twists of fate.

"Apparently, he took a bad gash from a rusted nail that had not been removed properly from a faulty gatepost. His blood turned bad and," Titus clicked his fingers, "gone to the after world."

"A rusted nail in a faulty gatepost, Mithras, what a damned useless way to die," Glaccus said, not enjoying an involuntary shiver that ran down his spine.

"He sweated for a couple of days in the infirmary, started seeing things, visions, you know, lost the power of speech and was found stone cold one morning," said Titus, "think I prefer a barbarian spear, myself. They found the mule who'd not pulled the nail properly and gave him forty lashes."

They paused to taste the sweetness of the wine and consider Pulla's fate.

"Where exactly are the Third at the moment, Titus?" he enquired, steering away from further talk of Pulla.

"Do you know, I'm not entirely certain. Somewhere between here and the one, two forts over, Litana I hear it's going to be called, I'm heading over there tomorrow to find them. But with the Sixth legion in the eastern sector, who knows from day to day where he'll put us? Tribune Albinius does like to shuffle things a bit," Titus smiled.

Glaccus scooped back more wine, there was, after all, a serious quantity in the jug.

"Tribune Servius will want you close at hand I expect Titus. He likes men who get things done efficiently. He is Boar legion to his bones, got the tusks to prove it," he joked, "and I know he was pleased with the patrol. The loss of men was unfortunate but otherwise he was pleased with the intelligence gathered."

Titus tipped his cup towards him in mock salute.

"Even so, promotion was more than I expected."

Glaccus smiled.

"Well he needed to replace Pulla and it was easy to put your name on the table. In fact, I think your name was already there. You did most of it after all."

"You suggested me?"

"Let's say I gave his horse an apple, so to speak."

Titus gave Hanno a broad grin but Hanno spoiled it.

"The other tribune of your acquaintance?" he murmured.

Titus had a sudden ominous feeling.

Hanno Glaccus went on, "the other tribune wants the name of, how shall I say? A man who can be relied upon for a nasty job he wants doing."

"To do what?"

"Not asking is the best policy on this one, I think Titus. You can thank me for putting in a word for you by taking on this little task. It has a nasty smell. Just have a think and get me a name I can relay to our feisty young friend," Glaccus hissed, "he doesn't want to let this thing lie. Stupid really, but when a tribune speaks, we all have to listen."

"As it happens there is a mule that might do. His name is."

"Don't tell me until you're certain Titus."

*

"Brutus Carruso I'm told you can keep your mouth shut?" Glaccus said.

Carruso nodded, taking the question to heart.

"Centurion Rebilis has recommended you," Glaccus barked at him, as if he was laying a curse. He placing his vine stick on Carruso's shoulder and tapping the lorica strips.

"Centurion?" Carruso blinked.

"Titus Rebilis is now centurion of the Third century, Fourth cohort. You did not know Carruso? Centurion Rebilis has whispered to me you are the very man I might need to do a special job. Not for me but for Tribune Paterculus.' Do this well and you will be rewarded."

He tapped his stick on the legionary's shoulder again.

"Foul it up and the tribune is likely to make you the first soldier of Rome ever to be crucified in Britannia. So be warned. All clear so far?"

Carruso banged his fist into his chest in salute.

"Good man, that's the spirit, come with me."

He led Brutus Carruso to the tribune's door in the principia and waited outside. The guards stood rigid while he passed the moments inspecting them. Carruso came out, his expression not as joyous as a chosen soldier's should be: he looked at Glaccus.

"Well?" Glaccus said, drawing him out of earshot of the guards.

"He wants me to."

Glaccus shushed him with a glare and an upraised palm.

"Kill Tesserarius Pinneius the next time we go into battle with the enemy sir. From behind like, if you know what I mean?" Brutus wanted to say but took the hint and kept his mouth shut.

"Carruso, you are now in more danger than you have ever been. There are forests in Germania where no Roman has ever set foot that are safer than you are right now. If I ever hear a gasp of what you have been told you will be dead within the hour. Believe me soldier, you are marked both as a man of the tribune and one of mine. Fail and I will have you killed. Speak and I will do it faster. Do it quietly and you will be rewarded. Brutus Carruso, if I were you, I would go back to my post and remember what you are to do. But do nothing for now."

Brutus Carruso crashed another salute with his fist to his chest.

This is all getting out of hand Hanno. This tribune is going to be trouble,' he told himself as Carruso walked away.

He turned and entered Paterculus' office. He saluted. Paterculus made a faint wave of acknowledgement. In his hand was a scroll, an order.

"The governor himself wants me to pay a courtesy visit to represent him. This local Votadini, Ferrdigon, you know him Hanno? He wants me to find out what's on his mind, if anything, give presents, wave the standards, pat the children," he groaned, "Servius is too busy apparently. Duty upon duty Glaccus. I won't have to sleep there will I Glaccus?"

Paterculus' horror changed his face to a child's.

"And then I have to report back in person to Governor Urbicus who is currently sitting in Eburacum."

Glaccus decided Brutus Carruso had to all intents never entered this room.

"How strong a patrol Glaccus, I would welcome your advice on this."

Paterculus was sounding the way he had on his first day at Carumabo. Glaccus sat down and waited a discreet moment to state the obvious.

"You need to take enough to intimidate but not terrify, sir. Cavalry preferably for speed."

"Bloody auxiliaries, don't want them Glaccus, d'you hear? Regulars only."

"A turma of regulars then. Thirty two men sir, and they'll have a decurion to lead them so you won't have to bother about that side of things," he suggested.

"Two I think, no make it three turmae. That will give me a hundred men. That should be more than sufficient."

"How soon sir?" he asked, keeping the desire to laugh at bay in his head, concentrating for all his worth.

"Tomorrow, see to it would you Glaccus? I have a vesuvius of paperwork to read today. Oh, and find me some suitable gifts. Some bright cloth for the women, if you can find any in this wretched place."

Servius read the monthly report of native Britons reporting for service to the ranks of the auxiliary. The numbers were pleasing. Rome was winning the war each time a native Briton chose Rome over their own people. Cohorts for the Germania frontier were here for the harvesting. Let savage fight savage and honest legionary stand to the rear and observe. His further order from Governor Urbicus also pleased him.

'Tribune,

I am advised your commissioning of research into lost patrols appears to have turned up no possibilities that cannot be accounted for. I have ordered Tribune Paterculus to attend other matters of interest to me. Proceed in his absence.

Quintus Urbicus.'

He clicked his fingers. Epeius stood alert.

"Get me Titus Rebilis," he told him.

Rebilis was quickly there. He got to the point.

"Pick your men, you leave the day after tomorrow."

"And the Caledons sir?"

"If you can't get there without incurring losses, retreat and we will rethink the problem. Otherwise, if you can get there, do as we discussed. Let me be clear Titus, I don't want losses. But I do want the problem cleared up. But should this transpire to be anything more than a man or a patrol, if there is any hint at all this could be the Ninth, remember they have been there for more than thirty years, we just didn't know where they were, do you follow?"

Titus nodded.

"You must use your judgement. If it is really the Ninth, you will send word to me when you have secured the valley. I will follow on to administer the funeral rites. But if you cannot control the valley, I will not endanger more men. In that case you will retire, and we will leave the Ninth where they lie. The helmet you and Pinneius brought back will be a proxy for them. And if that is false, I will say a piaculum for us all. It will be the only thing we can do. It is the wall that counts now."

"What about Tribune Paterculus?"

Servius shrugged, "the tribune is both right and wrong. We owe our soldiers a proper send-off no matter how late we make those prayers, but the world is full of the bones of dead Romans who never had an offering or a tear shed for them. Titus, this cannot be anything more than a salute, and a bow to the gods. It can't be anything more. Do you understand?"

"I think so sir," Titus replied doing his best.

Servius smiled at his new centurion. What a task to give him so soon. He knew it was not really fair, but it would be the making of him. Should Titus decide to retreat in the face of enemy opposition, he would be just as content.

"Titus. Titus. I wish Pinneius hadn't found that helmet. I have a dead man's armour and his spirit is asking me for revenge. I can't ignore that. But I can't make him live again."

Rebilis made a slow deliberate salute.

"I will secure that valley. And when I have done so I will send word so you can say prayers on behalf of the emperor. May I take Pinneius again?" he asked.

"Titus, you can take who you wish. You'll have a full ala of auxiliary cavalry this time. Go softly and fast Titus. The cavalry commander has been ordered to follow your orders, but you may need to be firm. Ordinarily he outranks you and you know what the cavalry are like," Servius said.

"I understand, tribune."

Forty-eight hours later Velio found himself on horseback riding up front behind Titus Rebilis, heading out of Velunia towards the crossing point of the Bodotria. Then north towards Pinnata Castra except that this time Centurion Rebilis intended to veer west of the Tavae river, staying on the higher ground and bypassing the old fort. Except that this time Marcus Hirtius was not coming with him.

The cavalry escort was the entire auxiliary ala of the Sixth legion. Sixteen units each with a legionary decurion commander and colour matched horses, answering in turn to the ala's praefectus. Velio was the solitary infantry soldier amongst them, aside from Titus Rebilis. His lack of ability on a horse was exposed but his rank helped a little. He could hear their comments behind his back but managed to keep his horse moving along. An infantry man, dressed as an infantryman, on a horse amid cavalrymen.

They were a flamboyant lot. Decorated horse harnesses, fancy scabbards for the long swords. Expensive chain mail armour. Glimmering war lances decorated with braids of enemy hair, feather bunches, strips of once colourful ribbon that had become stained and brown through time and use. Phalerae rank and bravery badges on display. The constant silver music of bridles, bits, and ornamentation hanging from saddlery.

Glory boys every one of them, with that arrogant way that worked wonders with the local women, he had no doubt. They spoke to their horses and made bets with each other for future races on the parade grounds when they returned victorious from this mission; as victory was the only option they could countenance. Every so often one of them would rise in the saddle to let his horse piss. Here was a section of the army of Britannia that knew itself to be fast and elite, the best of the best. The bonds between officers and men were different too. The legionary mules on foot, Velio's people, held their disciplinary order and rankings like it was tattooed on their foreheads; you could see it from a distance, and it only got more obvious the closer you got. The cavalry troopers, on the other hand, were chummier altogether with their troop commanders. There were a lot of Lucius this, that and the rest, and several Publiuses and Flaccuses; Priscus was another name that got up his nose. Flaccus sounded like a man who farted too much even for the army. Sounded like one of several services painted on a brothel wall. Velio patted the hilt of the Ninth legion gladius on his hip and sent prayers to Mithras and Fortuna that he would not have to depend on Lucius, Flaccus and Publius or Priscus to save him. The cavalry-loving girls at Trimontium were probably in a state of deep grief at their absence. Or possibly not. Two days ride beckoned, and the saddle was already feeling uncomfortable.

Titus ordered no fires be lit at the first night halt. The equestrian officer took a dim view of his cold supper. It was mid-summer and the temperature was falling down to something short of cool. Velio watched fascinated. It led to a short sharp exchange of pleasantries that had been simmering since the praefectus paraded his men that morning.

He was a typical small, bandy legged, barky-voiced cavalryman with a face like a badger. He wore the same chainmail as his men and Velio reckoned the lot of them thought they could conquer and vanquish at will.

"Why is the tesserarius with us centurion? He can't ride and he will slow us down," was the opening shot.

Titus took a sip from his ration water and replied, "he knows the spot."

Waiting to let that sink in he decided to save some time and get it all out in the open now

"He tells me that you won't be able to get horses up the path. It's too narrow and rocky. Your men will have to dismount."

"Leading the horses up will slow us down," the praefectus admitted.

Titus shrugged, "it's too steep to take horses up there."

"By 'there' you mean this valley? I will have to split my force and leave men holding horses. Is that what you are suggesting?"

"Tesserarius Pinneius tells me the horses will be of limited use up there."

Titus offered his water to the praefectus who shook his head.

"I think it's my job to decide what's too steep for my horses. The men left with the horses are vulnerable," the cavalry man growled.

"We will all be vulnerable," Titus said.

"My boys don't fight on foot. That's your job," reposted the praefectus.

"Your boys are here to secure the valley so that Tribune Servius Albinius can perform auguries for men we believe might be remnants of the Ninth legion. I don't care if they crawl up there on their hands and knees. And if it comes to it you might want your horses tethered on flat ground for a retreat if we are opposed in any great numbers. Trust me praefectus, this is not a training patrol along high ground waving standards to intimidate savages. These savages may be the ones who sorted out the Ninth. Ponder that if you will. The Ninth legion. I don't think your single ala is going to make them run."

He sat down on a convenient rock and watched the last flourish of the setting sun. The light changed colour and the sweet stink of pine trees and wet grass was strong and pleasantly overpowering. He inhaled it with real enjoyment. The smell of trees. The cavalry lines were spread before him, the horses quiet, the men digging a low defensive ditch. Mounted sentries on the higher ground. At their back was a low hill, chosen because it would help to shield any attack coming from that direction. On their left side, the pinewoods were now dark and moody, where they had been welcoming when they had arrived. In front and to the right was open heavy grassland, heather and rocks, streams and the unknown. In the further distance were the rising hills of the true wilderness. And they threatened.

The praefectus stood and clenched his fists, trying to find a suitable barb to respond with, patting his pugio dagger, racking his mind for a way to re-establish the social and military sense of order that Titus had wrecked without too much effort.

"I know what we are ordered to do centurion. I understand the sensitivities. You and me can share command but I do not want an unknown foot soldier dictating how I deploy my ala," he snarled.

It sounded lame but it was the best he could manage.

Titus faced him once more, feeling the upper hand was his.

"The tesserarius is not dictating anything, he's just relaying the intelligence of the ground he saw. I'm afraid you won't be able to take horses up to where he found the helmet. But if you disagree when we get there it will be your decision praefectus. Yours to make. And by the way, the tesserarius is not some foot soldier. He is known to me and Tribune Servius. That is another reason he is here" he said.

The praefectus flinched and Titus enjoyed the effect his words were having.

"Indeed, centurion you and I can agree on that," the cavalryman said.

Velio could hardly believe what he was hearing. This was going to be a tale for the barrack block.

The ala slept undisturbed, ate bread for breakfast and were mounted and moving soon after the early sunrise. A blanketing mist lay over the grass and trees. The column was silent. Not a voice to be heard. Titus rode with Pinneius at his back, wondering if Velio had managed to shut a few of them up with his first-hand account of what he and Marcus Hirtius had found. It would not have surprised him in the least. The praefectus sent a half turma of men with a decurion's second out in front as a screen. He watched them fading into the mist and signalled Velio forwards, irking the praefectus.

"Tomorrow perhaps?" he said.

Velio tried to ease the pain in his behind. This saddle was not the same as the last one he used with Paterculus' patrol. He wanted the sun to burn through the mist and give them a bearing to the hills. But the mist was thick and for the moment he was happy to settle for that.

"Do you think we'll get through without being spotted sir," he asked.

Titus paused and the praefectus eavesdropped alongside.

"No tesserarius, I don't expect we'll be that lucky. The question is, what will they do about us?" Titus said.

Velio grunted, "a wineskin on the altar of Bacchus if we get away with this then, sir."

Titus smiled. He could see Velio's eyes on the transverse coxcomb of his new helmet. The red feathered crest that steadied men and drove the relentless meat grinder of Rome's legions, time after time.

"It'll be a barrel, paid for by the governor I expect," he replied, "and a silver cup for Bacchus to drink from. So, Pinneius, do you think it will be tomorrow?" he repeated.

Velio looked at the mist again. Titus accepted his silence as an answer.

After a couple of hours, the mist began fading as the sun warmed it away. They both scanned the hills for a familiar landmark. The praefectus held his tongue as the horses walked on.

"I don't think we are far enough north to be level with Pinnata Castra," Titus gestured off to the right, "it has to be a full day's ride from here."

"How much further west are we?" the praefectus enquired.

"Not far, I calculate a few miles but we are still some way south."

"So how long before we get to this valley?" the praefectus worried.

"Could be late tomorrow or the day after," Titus replied unfazed by the predictable question.

"I'd prefer early the day after, rather than late tomorrow. Getting there early gives us time to assess the position before nightfall. It all hinges on whether we run into local opposition," he added.

"How exactly are we going to secure the lower valley sir? The upper part where we found the helmet and the bones should be easy enough, we have enough men, but the area below is huge," Velio fretted.

The praefectus decided to intervene.

"If I have understood this clearly, we will hold the entrance to the main glen with a couple of turmae of men, we will need horse holders at the foot of the climb to the upper valley, if, as you say we cannot get horses up there. I will use a holding force, perhaps three or four troops down the glen to give warning of any attack coming from that direction. That will give me eleven troops, say nine discounting horse-holders to secure the higher valley."

Titus thought about it and nodded agreement.

"It's simply a question of dividing the ala correctly. My job I think, centurion."

Velio said nothing but wondered what use three hundred dismounted troopers would be up in the high valley if war broke out down below.

Later, he drifted into thinking about home and the sea around Misenum. Father's garum business. The delicious pungent sauce used by all the civilised world. Legionaries around the empire dreamt of three, perhaps four things, but the important, and most unavailable three were good bread, good olives and garum-fish sauce. Money alone could not send them in quantities fast enough or sometimes even at all. The fourth somehow never seemed to pose a difficulty.

Father worked all day long on a low hulled boat with a hand sewn net, casting for sardines and sweet little lyre tailed fish. He had skin browner than tree bark and hands harder than iron. Though he also had a grip and caress as gentle as a lamb's when he chose. Velio used to hear him singing his old soft hunting songs, songs the fishermen sang in the evenings when they were all safe ashore. Well-fed and drinking wine while their wives and women smiled and sat close by their sides. Songs for when the sea was cheated for another day. Bearded, grizzled men singing their harmonious melodies; so strange that a bunch of ugly fishermen could sing together and silence the world for a few minutes. The sight and sound of his father in full voice was not embarrassing to think about now, because he knew so much more, but back then, he had been torn between joining in, or running off.

The sight of Da relaxed and happy with his friends, grateful to be safe and warm and dry made the old man vulnerable and less intimidating. He was as frightened of the unpredictable world as anyone else. It was simply that he wore better armour. Each piece of it hard and anvil wrought. The warm light of oil lamps and fires. The distant nudges of water down in the harbour where the faithful boats were stabled. Abundant food on the tables. Those were the good memories of childhood.

He heard horses passing wind and let go of the tinted, happy memory. The truth was, home had been a battleground. Garum was not his trade. The legions, passing by one day had whistled, and doglike he pricked his ears and sat up. Father had been out on the boat, where else would he have been, and the poison entered his head. He would be a soldier. The sea could wait. It was not going to go anywhere. The world had enough garum sauce for a day or two and Gaul sounded an interesting place to go and fight. Gold and women and the company of men who conquered everything before them.

A voice called to an unsettled horse. The cold night air of northern Britannia was as far away from Misenum as poor Marcus from this shallow billet.

'Rest easy Marcus. It's me who fetches the bread for Gallus now.'

Home; and dead Marcus. Two unhappy thoughts to keep him company in the night to come.

*

Paterculus was sitting on what seemed to be a milking stool at the grubby little fire pit in Ferrdigon's grubby little hall.

There was not an article of sophistication anywhere in sight. The man himself had decided to die right before his visit. A man he had only seen once from a distance, the day he arrived at Carumabo. Eilaver, the widow, was weeping fountains and to make his task just a little bit easier the gods had arranged the bloody mangled corpse of her son Enomani outside on the grass. The young prince's body found that day at the foot of the red cliffs. By the state of it he must have bounced his way over every rock. It was not pretty. Her lamentations forbade his prepared speech, and he was further distracted by an enormous bear skull mounted on one side of the circular hall. A male animal of prodigious size. Bigger than any he believed possible in the province.

'How in the name of Dis-pater am I to get out of this?' he wondered.

There was no point in continuing the visit. Continuing? It had not even started. He got up and passed by the widow. She did not notice him leaving.

Outside he took a deep breath and summoned the decurion of the cavalry with a flick of his head. He observed decurion's hand resting, out of habit, on the pommel of his sword.

"Decurion, keep your hand off the sword. The last thing I want to do is set these people off."

The decurion flushed and put his hand by his side, "sorry sir."

He shook his head dismissing the need for the apology.
The decurion made amends.

"Is it best we leave them to it, sir?"

He had twelve men in the small fortress and the remainder of his lead turma outside the stockade walls. Servius had dismissed Paterculus' desire for full legionary cavalry with an upraised eyebrow. All had dismounted waiting for food to be produced. This was a client tribe; the soldiers should be fed and watered, shelter provided for as long as the tribune asked. But there was a tension in the air. He spoke in a low voice to his second.

"The death of a chief and then his son can only be viewed, as a matter of logic, as a single act. These people are in the midst of settling scores. Sorting out who will be chief next. Rome's only interest is they stay peaceful and loyal."

There was something here that smelled of defiance. What was it? They would laugh at him if he got this wrong but there was something brewing. Anything that threatened the wall had to be stamped out. It was after all a tribune's duty to lead. He smiled a little smile.

"Mount up the men, I will leave the gifts. Give our respects and tell them we will return once a new chief has been chosen. We need to ensure his allegiance. Where is their high priest, I suppose I should speak with him?"

"Their priest is missing sir. I've been up here before. I know what he looks like, and I can't see him. Why would a priest be missing at a time like this?" the decurion said.

He paused for a second, "why indeed."

"I found out he's going to the fortress of Dunpeledur, it's to the south of here. Not far," the decurion added.

Paterculus looked at him, the decurion was doing well.

"Can we overtake him decurion?"

"We could if you command it sire."

"Remind me what's at Dunpeledur?" he asked.

"It's the capital of the Votadinii."

"Ah, I remember. Mount up and lead on, I want this priest. Hold back the gifts, this woman can wait. She'd probably throw them on the fire."

"As you command tribune."

"And send my order to the third troop to go now and detain the priest, we will follow on, but half an hour may make a difference, so I want those horses moving now."

"Tribune."

The decurion nearly ran to his horse. Paterculus cast around for a reason to delay, a courtesy that needed doing, or a word that required saying to Eilaver. The son's body was still lying as they had set him down, his arms at odds with his torso, his legs askew. Blood saturating his clothes. His eyes trying to see a sky that was not there for him anymore.

"Damn it," he muttered.

All the diplomacy in the empire could not make this hill fort into a victory of army-tribal relations. He gestured to the trooper holding his mount and spurred out bringing the remaining eleven troopers after him. The decurion sat on his horse down at the elbow shaped pond waiting with the remaining troopers. The other decurion, from the second troop had been brought up to date. His face was set for a fight.

"Are they despatched?" Paterculus asked the two of them.

"They are sir."

"Good lead on," he said.

The officer signalled four outriders to lead off and they picked their way down the northeast slope to the woodland below the hill fort. When they reached flatter ground they swung around to the south and pushed on. The ground was like long swells of the sea rising up and falling away in slopes and dips with innumerable small streams feeding their way to the shoreline down and away to their left.

"May I ask tribune, why you want Ferrdigon's priest sir?"

He didn't bother to reply.

"Should I send a rider to Trimontium to alert the governor?"

He did not turn his head from the path his horse was taking, he knew his horse skills were not comparable to these easy riding cavalrymen. He kept his voice low as the decurion leaned in to hear.

"Too many coincidences. The Votadinii are not at peace. Druids have a long history in these lands."

"The druids are gone sir, General Agricola sorted them out." the decurion answered.

"Decurion, do you think every blackbird of the forest can be lured with crumbs to its own execution?"

They thundered down a clear slope of waving grass bathed in sunshine. It was a pleasant afternoon gallop. He was beginning to enjoy it.

"I want to look this priest in the eyes and have him tell me these three coincidences are the games of their gods and not the hand of man. Most specifically, his hand," he said.

The decurion nodded swerving around a cluster of rocks that split the trail. They crossed the hoof marks of the third troop and Paterculus joined that course.

"Otherwise, this priest is not going to arrive at Dunpeledur with his head still attached to his shoulders. The Votadinii are going to remain a pack of tamed dogs whether they like it or not. We must catch him on the road before he gets there. We cannot have a distraction while the wall is not yet complete. It could get awkward. Don't you think?" he said.

"And if we can't catch up with him before Dunpeledur sir?"

Paterculus considered this.

"Then I will have to enter Dunpeledur and see their temper for myself. And they will see me. And if I have to go to all that trouble I may flog the entire third troop," he smirked.

The decurion recovered his wits.

"Then we will catch this priest on the last steps if necessary, sir."

*

Vusiavi saw Romans in the distance approaching the hill and made a quick decision that he did not want to be here when they arrived. Dunpeledur was calling. He came down from his vantage point, gathered up his few things and slipped out of the village. Enomani was stilling lying below the red crag, but he could not afford to wait for his discovery. The Romans were too close. He made his horse put the first few miles in at speed before slowing her as she tired, to a steady walk. Mixing walking and trotting he ruminated on how long it would take for the boy's corpse to be found. It might have been already. His mare picked her way and took every opportunity to stop and graze. He gave way a few times before getting impatient with her. The day was warm.

Enomani would never have raised a spear if he had lived to be sixty or seventy. He had raised and trained the boy, but the child was born without hatred, born weak. He had tried to instil some hatred into him, but what the gods left out, a priest was hard pressed to remedy. They must have had a task in mind for him but whatever mystery clouded that, it was not a task that included defying the invaders. A bed at the foot of the red cliffs suited his plans better. It was for the best. He remembered his druid guide's obscure wisdom.

'Decisions are like the dirk made from a stag's antlers; those antlers may point in different directions while the beast lives, but the dirk always ends up in a point that can kill you. So, it is with a decision, Vusiavi. A good decision can end up killing you just as easily tomorrow as a bad one can today. Remember that.'

He slowed to ford a shallow river, it was not too far now. What would the Romans make of Enomani's death? Could they be stupid enough to think it was all accidental? His first step must be to garner support from his druid brothers. Then a hearing before the council. To put his case. To shame them for their soft life while Veniconi, Dumnoni, Caledon and the other northern tribes still lived free and defiant. As the miles passed by, he smiled; all would be well.

Chapter 13.

To the Hidden Valley.

Velio stepped down from his saddle, rubbing his knuckles into the tight muscles of his lower back. Hurrying, he went forward to Titus Rebilis and the praefectus. The same black stream was tumbling down the same rock face he had scrambled after Marcus' death. It was still early. The air was still and the tall sentinel pines along the side of the glen that had so unnerved the tribune before were quiet. The sky was clear and blue. He shivered. This was a bad place. A place with its own gods. There would be one in the trees and one ruling the tumbling stream. He saluted both officers, pointing without being asked to the high hanging valley off to the left-hand side of the main glen.

"It's up there, sir," he said for the benefit of the praefectus.

The cavalry man harrumphed to himself and took a second look at the situation Titus Rebilis had just finished explaining to him. The ascent to the hidden valley was steep and narrow. His men could do it if he demanded, but getting them all down again in one piece would be more difficult. The glen was more open than he had expected. Now it was time to decide how and where to place his five hundred men.

"There is no reason to take men up there other than to confirm what Tesserarius Pinneius has previously reported. May I suggest, centurion, that a party goes up there to do just that. My men will hold this point and block off the lower end of this glen from uninvited guests," he said.

Titus smiled at that euphemism for the Veniconii.

"Once we have confirmed whether it really is the Ninth up there or just a patrol of some kind, I will send messengers to Tribune Servius Albinus to come. The rites can be made. Then we can all get the hell out of here," the praefectus continued.

Titus thought this through. The praefectus gave him a little nudge

"We only need to control the lower valley. We most certainly don't want to go up there in force and get ourselves trapped, with all our horses down here," the praefectus said.

Titus scratched his chinstrap. That was what he and Pinneius had been saying all along. He noticed Velio was keeping quiet. He untied his helmet and ran his hand through his black, sweat thickened hair.

"We will need to hold the valley for five to six days before the tribune could get here. We would have to hold it and not be seen," he said.

The praefectus frowned, "not be seen? Over five or six days? Impossible, I would have thought centurion."

"Exactly my point We are too few to hold off a major attack so we must hold this place without the Votadinii knowing we are here," Titus replied

"For five or six days?" Velio said.

If he could have clawed the words back into his mouth, he would have swallowed them.

Titus turned to him, "you have doubts, tesserarius?"

Velio stiffened to attention at the definite change of tone. But he was not feeling repentant.

"The horses sir," he replied.

"Ah, the horses. Well, praefectus, what about your men's horses? How do we hide them exactly for five or six days?" Titus asked.

"Sir?" Velio interrupted.

"Go on tesserarius," Titus said.

"We passed another valley just south of here. Posting a few men here would be sufficient to watch the glen."

"And we hide the rest somewhere close at hand, in that glen perhaps?" Titus added.

He faced the cavalry commander and reset his helmet. The praefectus looked up at the entrance to the hidden valley, the wide glen in front of them and the steep sided slopes.

"A good idea is a good idea regardless of rank," the praefectus admitted, "we just have to scout the other valley and hope the locals are asleep."

Titus raised his eyebrows.

"They know we are here praefectus. Have no doubt about it. They have been watching us since we left the wall. The only question is whether they intend to do anything about it."

He looked once more down the long valley to the point where it bent and curtailed further examination. A small but heartfelt sacrifice to the gods would not go amiss. This place reeked of the enemy. Why was there no challenge to the ala's presence? It all felt wrong.

Velio coughed.

"What is it now tesserarius?" he snapped.

Velio was tempted to say, 'what does horse taste like sir,' but common sense and discipline got the better of that potentially punishable comment. Officers never liked a smart-mouth. The praefectus seemed to intuit the thought.

"Your sergeant is wondering what he is going to eat for the next few days I suspect, centurion."

"Let's deal with that once we have inspected the higher valley. If you were mistaken Pinneius you won't have to worry about food," Titus retorted, "and as you rightly say praefectus we can all get the hell out of here."

Chapter 14.

The Hill of the Resting Lion.

Eilaver rocked herself to sleep, into a troubled dream of Enomani's face and smile. Her child was puzzled. His eyes and mouth, his glances, always never quite settled. She startled herself awake. Cold sweat was running down her back and her front. All over, the chilly sweat of fear. Like a shape that caught her side vision and when she turned, was gone, and yet had been there. Not imagined. Enomani seemed to hover around her. She felt him. But she could not see him. Because? Because her precious boy was dead. Enomani's spirit did not understand. She felt him pawing for her attention, as if seeking the breast of his infancy. Complaining, distraught, not yet gone to his forefathers without kissing his mother goodbye. The first born. The unique child. The child that tore himself out of her, a pain forgotten like a bad dream. Enomani, her first, had been the hardest.

The hall was quiet in the dark. Her earlier wailing sending them all scurrying away. The Roman soldier-boy had fled too. One day when he had grown a beard he might return, but the horror and confusion on his face suggested otherwise. She had warts and moles older than him. She sat down at the dwindling fire and watched the slow flames on the settled logs. At least the fire was at peace and the stones around it radiated warmth. All the colours of burning had vanished from the logs.

She poured wine into Ferrdigon's drinking horn and sat down at his end of the fire. Enomani's spirit sat at the opposite end; she and the girls usually took places on the sides. Except tonight, the girls were sleeping close together and their brother was not there. She drank the slow horn of wine. It was Roman but she did not care. Her son was dead. Vusiavi was missing. He had persuaded her that an iron needle through her husband's heart was the only way the people could hope to be free. How could she have been so blind? He did not want her to have the power. She no longer believed he wanted to share it with her. She stared at the empty seat where her son was sitting.

"Did he kill you too, my love?" she whispered.

How could Enomani have fallen from rocks he had known all his life? The crags were dry these last few days.

"Vusiavi," she said," Vusiavi."

When it was empty, she placed the drinking cup on the low flames and with a knife slit her thumb, dripping blood on top of it. He would follow Ferrdigon and Enomani to the reed girdled waters of the afterlife. Her blood was the sacrifice.

*

Duald grinned like a wolf with a doe between its paws. From the fastnesses of the glen scouts brought him reports of a cavalry column heading in his direction. He hoped. He waited. Then they told him what he most wanted to hear. They were coming towards his heartlands. Under the cover of the great pinewoods his men had watched the column halt and confer. The glen of sacrifice had drawn them back again. Despite the ambush he had sprung on them before, they were returning. More horsemen this time. He had no doubt they understood they had found the glen of execution. Grandfather had been both witness and participant. Now the Romans were coming back. But why? To gather the bones of cowards who died badly? To avenge them? No, years had passed by and the 'sons of the wolf' had never once come looking. He smiled. Grandfather had helped to give them that death. He remembered from the stories there had not been as many Romans to fight as they had first thought.

Grandfather would take stock in the flames and when he lifted his eyes his face would have changed to a hard mask, making him grimmer than the mountain, harder than the rocks, colder than the ice clogging the waterfall in winter.

They took the officers to the high corrie, roped by the neck like cattle. When they got there, there was a debate amongst the chiefs. Every warrior took a turn to select a soldier, drag him to the centre, kick him down to his knees, rip off the helmet and take his head. They did this one after the other, working their way through the feathered helmets until there were only four of them left. One for each tribe. Grandfather took the last one, he said it was the Romans' chieftain.

"I took his head, Duald, as payment for the land, the cattle and goats they stole, the trees they cut, the rivers they poisoned, the stone halls, the roads, the forts, the young men they took to fight in their army, the lives they ruined. They were so sure they were better than us. Everything we held dear was worthless because it was not Roman. I took his head in payment for all of that and I would do it again tomorrow."

"Did they beg or did they die like warriors, Grandfather?" he only asked once.

Grandfather nipped back, "they died, that's all that matters."

"Do you see them still in your head?"

"They were soldiers. They are our enemies, yours and mine. They do not share bread with us, and we don't shelter them, that's all you need to know. We will not surrender our way of life to them. They have nothing we should want. Our gods give us everything we need. Sometimes Duald, it is better to die than live as a conquered man."

He wanted to ask more but Grandfather was too fierce-faced, and he never found the courage to raise it again. But later Grandfather added something to treasure.

"You have distant uncles who live in a village built above the waters, in crannogs built on tall poles of pine. There they compose their great praise songs for the chiefs and live with one ear tuned to their harps. They fight no one. They carry dirks that they never use. I don't think they've ever seen a Roman soldier. The crannog walls are wattle like ours and you can look down through the gaps and see the water. You can see the sunlight gleaming off the water and the stones below. Your uncles built them that way on purpose. They don't mind the cold mist in the winter. They like the music the water brings. Poets and bards are useless in a fight Duald, but do you think the Romani would live in a hall like that?"

He sent messengers to Asuvad and Aulercas' father,

'There is wolf-meat on the table.'

And sat back to imagine life in a crannog high over the lapping water, listening to the birds and the wind on the high slopes.

*

Velio escorted Titus Rebilis and the praefectus and a support troop on foot past the place where Marcus had fallen and up the long narrow ascent to the hidden valley. It was mid-morning, perhaps two hours before midday, before he led them into the opening of the actual corrie. It was sunlit and warm. Velio looked out over the ground only he and Marcus had surveyed, since the dead fell here. He pointed to the low undulating grassy knolls.

"That's where we found the bones."

"Where did you find the helmet tesserarius?" asked the praefectus.

Velio took a slow look around.

"Somewhere close to where we are standing," he said, "I felt it with my boot."

Rebilis and the praefectus stopped and looked around. He saw the effect it was having on them. He and Marcus had spent their last hour in this place.

"Well," Titus Rebilis commented.

The praefectus nodded, "you did not see the man's head, his skull?" he quizzed.

"I didn't look for it," Velio replied," I picked up the helmet and showed it to Marcus. We stood about where you are now and looked around, then we split up and made our way down each side of the cliffs. We met up at the far end and we were walking back this way, we were getting out. That's when we found the bones in those grassy bumps over there."

Titus nodded as he spoke, as if he was guaranteeing the truth of every word. The praefectus turned to his decurion.

"Have the men spread out and set four lookouts back down the trail to the bottom. Let's not get caught out up here."

The decurion saluted and called out the orders. There was a general bustle as the troopers jumped to it. Titus waited until he had the praefectus' attention.

"Those bumps are where we should start. If the Ninth are here I want messengers sent immediately to Velunia."

"Indeed," said the praefectus, "well, lead on then, tesserarius."

Velio had brought a borrowed cavalry shield with him, forsaking the large infantry one strapped to his saddle. The slimmer cavalry buckler had a comfortable feel in the circumstances. He put it down and walked out towards the centre ground to the nearest green mound. He drew his gladius and began cutting down into the grass, leaning down to ease stones aside. Titus Rebilis knelt down beside him and pulled in similar fashion and after a few moments the cavalry commander joined in. The three of them digging like children for coins hidden by a playful father. It did not take long before Velio found what looked to be a thigh bone in the thin soil.

"Jupiter, thou Best and Greatest," Titus said in disbelief, "there really is something here."

He made a rigid middle finger sign against evil. The praefectus did too. None of them spoke as the enormity of it sank in. Titus sat back on his heels and took in the stone headwalls of the corrie. He began to understand what Velio and Marcus must have felt up here, the two of them alone with the unhonoured dead.

"The only question now is, how many?" the praefectus said, "it could be a patrol. One helmet and a leg bone."

"We found ribs and a bit of armour, over there," Velio pointed.

The praefectus stood up, dragging Titus out of his uncomfortable thoughts.

He turned to his second, "decurion, I want six men digging on these mounds. Look for bones and armour. Now, at the double. Get the rest standing to arms and watch the cliff tops for any sign of enemy warriors. We cannot afford to be trapped here."

The decurion's eyes searched the high rocks for barbarians.

"Immediately sir," he replied.

Velio stood up and went towards the furthest mound. Titus followed, curious to see what he was going to find next. He no longer doubted Mars and Jupiter had given this soldier an errand. Why they had chosen this young man out of all the garrison of Britannia to be the one to find all this, he had not the slightest idea. Velio halted and knelt down, digging again. This time he found armour, a breastplate gone brown and black with rust, its leather fittings and straps rotted away. He hauled it out of the ground and set it down. Titus was on it in a flash tracing the remnants of engraved decoration with his fingers. Velio kept on digging.

"Sir, there are heads and helmets here. Those bastards must have separated the senior officers from the rest," he spat.

Titus looked down. Four skulls gazed out of four senior rank helmets. Strands of horsehair plumes had survived where leather had perished, the faintly coloured hairs dirty with the rainwash of neglect.

"Help me Pinneius," he said.

His voice was raspy and thick. Together they laid them out side by side.

"Praefectus over here please," Titus shouted, waving to the cavalryman.

The praefectus ran over.

He took a look, "well done tesserarius," he said, "so it's at least a patrol. But look those helmets. It's no ordinary patrol. I did not believe the story, but you were quite correct. How many are there centurion?"

Titus bit his lip, "it's more than just a patrol. But is it the Ninth? We have nothing so far to tell us that. But if it is, I don't think all of them can be here, it's not big enough. But if these bodies here are anything to go by, we may have found centurions and higher ranks."

"They split the officers away from the men and killed them up here, sir?" Velio asked.

Titus nodded as he scanned the grass around them.

"We just need something with a Hispana mark, Pinneius, and I would be willing to bet the Ninth met their end somewhere near here. And who knows how many ranking officers that survived the fight were herded up here as a sacrifice and executed."

He blew out his cheeks and made a decision.

"Gentlemen we are not going to go on looking any longer for the rest of the Ninth. Once I've got proof these men here are Ninth this is what we will report to Tribune Albinius. Agreed?"

Velio was startled.

"Agreed. That is a sensible idea. Finding all of them does not matter. The tribune needs to perform the ceremony for the dead. You have all he needs here," said the praefectus.

"Should we remove any more bones sir?" asked Velio.

"Tell every man to look for the symbol of the Hispana," Titus ordered, "I want messengers riding to Velunia the instant we are certain. Leave the bones, tell the men digging to count heads and helmets. That's all I need. The tribune may want to cremate all the bones but leave them for now. Just get me proof this is the Ninth Legion."

"But who else can they be?" said the praefectus.

Titus dismissed the comment with an irritated wave of his clenched fist at the ground.

"Just get me proof," he snarled, "and don't argue."

The rest of the troopers got down on their knees and started digging. Minutes passed and Velio kept his attention fixed on the headwall heights. No ravens or crows were calling today. More bits of armour were uncovered. More skulls but not a single weapon. Then, pinned to a lorica fragment, a phalera-courage-award with a discernible name, cohort number and Ninth legion mark.

Titus took it, turning it over in his hand, gently rubbing the earth from the pitted metal. A sad vestige of a smile touched his mouth.

"Take this to Servius Albinius. Tell him we have found at least some of the officers of the Ninth legion and await his further orders. Tell him we will not be able to hold this place without immediate heavy support."

The praefectus took it, "my best decurion will take it for you."

"Thank you," he said and offered his arm to shake the commander's in a gesture of comradeship.

He turned to Velio.

"Well, Tesserarius Pinneius, it seems the army of Rome and indeed the emperor himself may owe you a debt of gratitude."

Velio saluted.

"Marcus Hirtius would have been proud to serve the emperor in such a way. I pray he knows what we have done here today," he said.

Titus watched the troopers digging in mounds around them. They were finding remains everywhere. This little stony corrie was a graveyard. He bit his lip for a moment and lowered his voice.

"Tesserarius. I believe you were led here to find them for a reason. You could have taken one look in the glen and walked away. Had you done so neither me nor Tribune Paterculus would have been any the wiser, nor would I have blamed you. It looks as if there is nothing here but rockslides and grass. But here they are, and they should not be left, lost and unaccounted for in this province. But, finding them and holding this place long enough for Tribune Albinius to get up here and then getting out of here again, is frankly not something I think either of us should place a bet on."

Velio blinked at the bluntness. Titus Rebilis continued, sotto voce.

"The last time we were a little fortunate to get out of the ambush sprung on us, wouldn't you say? They were watching us then, and they're watching us now."

He paused and looked up at the sheer rock faces on the three sides of the glen.

"There's no other way out, sir, if that's what you're looking for," Velio said.

"Are you sure? Have you looked?" Titus snapped.

"I'll look now sir."

"Good, do that. There may be a path up out of here. Anything that makes our escape less obvious is worth knowing about," he said.

Turning away he could see men placing recovered heads and helmets in a low pile. Part of him wanted to shout that those men should be laid out with more respect but, what was the point up here in such a place as this?

"How many now?" he asked the praefectus.

The cavalryman was looking paler than before. The enormity of the position weighing heavy. He cleared his throat and spat.

"About sixty officers of various ranks I should think," he barked in his abrupt way, "no standards recovered, no side arms, no shields or weapons. Just the men and their armour. Not all of them had armour."

"Stripped some of them first I expect," Titus assented, "the last men of the Hispana. Bloody awful way to die, up here away from the men."

"They probably led them away from the survivors."

"Fuck," Titus growled.

The praefectus looked at him. They were close in age. If they had been in the same unit, they might have been friends.

"I think we should burn the remains now and get the hell out of here," the praefectus said in his short concise way.

Titus looked at him, "we have just sent word to the tribune to come."

"Titus, if this was my command, I'd gather every scrap of wood I could and burn everything. In the unlikely event Servius Albinius decides to flog two of his officers that will be an unusual punishment, but I'll risk it. Take back the helmet of the most senior soldier we can find, and he can use that to propitiate the gods. He doesn't need to be here. Please Titus, think about it. We can't hold this place for the time Albinius needs. Four, five days?"

"It was an order," Titus reminded him.

"He did not say to me *'Minucius Basilus, I want you to sacrifice your ala in a pointless gesture.'* Did he say it to you?"

"It's not pointless."

"Titus, as commanding officer present, you have the emperor's commission to act in his place. Order me to build a fire. Select the token helmet. Say a soldier's prayer for these unlucky men. Tribune Albinius will thank you if you lead us all back alive."

Titus felt the power of the argument. Staring at the ground, he kicked the stones away from his feet. He waved Velio to join them again.

"Did you find another path out of here?"

Velio shook his head. His toes were bloody from attempting the rock face. There could be no discussion that he had not tried.

"The praefectus has given me his advice which I am inclined to take. Pick out the helmet that most looks like the legate's or a tribune's, a senior centurion will do. The rest we are going to burn."

Velio crashed out a salute, "as you command me, sir," he said.

Titus turned to Minucius Basilus, "very well, get them to build a pyre."

The praefectus answered with a quick nod.

Twenty minutes later the stacked wood began smoking underneath the layer of skulls and bones slotted amongst it. Titus had done most of that part. Velio handing the grim remains to him, one at a time. Basilis stood back with his men, helmet in his hands watching the heights. Tendrils of white rose up, swirling in the calm air. The wood crackling and spitting green and blue and grey. Titus fretted at its slowness. The smoke was going to betray them. At last, the fire began to turn yellow. There was a decent pile, he just wanted to burn faster. He stepped forward removing his helmet. He picked up a sizeable branch of dead wood and threw it onto the now vigorous flames. He cleared his throat still deciding what to say; when he spoke, the words came from his mouth, unplanned.

"Hail and Farewell, you men of the Hispana Legion. You fought Boudicca. You fought and conquered at Mons Graupius. You served the emperors and the people of Rome with honour and courage and loyalty."

Velio stepped forward handing him the helmet they had selected. It looked like it could have belonged to a tribune. Good enough. Titus carried on.

"The Twentieth legion will take this to remember you by. Rest easy, the prayers will be said for you. The Valeria Victrix, your friends in the legion of the Boar say, 'Hail and Farewell'. We will not forget our brothers in the Hispana."

His voice echoed off the stone cliffs. Titus stepped back.
" 'Hail and Farewell' the Hispana legion," voices said behind him.
Velio drew his sword and after a moment's hesitation said to Titus, "with your permission sir?"
He nodded. Velio took his Hispana blade and with it in his outstretched hands dropped it into the flames.
"Take this, brothers," he said, "so you do not go naked."
Minucius Basilus looked on with grim approval and said nothing. The fire crackled and snapped. Smoke was now rising high up out of the valley walls.
"Withdraw your men," Titus said, "and say a prayer we are not with the Hispana today."

Chapter 15.

The Veniconi Chieftain's hall.

By the time Aulercas and his father arrived at Duald's hall there were six fresh Roman heads hanging from branches; the heads of auxiliary cavalry scouts. A fine catch.

"We caught them a few hours ago near the same place as last time. They don't seem to learn," he cackled, shaking their arms and exchanging bear hugs, "how many men did you bring?"

"Sixty men," Aulercas' father said.

He walked over to inspect the trophies. Blood had ceased dripping into the puddles below each one. These were not novice soldiers. They had been, up until their deaths, tanned and moustachioed auxiliaries: Gauls.

"How many of them are up there?" he asked.

"Too many for just you and me to kill by ourselves, but if we can hold them in the glen until Asuvad brings his Dumnoni we will be enough."

"Is he coming?"

"I sent him the same message as you."

"Good."

A messenger came towards them, shouting as he ran.

"Lord, the soldiers are leaving."

"What? Already? Are you certain?" Duald shouted.

The messenger sucked in air, mopping his sweat soaked face with his sleeve.

"Lord, they were there for no time at all. A small number went up to the corrie, dug up their men and started burning them immediately, then they came straight back down. There is still smoke rising from the fire. They are already out of the glen and heading south."

"This is not like them. I'm afraid they may have escaped you Duald," Aulercas' father interrupted.

He thought for a moment, "do you think you can spring your trap twice Duald? Will they take the same path back to the wall?"

The messenger straightened up shaking his head.

"Lord, I do not think so. They are taking a more easterly route. They are not coming this way."

"The old fort?" Duald guessed.

"I think so," assented the messenger.

"They may slip past Asuvad. He is heading this way to join you here. We must try and catch them on the great moor, father," said Aulercas.

"He is right, if we push onto the moor there is a chance we can still trap them. The ground is wet, it will slow them down. I was certain the gods had delivered them to us again. But if they get past we won't catch them again," Duald said.

"Then it is time we attacked the wall," Aulercas' father stated, "if they start coming north as they did in the past, they will bring their war machines to wipe out our fortresses. We must attack the wall to send a message."

"Without the Votadini it will be against the side they expect to defend. We know the Votadini are not ready, but to succeed we need them to attack from the south. They have no one to lead them. Only Vusiavi is interested in taking war to the legions and he holds no power," said Duald.

"The cavalry soldiers, Duald. There is no time to waste in speeches now," urged Aulercas' father.

Asuvad was already moving with his men towards Duald's hall when a Veniconi came galloping towards him. He held up his hand to bring his two hundred warriors to a halt.

"The Roman dogs have already left the glen and have passed over the moors," said the messenger.

"But how can they have already left? Are the Veniconi sleeping while the 'sons of the wolf' go walking through their lands?" Asuvad said.

He was angry the prey was already moving.

After a moment he said, "will they take that same road back?"

Duald's messenger looked unfazed by Asuvad's outburst.

He shrugged, "I would," he replied.

"They must know they have been scouted by us and Duald sprang a trap the last time, so I think they will try to throw us off their scent by heading east towards the Tavae and then due south along its banks," Asuvad reasoned.

"You think they will make a stand at the fort if we can catch up, my lord?"

Asuvad shook his head.

"There is nothing left to defend there. And with the rains the river will be high. It will box them in. No, I do not think they will make that mistake, they will pass it and keep riding south."

He turned in his saddle to his men, "we ride to the old fort of the Tavae, the rest must follow as fast as they can."

He kicked his horse into a trot and set off.

Half a day's hard riding brought them to a spot where they could see the Roman column moving across their front. From the assortment of helmets, they were auxiliary not legion, riding in sets of four and eight, each large block of horsemen led by an officer. Asuvad counted sixteen of them. More than they had expected. They were moving at a steady canter, disappearing behind a fold in the ground and then reappearing over its crest; standards, heads, shoulders, horses and more.

"Well?" said Duald's man.

Asuvad hesitated, there were too many for his small force to handle but having brought them here and second guessed the enemy's line of retreat he could hardly call off an attack. The presence of Duald's man put his reputation at stake.

"We'll take them at the next river ford. We'll wait until they're split between both banks and then," he punched his horse's shoulder making it flinch, "we'll attack from behind. If we can panic them, they'll scatter. Be easier to ride them down. They won't stand and fight this far from home, and they won't want to come back across the river to fight when they can escape," he said.

"You don't think much of their courage then?" said Duald's man.

"No," he replied.

*

Titus saw the next river and reckoned it could be a feeder for the Tavae, they were close.

"Do we cross over?" Minucius queried.

He checked about for signs. They had been playing cat and mouse with trees and woodland for several miles. Always trying to keep in their shadow without getting into difficulties navigating a path through. No one liked riding through strange forests. The rocky, gushing river was blocking his preferred line of retreat.

"I think we have to, to find a bearing," Titus replied, "how we would get south with this in front of us I don't know. The pass through to the Tavae is perhaps three or four miles away. Pinnata Castra is on the right. If we can cross and then turn south, I'll be happy. If we can't, we will take the trail on this side that Tribune Paterculus and I used last time."

Minucius Basilis nodded and signalled his leading decurion to get the first troop moving. The horses picking their way over the slippery rocks. He rode to the rear of his command and spoke to the last troop.

"Deploy and guard our backs," he instructed, "we are vulnerable here."

"Sir," the officer acknowledged.

More orders were given. Ten minutes later Titus was on the safe side of the river with Velio, watching Minucius on the Dumnonii side talking with his men. His men were listening and smiling at what he was saying. Titus thought it sloppy to relax at this point, but the auxiliary had their own ways of command. There were five troops left exposed on the wrong side.

*

Asuvad observed from the safety of the forest.

"Wait until they are spread evenly as I told you. Attack on my command," he said, "quietly though, don't let them know we are here."

The woods concealed them as his men fanned out. Asuvad rose in his saddle.

"Now," he yelled.

The Dumnoni burst out of the trees, yelling. Minucius turned. The barbarians had got very close before they came out of cover. He shouted a warning but the rear-guard troop seemed to melt away in a torrent of them.

"Shit," Titus groaned, "Pinneius, stay here that's an order."

He kicked his horse back into the water and began to force his way back past the still crossing troops to the men under attack.

"Keep going," he ordered, "get to the other side."

To their shame they needed little encouragement to obey him. Minucius was causing some damage with his spatha to a ring of Dumnonii surrounding him, his elaborate plumed headgear marking him out. He was calling to his men, but pandemonium was everywhere.

The Dumnonii outnumbered them. Titus breached the riverbank and drew his gladius. Its shortness and his lack of shield didn't deter him, and he charged headlong towards Minucius, determined the cavalry praefectus was not going to be speared like a fish by these barbarians. He whacked aside two attempts to unseat him, taking forearms off at the elbow. The troopers were herding back to the riverbank, horses began losing their footing, sliding into the water. It was getting messy. Several men came back to help from midstream, but the rest were obeying his order to cross over. He felt his horse stagger with a spear in its shoulder. The beast ploughed on closer to Minucius' personal battle. Another jolt slammed into it and he went down, trapped by his left leg. He twisted his body up, raising the gladius to defend himself. From forty yards away Velio watched helpless. Two Dumnonii sprang on the centurion and stabbed him to death. Minucius fared little better. He tore himself free of his assailants and hauled on the reins to get his horse facing the river. A spear burst through the chainmail on his back, and he plunged sideways: dead. The Dumnonii were howling now, tails up and cutting into the troopers.

"Fall back," shouted one of the decurions loud enough to be heard.

The remainder fought their way back into the river and as it got deeper, the troops on Velio's side sent over a volley of spears. Some caught their comrades, but it was enough to cover the rest.

"Form line. At the ready," was the order.

The troopers lined up along the riverbank in a single consolidated line. The

Dumnonii in the river started falling to the spears and their attack began to stall. Asuvad faced his mortal enemies as they rallied and stood firm, facing him, daring the Dumnonii to press the attack. He raised his hand.

"Enough," he called.

Velio heard it. Around him the remnants of the five mauled troops swirled in a disorder of startled, whinnying horses. Officers shouted men's names trying to establish the butcher's bill.

"Silence," a decurion ordered.

The auxiliary muttered and swore but obeyed the command.

Asuvad raised his hand again in the sudden silence.

"Run to your wall Romani, if you think it will protect you," he taunted across the water.

"We should go over and sort those bastards out," Velio fumed.

"No. Hold your position. First Troop lead on," the decurion took charge.

His name was Priscus.

"What if they cross and follow us sir?" a trooper asked.

"They have an opportunity right now and they don't seem to want to take it," Priscus replied.

He took a long look at the men, unimpressed with their performance. The point of his sword was aimed at the Dumnonii opposite.

"You have left your commander over there. Minucius Basilis is dead."

In Velio's ears the cries of the Dumnonii were mocking all of them.

"Centurion Rebilis is also dead, you cowards. At least he tried to save the commander," he chipped in.

The decurion lowered his voice to a hiss, "I should send you all back to get their bodies."

He saw the other surviving decurions were angry too. Priscus' threat looked real. He turned to Velio.

"May I suggest you get moving tesserarius, just in case they give chase. On that horse you might want to be well ahead of them."

He smiled at the irony of Velio's salute. An imperial tesserarius saluting an officer of the auxiliary, what was the province coming to? He faced his men.

"We're going back for them," he said, "prepare to charge."

Turning to Velio he said, "I will catch you up, take half a turma with you. Stay safe tesserarius. But if we don't meet again, tell the tribune not all his auxiliary were cowards today."

Chapter 16.

The Principia: headquarters building, Velunia fort.

Servius Albinius had leading decurion Priscus of the auxiliary and legionary tesserarius Velio Pinneius marched in front of him. Priscus looked alarmed, as he had cause to be, and Pinneius, he looked as if standing in front of the senior tribune was just part of his daily routine drill.

Servius flashed a look at Epeius. The sound of an iron pen loaded with ink hitting a scroll to record the meeting lent a chill to the office. Carumabo was not much more than a fortlet to safeguard a military supply harbour. Velunia was a fixed point on the wall. There was a tangible difference. Servius Albinius was the difference. Pinneius was the junior rank of the two, but he was imperial legion. Priscus was the auxiliary. Despite Servius' rebuke to Paterculus about not squandering auxiliaries, that was their function; to bleed and die if necessary in order to spare the legionaries.

He regarded the tesserarius. Twenty-four years of age and two sorties north of the wall with enemy contact both times, all in the space of a few weeks. The man was gaining experience at an astonishing rate. Furthermore, he kept surviving the encounters. He wondered if Pinneius considered himself to be a lucky man? Lucky men were precious. Lucky men made for better general morale. Titus Rebilis had not carried his luck as easily or with as much care as Pinneius.

He pursed his lips and opened his hands in a "tell me what happened" gesture. Priscus swallowed.

Servius looked instead at Velio.

"You tell me first tesserarius."

Velio swallowed too, dry and nervous. He shrugged, deciding to keep it short, just the bare facts.

"We went back to the place where Marcus and I found the helmet. After a bit, Centurion Rebilis said he was sure it was men of the Hispana, sir. And a phalera was found. Most of them were officers judging by what was left. We dug up the men and burned their bones. The centurion ordered a tribune's helmet be brought back for you to auger. We got out quick and the centurion, sir, he said a prayer before we left, that the Twentieth would not forget the Ninth and they should rest easy. We got across the moors and were heading for Pinnata Castra when we got jumped by two or three hundred Dumnonii on horseback. They caught us crossing a river. We fought them off but Centurion Rebilis and Praefectus Basilis were killed organising the withdrawal. And that's about it, sir," Velio trailed off.

"Is this true?" Servius asked Priscus.

"That's is the long and sort of it sir," Priscus confirmed, "I ordered retrieval of the praefectus and the centurion's bodies."

He paused, "the river sir, it was not good. I ordered the men back over as I say but the enemy withdrew. They, ah, took the praefectus' and the centurion's heads with them. Sir."

He halted.

"Sir," he repeated.

The pen scratched down the words behind their backs. Servius waited until Epeius raised his head and reloaded his pen. He nodded.

"Questions," he growled, "two senior officers lost and most of the auxiliary survive. Are we sure the centurion and praefectus were not abandoned tesserarius?"

"Definitely not sir," Priscus spoke before Velio could answer.

Servius was about to shout for silence but Priscus floundered on.

"The withdrawal was as ordered by the praefectus and was a standard manoeuvre. The Dumnonii must have tracked us through the forests. The praefectus was waiting to cross with the rear troops when the attack started. Your centurion came back across the river to help."

Servius glared at him.

Velio straightened his shoulders, "it's no lie sir. The auxiliary did all they could. I heard Priscus order his men to go back and prevent the barbarians butchering the bodies."

"And where were you while this was occurring tesserarius?"

"On the wrong side of the river sir," Velio admitted.

"Casualties?"

"We lost fifty-eight crossing, or waiting to cross the river, eleven wounded made it across. There were no losses after I rallied the men and went back. The barbarians withdrew. I decided not to pursue. It would have been the wrong choice to take the men deeper back into enemy land when our intention was to get back here. The officers were not betrayed."

Priscus was in full flow and Servius wanted to know everything.

"I served with the praefectus from the day I joined the cavalry. He was the best commander of cavalry I have seen," he stated.

Servius saw he was getting down to the bone of it. Betrayal was the fear running in the blood of the army. Since republican times and through the bloody birthing of the empire men had been given cause to wonder if they were fighting for the right general. Scratch the skin of every legionary and that fear welled up. Priscus seemed an honest soldier. He let it lie. Priscus' going back after rallying his men was not the act of a treacherous man and Pinneius had witnessed it.

"And the tribune's helmet for the augury?" he asked, fearing the worst.

"It was in his saddle bag," Velio said.

"There was nothing in the centurion's saddlebag," Priscus said, "I checked it for his personal things. In case they should be sent to his family. The praefectus' too."

"Are you telling me they had time to take his head, rummage through his saddle bag and steal the helmet all before you got your men together decurion?" Servius shouted, unable to contain his frustration, "perhaps you took longer to gather your men than you are telling me decurion?"

Velio kept quiet. He stole a glance at the decurion. Priscus was on his own now. Priscus was pale. He had never stood before an angry tribune in his life.

"Not so, sir," was all the lame defence he could offer.

Velio shuffled his boot on the wooden floor. The hobnails made a noise. Servius switched focus, Priscus did not dare breathe.

"Well, Pinneius? Tell me something. Tell me this is not an unmitigated bloody disaster."

Velio did not understand what 'unmitigated' meant.

"Centurion Rebilis did say a prayer of sorts when we burned the bodies, more of a promise I suppose, to the Ninth. The bodies were burned, and you do have a helmet from the first patrol," he argued.

"Let me be clear. You are telling me that Titus Rebilis made a promise over the bones before he burned them. Is that correct?"

They both nodded. Servius looked at Epeius. He nodded in support.

"You don't need to record any more of this, Epeius."

'Titus Rebilis may you walk among friends in Elysium,' he said to himself.

A deep sense of relief flooded through his chest. Titus had managed to do enough before he was killed and Pinneius was bright enough to understand. It was not the complete disaster he first feared.

"Anything else to say? Decurion?"

Priscus shook his head, his long shoulder length hair was matted with sweat and grime. He looked chastened by the loss of his commander and so many of his ala. Servius had cooked him.

"There will be promotions required to replace the officers lost. I will expect your recommendations Priscus on my desk in two days once you have had a chance to think about it. Be certain you never lose another commander and still survive yourself. A new praefectus will be appointed. I will inform him of your actions Priscus."

He turned his attention to Velio, "tesserarius?"

Velio wiped his dry lips and decided to say his piece.

"Only that the Dumnonii shouted something at us across the river and they did not pursue us when they could have."

"And you take that to mean what exactly? You speak Dumnoni?"

Velio shrugged.

"What do you think decurion?"

"I don't speak Dumnoni either sir. It could have been anything. They moved back into the forest as soon as we began crossing back."

Servius raised his hand. He did not want to hear it all again.

"Give reports on your wounded to my clerk decurion. Otherwise dismiss," he decreed.

They turned and marched out.

Epeius put his pen down and looked at the tribune. For a few seconds Servius looked back at him saying nothing.

"A praefectus and a centurion. What a bloody mess. How do I tell Urbicus that Epeius?" he said.

Chapter 17.

Eburacum, home of the Sixth legion.

Quintus Lollius Urbicus, Governor of Britannia, spent all morning in his palatial quarters dealing with correspondence, grew weary, left his office, touched his heart as he passed the open door where the eagle and standards of the Sixth rested and left for his residence. The legate legionis commanding the Sixth was his neighbour. Their wives were not great friends. That was unfortunate. It would have been nice, he felt, if they could have been. The only bit of domestic harmony Urbicus felt he could rely on at the moment did not extend beyond his own villa walls. He brought with him a scroll from Servius Albinius and sat down in his outer courtyard, by the fountain, to read it. Faustina saw him sit and told her housemaster to prepare food for her husband. Quintus so rarely took time to visit the house during the day. He would not have eaten since breakfast and might well get up and walk back to the headquarters building at any moment. It could be dark outside before he came home. He was wearing himself out. She took a goblet of watered wine and approached for him to notice and put the message away if it was something she should not see. Instead, he smiled up at her offering and exchanged the letter for the goblet.

"You'll stay and eat Quintus?" she asked.

"As you command," he jested in return.

"What is this?" she said.

"It's from Servius. My wall builder."

"What does he say? Bad news darling?"

"No, quite the reverse, you can read it, but just you," he said.

The water in the fountain glittered and rippled in the sunlight. He trailed his hand in its coolness as she read. The watered wine was mixed to his daytime strength. He waited for her to finish.

"It means we can put the evil curse that the loss of the Ninth cast on the army to rest. I will order Servius to hold a discrete ceremony at the fort and that will be that. A short note to Rome to update the emperor, and all files can be closed. Whatever stories that legion left behind are now just stories. This legion here, is what matters now," he said.

He withheld the loss of a centurion, an auxiliary praefectus and nearly sixty men. That information had come under a separate cover for the sake of security. A centurion and a praefectus was a somewhat expensive price to pay. One he had not expected. Now, no doubt he would have to fend off Cornelius Vatinus Paterculus who would be demanding to know why he had not been involved.

"And the wall, will that be as good as the emperor demands?" she wondered.

"The wall is resting on the work Agricola did. We are using some of his old forts and towers and bits of ditch, improving them of course and filling in all the gaps. It's not going to be as straight and pretty as Hadrian's stone-work, but it'll do the job very nicely I'm quite sure and hopefully it won't take half as long to do."

"The emperor will promote you once you have it done darling, he must, he really must," she said with pride.

"We have to see how well it works first," he replied.

"How so?" she asked.

"In Germania we tried something similar. You see Hadrian's is not just a single barrier. It's designed to make the barbarian stop and think before he attacks. Make him think twice I mean. It's also got a purpose as a levy point for grain and livestock."

She sighed; all of this boring policy talk.

He flowed on.

"In Germania we created a defensive zone through which people could be allowed to pass, or be prevented from crossing. It was a military corridor across the country. But here is the important thing if you are a barbarian, my dear. There is no single place that you could say, 'this is it. I'm through the defences' so the German tribes had no marker to help them."

"I'm not sure I follow the difference?" she said.

"It's easier, less effort to create an area of ditches and watchtowers, small forts and roads that stretch back several miles than hack stone out of quarries and construct a single solid wall that is actually surprisingly hard to defend. The sheer length of it makes keeping men at watch all the time an impossibility. No, it's all about the signalling you see. That's what makes it work. The plan is to create a self supporting zone. The signalling network allows less men to guard it than the numbers needed to adequately defend a single solid wall which, once its breached, leaves us open to attack. We can move men quickly along the roads behind the rampart. Oh, they'll see the new wall and think once they're through it they can pillage and murder, but it won't be that simple."

"I think I like the idea of another big stone wall. Keep the barbarians even further away from decent civilised people than they are now," she complained.

"Well, we did try killing as many as we could, Agricola had a good go at that, but damn it they're a lot harder to stamp out than the Gauls. At least the Gauls gave up and broke bread with Caesar eventually. Didn't want to of course but that's beside the point," he concluded.

They sat together while he ate his midday meal. Faustina pushing food at him across the table, making him eat. He was too thin. His mother would scold her as a bad wife if she could see him now. Too much worry. Far too many demands from Rome. Why did the emperor not come out here and see how much was being done in his name? Then he would have less need of all these reports Quintus laboured over.

He ate enough to pacify her though his stomach started its knotting games at the load. Pushing the plate away he took a final sip of the watered wine, throwing a titbit to their dog, leaned over and kissed her cheek.

"Must get back to the sweat shop darling, these things won't do themselves."

She gave him an appraising considered look. He was going to work himself into an early grave and this man she loved so much was not going to take the time to imagine what the impact of his death would have on her. Duty to a far-away emperor whom Quintus had only met face to face once would rob her and the children of a lifelong companion. She would lay his ashes in the sweet loamy ground of this strange, compelling country and what would she do then? Be the pitied widow of a provincial governor? What would such a life be like? Empty and joyless, humourless; or have a second life as some politician's wife, somewhere far from this legionary fort and its burgeoning civilian sprawl?

She realised with a start of surprise how much she loved the little wending river that came its slow way from across the flatlands to join its bigger sister here at the fort. She liked the way it passed unhurried through the reedbeds. The little river had a character of its own. The ducks and the birds made it live. Otter and beaver; fox prints in the mud. There was an immense peace in its soul. It must be a female goddess. One that was blythe and kind. Upstream past the small hubbub of the harbour wharves, the tranquillity of the meadow grasses and the short summering flowers, with butterflies beyond counting, would not let her go. It was all just as beautiful in the soft rain. The river had her entranced with its spell and there was nothing she wanted to do about it. It would always run past here to its fate with the sea. Sweetness consumed by salt bitterness. Like tears war and walls would not prevent.

She had come here with Quintus, expecting to hate it. To be cold and miserable for twelve months just because he liked to swap his centre of command periodically. From here she could board a ship, cross over to Gaul and return to Rome. She turned her attention to convincing the children they would make new and better friends. Against all expectations, she loved it. The people were kind and the regular legionary guards at the front of their quarters could be wicked and funny when they thought no one was around. If Quintus were to die here, if she lost him, he would lie in good company with his soldiers, and she would never leave.

Tomorrow, she decided without knowing where the idea came from, she would walk upstream, find a quiet spot and make a small sacrifice to the nameless goddess of the river. She felt her feelings begin to flood and looked up, telling herself it was silliness. But she determined to do it. Now he was looking at her. His eyes thoughtful and concerned.

'Oh, Quintus if you only knew.'

"Remember we're eating with Aristius and his family tonight. All the children will be there. Please don't be late, you know how she likes to bait me about keeping the manners up here," she said, pulling herself out of the unbidden sadness.

"Letitia just does it to annoy you," he chided.

She was wearing that delicious, furrowed frown that had been one of the first things that had attracted her to him.

"You'll abandon me to talk about horses with Aristius and I'll be left with her. You know you will, you always do," she said in mock anger and took a drink of her own un-wined water. She patted the dog as it laid its head on her lap. It gazed up at her with deep brown eyes.

"She is such a terrible snob," she went on.

Her premonition, of sorrows yet to come, faded.

"And you outrank her, so let her chew on that," he answered.

She smirked, delighted at the barb. She was so cheered, the servant girls felt brave enough to begin humming as they worked and her body slave made a better effort arranging her hair than normal.

Chapter 18.

Votadini lands south of the Hill of the Resting Lion. Close to the Votadini capital of Dunpeledur.

Paterculus had the Votadini priest pushed down on his knees. He was scowling like a dog through a reddening, bruised cheekbone. Four troopers surrounded him with their spears pointing at him. Paterculus reckoned he had arrived in the nick of time. It was too close to the hill fort of Dunpeledur. He wished the troop had pulled him a few miles away north. Votadini eyes were everywhere.

"Do you want him chopped, sir?" asked the seizing decurion, "bloody priests are a menace. Suetonius had the right idea," he said.

Paterculus checked for a moment, amazed that a druid massacre nearly a hundred years ago by a long dead general was remembered by an ordinary soldier; but then this was Britannia and the normal conditions of forgetting the past did not appear to apply here.

"Bring him with us," he ordered, "it's a little too open here."

He led them back a few miles to a spot where a small pretty stream flowed past a stand of mountain ash, over shallow rocks, pooled and meandered on its way, like a child out for a day's expedition. Dismounting he took a drink from the stream. It was cold and refreshing. The troopers waited for his permission before watering the horses. Vusiavi was pulled down, both hands tied behind his back, and he half tumbled off the horse, hitting his shoulder on the ground as he landed. There were some caustic jeers.

"Over here," Paterculus ordered.

They set him on his knees with his feet overhanging the bank of the stream. Behind him the clear water passed three feet deep with darting minnows fleeing from his shadow.

"Latin? You speak Latin?" Paterculus said.

Vusiavi deigned no reply. Paterculus ran his tongue around his teeth pondering whether a quick bout of violence was likely to elicit co-operation.

"If you don't answer me, I'm going to let my men drown you in this river. You people revere rivers and pools I hear. It's your choice whether you taste the water today," he said, "so do you understand Latin or not?"

Vusiavi understood him well enough.

"Is it a bad omen to be found drowned I wonder, in a place where your local gods gather? To be found floating in the water I mean. Is it not a desecration of their place? I think it would be a desecration. What do you think decurion?"

"He'll be right at home sir."

Paterculus watched Vusiavi's face. It was not the ignorant expression of a man who lacked comprehension. If anything, there was a degree of brute intelligence in there. That being the case surely the brute could reason his death was clear too? Vusiavi shook his head.

"Decurion get some of the men to piss in the stream so he can see what I think of his gods," Paterculus said.

The decurion's face darkened a shade. One did not piss on the local gods. He knew his lads had adopted some of the native deities themselves. The tribune looked at him. He looked back asking permission not to follow the order.

"Local sensitivities, decurion? Very well I'll do it myself."

He walked over to the water edge, standing close to Vusiavi's shoulder, hitched up his riding toga and began splashing a stream of urine into the stream.

Vusiavi flung himself sideways with a roar of anger, knocking Paterculus over into the stream. Vusiavi followed headfirst determined on vengeance.

The decurion and two men were on him before he could reach the tribune who came coughing to the surface. Vusiavi had changed into snarling snapping wolf of defiance and rage, curses tumbling out of his mouth. All in a tongue Paterculus could not comprehend. The decurion got it and kept his mouth shut.

Paterculus accepted a trooper's helping arm up out of the river. He stood and dripped. A dry cloak was proffered. An odd smile danced upon his lips.

"That was fun," he said.

In the stream Vusiavi was ready for his death. The two soldiers holding him knew it and so did the decurion. The pretty little stream was the only noise. The birds in the trees held their breath.

"Do you speak Latin, Votadini?" he repeated.

Vusiavi uttered more oaths and curses.

"Very well, decurion you may chop him. Take his head and take the horse's too. There must be a tree that's suitable somewhere around here."

A courting couple watched three troops of cavalry moving through the open ground. Northwards, back towards the distant hill of the lion. Out to sea storm clouds were shedding grey sheets of rain on the water. The lad was fifteen, the girl fourteen. Approaching the stream, they stopped when they saw the decapitated horse and its blood. He gestured with his hand for her to wait and went to the water's edge.

A man was lying face down in the water.

"What is it?" she asked.

"We must get back," he said, "it's bad."

Chapter 19.

The high council in Dunpeledur was sitting in session. The news was grim. From the mouths of a youth and his girl the king heard words that shattered everything the Votadini had worked for over the years. Rome had taken a Votadini head. Taking just the head and ignoring the corpse was a clear and deliberate act to provoke a response.

"Who was he," asked the king, "warrior, kinsman, who?"

There was a shuffling on the benches. The hall was full. It was not so very different from Ferrdigon's hall, it was not even that much larger; just far more powerful.

"Lord when we pulled the body out of the river there were still woad marks on it. It looks like the body of a priest. It might be Vusiavi, priest to Ferrdigon but we can't tell for certain."

"They took the head of a priest?" the king said, incredulous, "why would they provoke us? What have we done to be insulted? For our gods to be insulted?"

He became angrier. He raised his voice.

"He must be avenged, there can be no debating. The head of a priest and the defiling of the river. Of all the rivers they could have defiled, they have defiled our most holy one. There is no man here who can believe it was an accident. We have no choice. These two things cannot be allowed to go unpunished."

"Lord, we have not fought against the legions before. Not one of us in this hall was alive the last time Votadini warriors raised the spear."

"We will not fight alone. Send messengers to all the tribes we have made pacts with. Send them to our enemies as well. Let them all know the Votadini want revenge for this desecration."

"As you say my lord."

*

Asuvad the Dumnoni also heard the news as it spread. Aulercas and Hercuscomani, his father, heard the news. The Novantae, Selgovae, Taexalii heard the news. The Epidii heard the news.

'The peace loving Votadini go to fight the sons of the wolf.'

"It is a good time Asuvad," Heruscomani said, "Ferrdigon's death was a perfect blood offering."

"Enomani too might have given his blood, I suspect," Asuvad assented.

"You will bring the Dumnonii to war with us?" Heruscomani checked his friend's face for confirmation.

"You've decided already?" Asuvad queried.

"Yes."

"Then provided our king commands it, we will support the Votadini in their vengeance. Dunpeledur cannot see the wall, but it sees the horses and waggons on the road that takes you there. I would not have believed the legions would have given us such a cause to fight. They must want a battle. It must be a trap. They are trying to trick us."

"Asuvad, they are asking for war. And we want the wall pulled down before it gets any longer or higher. So, we give them what they want. War and blood and heads hanging from oak trees. Like the old days my friend. This time we will chase them away forever," Heruscomani crowed.

Chapter 20.

Bergessia fort.

Velio was in a foul mood. He could feel himself growing more taciturn by the day. The men of the century displeased him. The training of the Fourth Cohort displeased him. He could flourish a gladius like an extension of his arm. Other men fumbled and bumbled, hacking not gliding, battering not sweeping. It was not difficult.

"Stay on your toes, don't overextend unless you are certain of making a kill because if you miss him, he will have you open and unguarded."

Things that were so easy. He lost his patience more often. Now that Marcus was gone the fun had gone out of soldiering. Marcus had asked him once, when they were both in a stupor, why he left Misenum to join the legions. Rome no longer required its legionaries to be citizens of Rome or its neighbouring towns. The legions were manned by recruits from across the conquered world. Velio tried to bat him away.

"Stupid question, I just did. Fancied a change, y'know?" he said.

"I'm not buying that Swords, there's more to it than that," Marcus persisted.

"Shut up and give me the wine, you're going to drink it all and we're broke after this is done."

"No, tell me why first. Why did you enlist when you didn't have to? You could have been a rich garum merchant, selling fish sauce around the empire. You could have been the king of fish sauce, with your own boat to sail in a sea of sauce," Marcus grinned.

"Shut up you bastard and give me the wine."

Marcus fell off his stool, it had got to that point in the evening. He reached out to haul him up, Marcus resisted being hauled and pulled Velio after him. Lying on the tavern floor they looked at each other.

"Get more wine and you can pay."

"So, you admit you don't have an answer to my question?"

Marcus dragged himself back onto his stool. Around him ordinary soldiers grinned at the sight of two drunk tesserarii. Dangerous to be too amused.

"Just buy the sodding wine and help me up," Velio said.

Later when the wine jug grew lighter Marcus returned to his theme, to pick at Velio's scab.

"Why'd you join up Velio, c'mon just tell me. I won't laugh, I promise. Mates don't laugh at each other?"

"Course they do, you dull ox."

"C'mon don't be a forum dancer, tell me."

"Because I like the feel of a sword in my hand," he exclaimed, goaded into admission, "and I thought I could probably outfight any man alive with a sword in my hand. It just felt like it belonged, that's all. Pathetic, isn't it?"

"And now you train other men to be as good as you?" Marcus laughed.

"No one's as good as Swords Pinneius," chipped in an eaves dropping mule.

"Piss off or bring us more wine," Velio replied unperturbed.

Brutus Carruso came walking into the barrack room one day and asked Velio, with some diffidence, if he could get some additional training so he could have another shot for the place left open by Marcus. Velio stood and looked over the bigger man. In a fist fight he would probably lose. Carruso was a bit of a bear. Just not quite a hulking bear, a nimbler bear perhaps and quite capable of meat pulping most men around him.

"You sure about this? I can tell you your faults right now and you won't like them," he probed.

Carruso shifted his weight, "I want to try, and I'd rather not hear your list, just make me better."

He got that straight away. No point in humiliating the man, just work on the pieces one by one and make them join together in a better soldier. Bread and olives. He went outside and found a space close to the rampart wall. Carruso squared up expecting a one on one. Velio shook his head.

"Show me the standard defensive parries, use the dead-gaul over there," he said indicating a six foot post of oak set upright into the ground, its surface chipped and chiselled by the strokes of real swords.

The Gaul is dead because we keep on killing him – a soldier's joke.

"A wooden gladius will do for now Brutus, we're not tribunes are we? Stand close as though he's attacking you and defend left, right, high and low," he said as a matter of routine, without thinking.

Carruso obeyed and stood within eighteen inches of the 'dead-gaul.'

"No, closer still, defend like it's your last chance," he prompted.

Carruso stepped closer and at a nod from Velio chanted the parries as he made them.

"Again. Reverse order this time," he said a moment later, "not bad, now do it to my order," and he called out the parries in repeats and at an increasing speed.

Carruso flashed the sword but kept hitting the dead-gaul as he switched his sword from left to right and back.

"No, defend, don't attack. I'll tell you when."

Carruso sweating and worked.

"Halt. Now show me the attacking strikes. Body high, low, left, right, head and knees, left and right,"

Carruso stepped back half a step to make space and launched a blistering, violent series of blows.

"Now listen to my commands and strike only as I command," he said and went into a standard pattern of attack mixed with defence.

Carruso was wet with sweat and gasping for air.

"Hold" he said, "drink," and threw him a water skin.

Carruso drank and offered the skin back. He decided to drink.

"It's all there Brutus," he judged, "you only need to quicken it up. And maybe you think too much over every stroke. If you let your eyes and the arm do the thinking, you'll get faster. I think that's fine for today. Come back when you can, and we'll start getting that arm to go a bit quicker. You can afford to use your fingers and wrist more to guide the blade, you're not going to drop it, so relax."

"Thank you tesserarius," Carruso replied with a shade too much politeness to ring true.

As he walked off, Gallus Tiomarus sidled across and stood beside Velio.

Tiomarus was a bearded and lean customer with vivid white battle scars on his right forearm that though old, still managed to put the fear of the gods into most men who saw them. He referred to them as 'my apprenticeship.'

"What brought him over here Velio?" he asked.

Velio shrugged at his training commander.

"He said he wants a shot at Marcus' position," he said.

"I remember that one from the recruiting day. He was one of the ones who fancied a go at you."

Velio nodded, "he's slower than my mother making bread when the old man was hungry."

Tiomarus took a drink from the water skin and as he closed the wooden bung into the neck he murmured, "I'd watch that one if I was you Velio. He doesn't like you and I have a feeling he is quicker with a sword than he lets on. Even faster with a dagger if you follow."

Velio swung round.

"He's a plodder. Feet of lead, arm like stone."

"And if he hits you, you'd know all about it. Just be careful that's all. Marcus is a loss to me, to the section. I don't want some knucklehead having a go at your back on a dark night in the lines. Hear me?"

"I hear you Gallus. Thanks."

"Did he pay for the lesson?"

"I gave him that one for free."

"Velio, what am I going to do with you? You're going to put me out of business. Go and get me some bread."

Gallus stood while his favourite young instructor trudged off to the bread ovens. As he went the young man raised his hand to numerous greetings and salutes. He had heard what Velio had done with his precious Ninth legion blade on the last patrol. Velio adored that old blade. It showed in his eyes when he held it. Gallus knew what it was to have a weapon that felt so comfortable no thought was required to use it. Effortless and tireless. And Velio submitted it for sacrifice without second thought, in honour of men he could not have known, in a legion that was not his own. It was a gesture that made Gallus proud. Velio Pinneius was going to be a good 'un. Of that fact Gallus would risk a hundred denarii.

Brutus Carruso walked away from the lesson knowing a quick murder within the confines of Bergessia was out of the question now that proper timbered buildings were replacing the tents. The legionaries would be moving back soon for auxiliary cohorts to come in and take up the permanent garrisoning. Centurion Glaccus had made it clear he was as likely to order his death if he fouled this up as any friend of Pinneius'.

The tesserarius had returned from two successive patrols north of the wall, unscathed, whilst others around him had not been so lucky. Now his commander Centurion Rebilis was dead. He decided he had a real problem.

*

Paterculus brought the three turmae of cavalry back to Velunia. The ride gave him time to consider what to tell Servius. There were a variety of possible truths that laid him open to some risk. Since arriving at the post in Carumabo he had been paying close attention to Servius and his favoured senior centurion Glaccus. Though the full complement of the Second legion was seconded to the construction task, there were only vexillations from the Sixth and the Twentieth. And yet it was as if the Twentieth legion dominated everything. The Sixth and the Second were being treated as subordinate to the mighty Boar. He had expected more consultation with the commanders of the three legions. But Albinius was behaving like the fabled kings of old Rome. His first posting was turning out to be a lot more complex than he had anticipated. Dere Street brought them to Carumabo and from there he took the coastal road to Velunia amid busier traffic.

In the end it was all an anti-climax. Albinius appeared to stop listening as soon as he heard Ferrdigon was dead and a tribal succession struggle was underway. He decided omission of his diversion towards Dunpeledur and the priest's execution could wait for another time. Albinius' map of the wall was, as usual, spread across the desk and annotated with ink lines and notes. He could see it was new. The last one so written over that it had become useless. Servius was not a tidy scribe. The new one looked as though Epeius had inserted all the previous corrections. How long it would remain legible was anyone's guess. The wall had been started in the east and the work there was nearing completion. The benefits of digging in light sandy loams. That section of the map was tidy. The mid sector progress was satisfactory but still behind the east; a fair bit of notation on the map for that section. But the west was slow going.

Heavy clayed ground and hard rock cutting there. He could see the dangers of an unbalanced construction that exposed a weak sector. Servius for once took him into his confidence. They would eat that night and discuss the progress. Just the two of them. Not even Glaccus. No scribe, just the two tribunes. Paterculus headed towards the bathhouse with a quiet joy in his heart.

Chapter 21.

Hill of the Resting Lion.

Eilaver received the visitors from Dunpeledur sitting in 'his' chair and wearing 'his' silver torc at her throat. Dunpeledur sent greetings to the new chieftain of the hill and brought the king's expectations of homage. She said the right things to his emissaries. The Votadini were a joined people. His kingship was not under any challenge from Eilaver. Ferddigon and Enomani were now lying side by side on the small outcrop on the opposite side of the pool. When she flexed her right to sit in her husband's place it had caused scarcely a ripple of comment in the stronghold. That part of Vusiavi's scheming had been correct.

Dunpeledur's words to her were stark. The Romans had defiled a pool by placing a murdered Votadini in its waters. The woad marks sounded like they might be Vusiavi's. For a few seconds she drifted away from the messengers' voices, feeling her anger change inside. The traitor was dead. Her lover was dead. The three men closest to her in life were dead. The messengers were still speaking.

The king was inclined to retribution because of the priest and the way he had been killed. He demanded her allegiance. He wanted reassurance her small hilltop could raise seventy men of fighting age from lads to grandfathers. She nodded, that number was possible. Getting word to allies across the wall was getting harder with each passing day they told her, but already the tribes were sending word they would ally with the Votadini.

She sat back amazed when they finished. She had spent her life aching for her people to get off their knees and sever all ties with the Romans. No trading, no exchanges, no acceptance of tributes demanded. No soft surrendering of an annual portion of the harvests to fill their granaries. She had dreamt of pushing the red cloaked army back beyond the southern wall for so long that it had faded into just that; a dream, a shadow yearning for something at times even she conceded was unachievable. In a few month's time she and her people would be trapped between two walls. The little independence they had would be lost. The children would learn the Roman tongue. The best things of their way of life would vanish. They would be prisoners in their own land. Dunpeledur could command more than a thousand warriors with a click of the fingers. It was hard to know how many more men the king could field if he chose to plan a campaign. Vusiavi had managed to sire courage in the mind of the Votadini king. Astounding.

"Seventy men, yes let me think," she said, stalling.

"What is there to think about? Your king asks for your obedience. You rule here now, do you not? We see no unhappiness in the faces because you have Ferrdigon's torc and his seat."

She touched the torc that still felt strange on her throat. It was heavier than her own bridal one, now passed to her eldest daughter. It had been made to be worn. It should adorn a chieftain's daughter. Now that Enomani was dead, she would be the one to follow Eilaver.

"What is there to think about?" she reposted, "we would lose everything if we joined the king's army and he failed. The wolves would bring their horsemen and their war machines up these slopes and destroy us. That is what I think about. Will Dunpeledur come and stand with us then?"

"Dunpeledur has always been the heart of the Votadini nation. You know this, we all know this. Dunpeledur cannot be allowed to fall. And if we raised war against the legions and lost, this hill of yours would be a lesser price than Dunpeledur hill. There can be no argument on this. The king's fortress must always be first. Every man and woman will be required to defend it."

She looked at them. The king's greeting had soured to this demand for fealty and men.

"You are fools, if you think you can you hold Dunpeledur at our expense. If the legions march, they will not bother about my small village. They will be coming to you. Have you not seen what they are building? What can they do? Your ramparts will not hold them long. A day or two perhaps but no longer," she snapped.

"Longer than yours," they smiled.

"What ramparts have I here? A ditch and a wood fence," she spread out her arms.

"Exactly. That is why Dunpeledur must be protected by every Votadini warrior. If Dunpeledur were to be taken, we would end up as slaves or be sent across the sea to fight in their army."

"You will not hold them. That is why our forefathers chose peace with the legions. Even the tribes in the north do not stand against them. They flee into the hills through the high passes. You know this to be true. It is only by bending that we can withstand the storm," she paused, "or by uniting in total war. Does our king have stomach for that?" she challenged.

"So, you will not come to the king's call?"

"My seventy men will not decide the king's war."

"But will you let them fight?"

"If they fight and we lose they will bring the wrath of the wolf up here. It would be the same if I led them."

"Then lead them and let our gods fight their gods and then we will know which are strongest."

She considered this.

"You ask me to throw my village at the Roman army. I might as well throw stones."

"They have insulted our gods, violated our rivers, defiled our land with their wall. How much more will you take before you stand and fight. I know Ferrdigon was an old coward, but I always thought you had spirit."

She bowed her head, "very well, you may tell the king, Eilaver of the Votadini on the hill, will bring her people to his cause. But he must come to mine if I have need."

"If you have a time of need Eilaver, the king will never desert you. He understands you want to be free of their yoke. Trust me, so does he, but to fight and fail would be a disaster for us all."

'Success,' she thought, *'they promise war.'*

*

Heruscomani still lamented Pasnactus. The whole family were grieving for him. His daughter had taken a knife to her arm and only by Aulercas' youngest sister's quick wittedness had she been prevented from following her husband to the afterlife. He sat and brooded, admitting he was the first to tell his children that life was not fair; it was a struggle. If life had been fair, they would live in peace, grow their crops and animals and feel the sun on their faces. Instead, they were facing their greatest challenge. Trust. It all depended on that. If any single tribe shied back from the trial and retired within their halls, the war of the Votadini would shrivel like a pear in late autumn. Attacking the wall would be a chancy thing. For one thing, it girdled the two great rivers but there were more Roman troops concentrated there than anyone alive had ever seen. Except perhaps the elders of Duald's clan. Their old knowledge of the battle of the blue mountains was revered, but not helpful. A memory of defeat was never helpful. Victories were potent as bulls. He knew Asuvad would be reliable. Headstrong but reliable. Duald would defer to the name of Heruscomani. Pasnactus would have been an able commander.

The Votadini would attack the wall from the south, where danger would be least expected. They would be the blade in the groin of the Romani defenders, lethal, but they must press home to the hilt. They could be decisive if they held their nerve. Or they would be dead. Only if the Novantae and the Selgovae could be persuaded to push northwards would that thrust be strong enough. And if the flighty Taexalii could be persuaded to come in on the attack from the north side then it was possible the wall could be over-run under the sheer numbers and the forts burned.

What chance the Votadini really had the balls to fight? They were bragging of war, but they had no experience. He stroked his beard and toyed with an idea that had dogged him since word had come out from Dunpeledur. Everyone was whispering of a mighty attack from both sides and that brought significant problems of striking as one united spear. But, what if the north attack came a day before the south attack? So that the garrisons were hit twice on successive days, but the second day would fall on their weaker open side. The wall faced north after all. And if they breached it and took a fort or two, cut the signalling lines, what then? Could the line be rolled up, fort by fort until it was all burned? He wondered what songs they would sing of him if he pulled this off?

The cold air was making his right shoulder throb. He huddled closer to the fire and wrapped his cloak tighter. This war-talk of the Votadini was a helpful distraction if it made the Romans turn in the wrong direction. If Votadini, Novantae and anybody else made an attack from the south that feint was worth gold. But he and the northern tribes should attack in their own time. If the warriors on Ferrdigon's hill stayed out of it, the Romans might excuse them in any reprisals. It all depended on the high kings of the tribes agreeing to combine in an army already split on opposite sides of their enemy.

*

The horseman approached Velunia's Decumana gate. He was twenty eight years old and carried shield, sword, spear and helmet. He had a heavy silver torc around his throat. His breeches were of fine woven, patterned wool. His under garment was decorated at the cuffs and around its low collar fringe. He wore a heavy leather, knee length, jerkin of bull hide incised with decorated motifs of animals, rivers and complex spirals that closed in to a single dot. At his middle was a leather belt studded with silver. His face carried his tribal woad and his hands were broad and tanned. The gatepost sentry picked him up at half a mile distance and had him under surveillance for five minutes before he called the duty optio.

"What tribe?" called up the optio before he got off his stool in the guard room.

"Don't know sir," replied the sentry.

"Well, you bloody well should. Is he a friendly or a hostile?"

"Doesn't look like much to me sir."

Two minutes later as the horsemen pulled up fifty yards out from the gate, checking for archers, the optio said, "Votadini, peaceful. Take a good look. Next time make sure you can recognise a Votadini when you see one, you useless mule."

"Sir."

The man dismounted and led the horse to the gateway. By his actions, he was not afraid.

The optio looked down at him from the gantry over the gate.

"Who are you?" he began.

The warrior returned his look.

"I am the cousin of Enomani, son of Ferrdigon, chief of the Votadini on the hilltop. I come asking for justice. He has been murdered. He was the rightful heir to the chieftainship and it was taken from him. The Votadini are friends of Rome and its soldiers. We have been your allies and traded with you for many, many years. And you must know this to be true."

It tumbled out of his mouth, pent up and full of bitterness. The optio reassessed the man below him. He was tall and well groomed, his clothes were not common cloth. The optio looked up and beyond to the horizon checking for trouble. The open grassland and the low rises of ground lay passive and domesticated. Smoke rose from groups of Votadini households and cattle were grazing by the stream where the road to Carumabo crossed it. The Votadini appeared to be alone.

"Interesting. What do you want me to do, if as you say your cousin is dead? Do you want to be the next chieftain of that hill-top?" the optio said, playing for time, wondering where the centurion would be about this time of day. Diplomatic relations with the tribes were not his responsibility.

"I want you to fix it," Enomani's cousin said.

"Fix it?"

"Can you do that?"

"Do what?" the optio queried.

The sentry beside him thought about interrupting with the offer of his javelin.

"So, you can't?" persisted Enomani's cousin.

"Speak plainly, what do you want? Or go back where you came from," the optio snapped, wearying with this conversation he couldn't get his head around, that seemed to be going nowhere.

"If I go back and you do nothing, remember when all this is over that I tried to explain," the warrior replied.

"I'm sorry your cousin is dead. I'm sorry Ferrdigon is dead. Do you want food?"

The Votadini shook his head.

And after a moment's pause, "what is your name Votadini?" the optio asked.

"Ferrdigon's nephew and Enomani's cousin. That is what my name is, optio."

The warrior pulled his horse's reins and it whickered, tossing the long mane. He looked up at the impressive gateway and made a final appeal.

"Romanum auxilium mihi." Help me Roman.

"I'm sorry, I cannot help you," the optio replied.

He watched the warrior riding towards the low hills southwest of Carumabo. The rider did not look back. He did not hurry. He took as long to ride away as he had taken to ride up to the fort. The sentry made the stiff finger sign. Something was coming. There was something about the way he had made his request - I want you to fix it – that was not normal. The local tribes-people did not make these sorts of submissions. They took the benefits the soldiers' money brought but they did not ask favours. They were passive, docile even, but even a humble mule could tell they did not pray to the new gods, the gods of Rome. They endured.

For all his feigned disinterest the optio was a little concerned. But what could he tell a busy centurion?

I've been speaking to a high ranking Votadini with a complaint I didn't understand? Who did not ask for anything clearer than "justice" for two dead men?'

Well, the green grass of Britannia was amply fed by the blood and bones of dead men. Two less Britunnculi bastards was all to the good as far as he was concerned.

He turned to the sentry, "carry on," he ordered.

"What was all that about sir?" the sentry asked, pushing his helmet up over his forehead.

"Don't you worry about it my lad. Just make sure you can recognise a Votadini 'cos next time he might be one of them unfriendly ones."

*

Paterculus sat before Urbicus and decided telling the governor about his little diversion to Dunpeledur would be best. He had already delayed reporting on his mission to the Hill of the Resting Lion since Ferrdigon, the object of that visit, no longer featured in Rome's plan. Servius had sent him to Eburacum post haste once he realised the Votadini might be in a period of upheaval. Tribal dynastic changes could be swift to turn sour. Germania had taught Rome that much and Servius refused to take chances. Confessing to the diversion would go a-ways to explaining his delayed appearance. One did not keep a provincial governor waiting. Paterculus carried a written version of his actions for the records.

The principia headquarters building in Eburacum was a splendid affair; an open courtyard with portico-ed columns, a drinking well, leading to the inner courtyard, leading to the inner sanctum of sacellum and administration rooms. Mosaic floors everywhere. Splendid and exactly the sort of location he should be in. If there was an Elysium for young tribunes, this was what it must be like. And the sun for once was hot.

The governor was in an amicable mood. The headquarters staff came and went about their tasks with their correspondence with polite nods and salutes. There was not the faintest sense that any problem in the country could not be resolved on the orders of these men. It was intoxicating and gratifying to absorb the miasma of power emanating from within these walls. It was nothing like Velunia where an air of tension seemed to simmer in the background like the scents from Servius Albinius' kitchen. Why in the name of Mithras did he have to be stationed so far north of here? Perhaps a transfer might be engineered?

He sat patient in a chair reserved for only the highest profile visitors and waited for Urbicus to despatch the last tasks before him; revision of field punishment and mining reports.

"Silver, lead and tin Cornelius, it's what makes this damn country worth the effort," Urbicus said with a smile.

He beamed at the use of his given name by the governor.

"Every province must pay its way," he agreed.

"And timber of course. The timber is inexhaustible."

Urbicus waved his hands like a man who owns the world.

"So, tell me now, tribune, how is that Ferrdigon chap eh? Still hiding like a good little dormouse on his little hilltop thinking we have forgotten about him? Still pays his dues on time I hear. Good fellow, not that I've ever met him of course. I leave that to you chaps to keep the wheels turning. Interesting place though. Excellent views of the plain and the estuary. I was thinking we should perhaps put a signalling station up there. What d'you think? He wouldn't object, would he?"

He felt his heart picking up speed. He coughed. This was not what he had prepared himself for.

'Damn the man, why couldn't he stop meddling in the frontier? Well best to spit it out.'

"Governor, the Votadini Ferrdigon is dead, I suspect he was murdered by his people. I can't say why. I was accordingly unable to make an assessment of the situation. To add to the mess, his son has either fallen or been pushed to his death, there are high cliffs on the hill, I don't know if you are aware?"

Urbicus nodded, a careful neutral look settling on his face. His hands rested on the desk, fingers intertwined. He let the tribune speak.

"I believed it to be no coincidence and the morning I arrived Ferrdigon's personal priest took off for their capital fortress at Dunpeledur."

"And so you did what exactly, tribune?" Urbicus purred.

"I followed and apprehended him governor. It was my intention to bring him in for questioning. Tribune Albinius has made plain to me how important the continuing acquiescence of the Votadini is to our construction of the wall," he dissembled.

"Just so. And this shaman told you what exactly?" Urbicus probed.

"He tried to escape from my patrol, he was killed evading arrest."

The lie slipped out almost without him planning it. Urbicus put his hand to his nose and breathed in, a deep sound; considered, calculating. He rubbed his jaw then let his hands entwine once more.

"Killed evading three turmae of cavalry. Well, he must have had the power of his gods on his side, don't you think?"

Paterculus had braced for the reprimand that must be coming. Sarcasm was not what he expected. Urbicus moved his lips in a small grimace of displeasure. There were a few moments of silence to contemplate the beating of his heart. Urbicus sat back steepling his fingers, the gold rings on them chubby and bright.

"I offer you my apology Governor, for failing in the task you set me to perform. I judged the apprehension of the priest to be wiser than letting him run to hide in Dunpeledur. As for the Votadini, they did not strike me as a threat.

Too many years of peace has softened them up. From what Servius Albinius tells me there is not a Votadini alive who has ever raised a weapon against the legions," he said.

Urbicus nodded a political assent, though Paterculus did not like the grey steel in the governor's eyes or the pale pallor of his mouth.

"What is done is done," Urbicus said, "you will watch the Votadini on the hill with extra care. Get a signalling station built up there as soon as you return. That'll cool them down. Send me word when it is operational. I want relays to Trimontium. Should there be any symptom of revolt from either the lion hill or Dunpeledur I want to know."

"As you command governor."

"And Cornelius, don't kill any more priests."

Paterculus took the reprimand and kept his mouth shut.

*

Servius Albinius took the news of the governor's desire for a signalling station on the Votadini hilltop on the chin. It was an ideal site but building a station right in the midst of a client tribe's ground was pushing things a little. He was glad the order had been given to Paterculus. It was his problem. All he had to do was offer wise counsel if asked. It seemed Paterculus had pondered on it too during his long ride north from Eburacum. His return was a lot less bullish than normal. He gave Paterculus one piece of advice.

"Take the timber in on waggons. For the love of the gods don't go in and start cutting down trees under their noses."

The only feasible approach for waggons was from the north and northeast sides where the ground was less severe. But woodland crept up those slopes from the plain below. The other aspects, its formidable cliffs and heights, extensive marshes lent it an impregnable air.

Paterculus summoned an architecti from the Sixth legion and sent him off with an escort to reconnoitre the heights from a distance. There was no need to go up there yet and stir things up. When the report came back it sounded promising. A line of sight to Carumabo fort and harbour, a line of sight to the lone rock that marked the distant mouth of the estuary and lines of sight to various points on the southern horizon. Why had no one acted before now?

"Servius, why has no one acted to do this before now?" he asked over a second dinner.

"Did the architecti go up onto the hill and see for himself?"

"He was pretty confident it was not necessary. Though there is that other scarp and rock that could be used as an alternative," he replied, "what is your gut feel for this Servius?"

Servius took more food from the platter and lay back on his couch. He looked bleak Paterculus thought. It didn't bode well.

"What Quintus does not want I would hazard, is war on both sides of the new wall. Frankly Cornelius, your disposal of the priest was not something I would have done. These people are obsessed with priests and trees. You know the Dumnonii have attacked along the middle section of the wall to test us out."

"But they were easily repelled Servius."

Servius raised his hand to hold him back.

"I consider those attacks to be more of an exploratory nature than fully committed. They were no more than a dog marking its territory."

"Pissing on every tree you mean?"

"Apt, Cornelius don't you think? But our wall is not on schedule in the west. If an attack were to come there and gain a foothold we could have need of every legionary in the north."

He chewed a morsel of goose. Servius' cook was indeed a good one. He laid the leg bone down. Servius had a red drip of wine on his immaculate toga. It was gratifying to witness that such a powerful man dribbled wine like other mortals.

He pulled himself together, "he gave me a direct order Servius. I cannot simply ignore it. If he said built a signal tower at the most suitable high spot, I would have discretion, but he did not say that, he said build it on the Hill of the Lion. What can I do?"

He leaned forwards hoping against the odds that Servius would throw him a lifeline.

"Obey, Cornelius, at all times obey. And pray to the holy 'Mothers of the

Parade Ground' to protect us. The Votadini can be pacified with beads and baubles, we'll impose less taxes for a season or two perhaps. Because if they rise and join a general uprising against the wall we, my friend, will be in for a tough time of it. So go carefully or give a rich sacrifice to Mars. I don't see a third way. More wine Cornelius?"

Chapter 22.

Hill of the Resting Lion; one week later.

The architecti, was less than impressed by the hill as a site for a signal station. At least it gave him a different challenge from working on the wall for a while.

"Who are we going to signal exactly?" he asked his centurion with his tongue in his cheek.

The centurion gave him a black look.

"Get a signal station built that can send and receive from Carumabo and also faces southwest. That's my order and now it's yours. Get on with it."

"There is no other spot you would prefer?"

"As long as it can do what I have instructed, I really don't care. Just get on with it. The tribune wants it done sharpish," replied the centurion.

The architecti knew when to take the hint and stop asking. He took a short walk on a low knoll opposite the Votadini fort. The lion's head and shoulders blocked the view to Carumabo, so that was no use. It would have to be on the other side of the pool, high up, where the access was more difficult. And he was not permitted to cut a fresh road up there because it would upset the Votadini too much.

'I think telling them we're putting a signal station here might have already achieved that, thank you,' he thought.

He descended and took a walk up the opposite slopes gathering a little following of children from the fortress. He smiled and waved and did not linger. There were some promising ridges that had the line of sight required and were away from the precipitous cliffs on the northwestern edge of the hill but the whole hilltop was solid rock. It kept breaking through a thin layer of earth and tough grass. Bushes clung on the soil. The tops were too bare for trees of any size. All his timber would need to be carted up here. Cutting a foundation into this would be a long job and the rock was not the kind that would release in straight lines when split. The alternative was to bring pre-cut stone up here to form a base. But time was not his friend.

'*Gravel base then to get it level, with a timber bed?*' he speculated.

He did not like that idea much.

'Turf, like the wall?' he mused.

A tower built without a proper foundation was an anathema but as he looked around he became certain that to do this to the required legion standard would take time and effort. He now had a small audience of wide-eyed children perched on the grassy slope above his head watching every move as he picked his way along little paths, to and fro searching for what he needed. He did not mind the company. He settled on a flat shelf of rock for the new tower and decided some of the heavy gateposts used on the forts would be the best size for the job. They would be heavy enough not to move once he had them in place and provide a sufficient base to build a low tower for the signal guard. Given the position, he could compensate for the lack of foundations by building it lower than the usual height.

'*Bloody miserable job, stuck up here for days on end with the Votadini watching every single thing you do.*'

For the actual signalling platform, he could use some of the stone lying about to set a level and use gravel as infill. It was a quick and dirty fix, just like his centurion ordered. He headed back, giving the children a cheery wave as he went.

A few days later, when it was finished, he gave it a final walk round inspection. His men had done a decent job of making the tower secure. He was not concerned about the signal beacon. From these heights its flame would be unmissable. He hoped it never needed to be lit. The timber accommodation pricked his professional pride but, it would do the job. He nodded to the decanus of its first guard.

"It passes inspection," he said, "may Fortuna smile on you."

"Sir," snapped the decanus.

A week later Paterculus sat on his horse watching a waggon progressing up the incline with its mule train stretched out ahead. It had gifts for Eilaver and her people, so it was bearing a small load, but the steepness of the slope was deceptive, bringing home to him the long climb up for any transport waggon. He wheeled his horse from the odd shaped pool and kneed it up the steepest part of the ascent to the gates of the village. Smoke from the fires was hanging low, courtesy of the stillness of the day, drifting out in widening plumes from numerous small halls. His cavalry decurion and his guard had already been up there preparing the ground and Eilaver and her council were waiting for him. From where he was, the signal tower lay hidden by the contours of the hill, but evidence of its presence was everywhere in the scored cart tracks of iron shod military waggons. He decided a bit of bravura was required. They were likely to be a bit unwelcoming after the disruption. Stamping all over their homes, that sort of thing. Well, what did they expect? Bloody savages the lot of them. Like as not to poison your wine with piss and steal your horse as soon as your back was turned. He pulled himself together.

"Greetings Eilaver. The Emperor Antoninus Pius sends greetings to you and your people. He sends gifts because you have pleased him and because you are counted as his friend and friend of the people of Rome. Cornelius Vatinus Paterculus, tribune of Rome, greets you and says 'Hail, Eilaver queen of the Votadini of the hill.'"

'Queen, too much?' he mused, *'but if it keeps her happy then so be it. The things I say and do for the glory of Rome?'*

Eilaver was looking more composed than the last time he had seen her, all things aside. She raised her right arm in a quasi-Roman salute that just managed to fall short of a genuine gesture of obeisance. The mourning had been covered. He had to admit she had a certain uncouth beauty. She was older than him by several years, but they bred young here the same way they did at home. By no means had it spoiled her looks. The thought teased him like a feather.

'What if she is amenable to? No, Cornelius behave.'

"I welcome you, Tribune. You and your soldiers are friends to me and my people. Will you stay and eat with us? We have good wine for you today," she replied, divining his base interest.

'Good, because it's Roman wine,' he jibbed.

He raised his hand in benediction.

"Thank you. I will be happy to. But first I would like to see the signal station.

We want to send a message to our men at Carumabo. A test."

He looked. Was it her mouth or her eyes that tightened first? He was positive he had seen a reaction. She made a little bow.

"As you wish tribune, my men will go with you. Your men can water their horses down below."

"I thank you, they already have," he blundered.

Her eyes changed again for him and this time he saw, too late, his error. It was a look that said, *'I know you have already watered your horses in the holy pool without asking me, because I watched you do it.'*

Permission to water the damned horses, whatever next? What did these people want from him? He decided to ignore it.

"Well, lead on my lady. Decurion, bring four men and follow me."

He dismounted and stamped his boots a couple of times. The ride had been a bit harder on the backside today for some reason. She waited while he performed this act. Her eyes were unfathomable now, almost placid but he still felt he had erred about watering the horses before coming up. They were so sensitive about these things. Down below, the escort started manhandling the crated gifts up to the fortress. Behind her back he saw the interest in her people's faces.

They walked over the uneven slope of the hilltop following a slender path worn into the very neck of the lion's head. A steep fall below, was the gorge the construction details used to haul up the architecti's timbers. There appeared to be steep sided rock faces and treacherous slicks of scree on all sides. It was a place of gouges and sculpted outcrops. He had never seen anything like it. There would be a local god here no doubt.

'A small sacrifice of appeasement for the tower might not go amiss and might even pacify the Votadini woman. The tower guard can do that,' he thought.

There was no need for that to delay him. No need to make too big a thing of it. But Governor Urbicus could not have imagined a trickier place to set a signal tower. The fall away to his right-hand side was precipitous and fatal. Were they taking him on this path on purpose, trying to prove a point? Etiquette forbade he make an obvious attempt to keep his balance. It did not do to show any weakness. They reached the spot the architecti had chosen for the tower. He stepped inside, noting the small bunks in the cramped quarters and up the stairs to the upper platform. It was a tremendous view of the countryside, really quite something. He came back down and went further along the path to where the signal platform lay primed and stacked with logs and brushwood. Getting logs up here would be hard work for the mules. Six legionary tower guards stood at attention as he gave it a cursory check.

"Torch," he ordered and put out his hand, "let's see if the Tungrians are awake today."

The men laughed. He reached up and set a torch to the kindling brushwood. A good soaking of pitch ensured it took and coloured up, the fire blooming under the upward draughts of air. He handed the torch back and said, "well done," to the decanus in charge.

"Sir," he saluted back.

Paterculus noted the looks of relief. He did not mind their fear. Having a reputation that made them wary was no bad thing.

Carumabo fort had been sited on a sloping field that tilted down towards the river-mouth and the sea, out on a limb, dedicated to its sole purpose of protecting the supply port. All its messaging came and went by horseback. The navy took the blame for recommending it. It was, they said, a safe anchorage in an otherwise open and windswept estuary with dominant winds from the west: most unhelpful. Its relay signal station was up on the first rise with a clear view landward. There would always be a delay in sending and receiving. To top it all, only the most basic, single beacon light could operate at the extreme distance. Paterculus turned to the small audience of soldiers and Votadini.

"And now we wait for Carumabo to light their torch," he smiled.

Within fifteen minutes a tiny pinprick beacon flamed in the distance. He had to squint to see it. Back on the signal tower one of the guards stood pointing with his arm outstretched. He smiled, guessing the Carumabo tower guard had acted on their own initiative, it was too quick a response for a rider to have reached the fort and returned with permission to light the test beacon.

"My word, they are indeed awake. Success," he announced, "let us eat."

"What do you want me to do with the fire sir?" asked the decanus, "should we save some of the logs for next time, sir?"

"Oh, just let it burn itself out. It'll be good for Carumabo to know where to look exactly for new signals, and for your men too," he replied.

Eilaver, pretending indifference, turned and walked back towards her hall. Overhead, the "kiiiii kiiiiii," calling of hawks caught her attention. She looked up. The hill and its woods were a hunting ground for owls and hawks. Ferrdigon's bird had gone with him on his journey to the ancestors. And Enomani's with him. She missed the birds bobbing their heads each time she or Ferrdigon passed the stances in the hall. She would have to get another one. Perhaps a small one.

A pair of speckled brown buzzard hawks were circling the high top of the hill on unmoving wings, riding the up winds. It was a good omen. She pursed her lips and wondered why seeing them unfettered by the cares of men below was not warming her as it did on any other day. Was it because of Enomani? Was their free flight a reminder of Enomani? He should be ruling the hilltop people now. She swallowed down the emptiness and held back her tears, walking the narrow path to the hall.

There was a point, Paterculus admitted to himself, when he should have summonsed his men and led them back, job accomplished, gifts handed over, to Carumabo fort for the night. Velunia was too far away to reach today. He and his men were being well looked after, given the earlier frostiness of Eilaver's reception. The troopers were behaving with commendable restraint. He heard genuine laughter and songs lilting. The Votadini ones sounded a great deal more musical that the soldiers', but the sound was evidence of friendship. He relaxed with what really should be his final cup of wine of the evening, this one poured for him in one of Ferrdigon's own drinking vessels. For a moment he wondered if it would be bad practice to drink from it, and moreover why it had not gone with its owner to whatever passed for Elysium to these people? She smiled at him from across the fire ensconced in her husband's oaken throne.

'She is trying to make amends,' he mused. She must have got over the death of her husband and son, though it did seem unusual to be so cold hearted about it. She was not a bad looking woman and by no means beyond her best days. She was making the effort to entertain him. There was a possibility of a little fun. The men would be happy not to leave here and get back on their horses for a ride to the slim comforts of Carumabo.

'A little fun,' he smiled back at her, *'what better way to cement relationships with the local chieftainess than by a little fun?'*

He could imagine recounting the tale to Servius.

'Did it go well?'"Servius would ask.

'Fine, Servius fine. They didn't mind about the tower really and the woman kept me warm in her bed all night.'

He settled in for a convivial afternoon that became evening.

"You and your men must stay," she insisted, "the tracks will be too dark soon and the marshes down there are dangerous if you don't know the paths. Your men can bed down in the barn, or wherever else they find a welcome," she grinned the first real come-on.

Another bout of singing and a lyre-harp began sounding, like water flowing over stones in sunshine. It transformed Ferrdigon's hall into something joyous. The fire was stoked up with more wood. He untied his neck cloth and loosened a couple of straps as his armour dug into his stomach. He accepted more wine, unbothered about drinking from a dead man's prized possession now. At some discreet moment, he realised she had sent her people away. The hall was empty except for the two of them. They had drifted off and he had not noticed. The darkness of smoke hole in the roof told him night had fallen outside.

"You must be tired tribune," she said, "we are the last ones still awake."

"Cornelius, it's Cornelius. That's my name," he smiled at her.

"Cornelius," she acknowledged.

She led him up the steps to the sleeping platform. The dying fire below was throwing small shadows across the hall. The effect was not at all unpleasant. Her bed was covered in a mixture of thick and soft animal pelts. He put down his helmet, laid his gladius by a stool, unfastened the buckles of his breastplate, and let the armour slide down to rest on the floor. He removed his ornamented greaves and untied the lacing on his caligae. She saw his boots come off and smiled. The dress came off her shoulders in reply to his complete disarming and she slid under the skins and smiled as he dispensed with his toga and undergarment. In the faint red hue of the firelight he slipped under the skin and pulled her to him. She smelt of flowers. Her hair smelled sweet. She lay back and smiled up at him and said, "Cornelius."

He was young and virile, and he pumped her more than Vusiavi had done. She smiled and gasped and dug her nails into his back, panting to encourage him. He thrust into her with no more attempt at gentleness than if she was a backstreet woman in an Aventine whorehouse. Every anger and every frustration in his life that he had concealed, even from himself, drove him into her, again and again. And again, until he exploded inside her with a loud grunt of pent-up satisfaction that the gods themselves might hear.

When they stopped, he rolled off her and went to sleep with a contented sigh. Had he been Ferrdigon or Vusiavi she might have taken it as a compliment. She lay still for several minutes in the gloom listening to his breathing settle into a deep rhythm. He was not many years older than Enomani had been. She kept her eyes on his face and reached a hand for the thin sheath lying on the floor by her side of the bed. Her fingers searched before they found it. Pulling it to her mouth she held the tip of the leather to her lips and pulled the narrow iron needle out. His face was calm. His was chest rising and falling, slow and even, relaxed.

'Like a man who's enjoyed himself,' she thought.

She put the small, rounded hilt-end of the pin into the palm of her hand, and placed the needle point over his heart, the same the way she had done to Ferrdigon. This time it was different. Ferrdigon had died in her angry rage. This Roman was different. Killing him was not the same thing at all. It was not so easy. His crimes were against her people, but they were not the intimate crimes of Vusiavi, taking Enomani and Ferrdigon from her with his mouth poison. The spear had to be raised. This Roman would give his life as a sacrifice to her war. For the insult of watering their horses in the pool. The arrogance, the casual arrogance that he could bed her without so much as a shred of courtesy. Those were his personal crimes. He had bulled her worse than Vusiavi. The folds of her palm hid the end. Breathing in, she conjured up Vusiavi's face in her mind and pushed it home with every single grain of iron in her soul, the same way he had pounded his hips into hers, whilst promising a life of power together,

'Vusiavi, murderer of my boy, my precious boy, Enomani, here is my revenge and here is my curse on you. May the gods hear me.'

The tribune froze in his sleep. She waited, praying he would not be strong enough to open his eyes or raise a hand. Her prayers were answered. The soldier lay. Dead without a sound. Pulling out the blade she repeated the trick with her fingertip, sealing the wound and lying back to wait for the dawn. The hours took an age to pass. Her arm went numb, but she bore it until at last faint light filtered into the hall from the sky. The hole in the roof announcing it to her. The fire was still burning with a few tiny, low flames licking and curling the red edge of blackened logs.

His face was white now. His body was still warm, but she could feel it cooling. She pulled her fingertip off the tiny wound and hoped no blood would seep. None came. But this too was different. The soldiers would not just look at their naked officer's body and accept a natural death. She had to get him clothed. She had to get help. With luck she might prevent them realising his death was premeditated. She rushed to dress and drank water by the fire, stirring it into life with an iron rod and some small, chopped pieces of wood to get it going. Gazing up at the platform where he was lying, the choice was stark. Get him down here, get him dressed and make believe he had fallen asleep by the fire drunk and had passed over during the night or, leave him up there and pretend. Pretend what? He slept down here last night while she slept alone overhead? No, no one would believe that. Getting him clothed would conceal the wound. She doubted they would dare to undress their leader here and look for wounds. They would wait until they returned with his body to their fort. That would buy a day or so of time. If the wound held shut, they might not even spot it.

Or, she acted now while the soldiers were asleep. Send them all following him to their gods. All or nothing. Burn the signal tower and bring revolt, like a slap in the face to the king in Dunpeledur; make him act.

She went back up and looked again at his body. It was a tiny wound. The craftmanship of the iron needle amazed her. She wondered if she moved his corpse whether it might yet leak and betray her. There really was only once choice now. Ferrdigon's champion must put all the tribune's men to the sword. There could be no survivors and the bogs beyond the loch could have their bodies.

Vusiavi had never bothered to take on an apprentice. Had he lived longer he might have done so to preserve his craft, but he had been casual the day he rode off from the hilltop and had not seen death walking at his side. She slipped out the hall to the hut of her champion, tapping on the door. It swung open in seconds and he stared down at her.

"My lady Eilaver?" he rumbled.

The sun was creeping higher. She had no time to plot with him.

"Come with me," she said.

He took a short time over the tribune's body.

"They all have to die," she hissed, "it's gone too far for any of them to leave here."

"I have the answer," he said soothing her.

His face was firm, "are you certain this is what you want me to do?" he asked.

She nodded, "we must be quick, they will waken soon."

"Stay here until you hear it beginning," he advised, "keep a distance from this and you will have an excuse if anything goes wrong."

Bending over he hoisted the dead soldier over his enormous shoulders and took him out of the hall. She sat down by the bright fire and folded her legs beneath her, waiting, straining to hear the second her warriors struck. The light was getting too bright. The Romans must be awake by now. They could not all have been stupefied by drink. It only took one to scent trouble and she would have thirty armed cavalry men on her hands in a small fort that had women and children within its walls.

Mayhem was breaking out in the stable barn. It had begun.

Hammering and shouts. Curses in Latin. The first sounds of horses panicking. The noise swelled up like a thunder cloud over the sea. She felt quite calm. Ferrdigon's sword had gone with him to his grave but against the wall several of his lesser spears remained. She chose one that had been a hunting weapon and took it with her into the compound.

The soldiers in the tower seemed to have guessed what the noise meant. Had one of them escaped the compound? The glow of a fresh signal fire was already visible over the crest. She had not planned for that.

At the barn her champion was standing with a circle of men setting fire to its timbers. Nails were going into crosspieces over the doors. Men and horses were going to burn alive. Paterculus had brought a single turma of cavalry, only some of them would be in the barn. The luckier ones, including the tribune's decurion she guessed, might have found more accommodating places to sleep. Fighting was spreading as her new champion set about his work, bringing others with him. Around the barn the Romans were kicking their way free. In other corners, huts were becoming scenes of bloodshed, shouts and cries of rage and pain ringing out. Children screaming. Women screaming. The stable entrance became a battle where neither Votadini nor cavalrymen were gaining an upper hand. It was too small for more than a few to engage, the rest were noisy onlookers. The shouting was incredible.

"Throw them back and bar it shut," she screamed.

Her hatred consumed all reason. The champion pulled men out of the way and held back a sudden rush by the soldiers. They seemed to melt before his sword. The door was heaved shut and barred again. More hammering of nails. Shoulders holding the doors shut as the fire took a firmer hold. The Romans pounding on the door and walls. Swords jabbing out through the gaps like wasp stings. Her champion looked down at her, his eyes blazing with fury but he took her shoulder and said in her face, "you are losing the barn. You will lose everything."

"Are you afraid to kill Romans?"

"Not me. I fear no man."

"Burn it, burn the tower. Burn them all. They killed Vusiavi. They killed my priest," she shouted at him.

He nodded and waved his arm at the warriors, "keep it burning and get ready when the door fails."

In the other parts of the hill-top, the turma's last resistance was snuffed out. She sat on a nearby woodblock and watched the horror unfolding in the barn. She looked up at her champion,

"Burn all the bodies there are. Put the tribune in with his men. Send word to Dunpeledur and the Dumnonii and the Veniconii. Tell them Eilaver has raised the spear and we will attack the fort at the river."

The barn was now an inferno, the screams rising to an awful crescendo. The horses, the poor horses, she wanted to put her hands over her ears; then it went quiet. And the silence was somehow worse than the sounds of dying.

"We saved some of the horses. The barn was not big enough for them all," a warrior said.

She nodded.

"But they are marked with the brand of the legion. We cannot keep them my lady. They would betray us," the warrior continued, matter of fact.

In a voice that she scarcely believed was hers, she said, "then you know what to do with them."

"Do we fight alone now my lady? Is this how it will be? We have not enough men here to attack the fort. I hope Dunpeledur comes quickly," Indutus her champion said.

He did not take his eyes off the blazing barn as the unstoppable fire roared louder and louder. The carnage inside was not a death he would want to face. There was no honour here. She fought with a rage that was not clean. Her act defiled the warrior tradition. Ferddigon would have understood. Burn them once you have killed them, if you must, but to burn men alive was wrong.

"I will send word to Dunpeledur," she assented.

"As you command, my queen," he replied.

"Thank you," she acknowledged looking up.

She realised there were tears on her face and she wiped them.

"This was always coming. We could not have lived here trapped forever behind their wall. You know this. They would have our children speak their language. The Votadini would become slaves in everything but name."

She stood up and turned to go.

"I must see if any of my people are hurt."

Indutus decided not to point out the fact they both understood sufficient Latin to make her argument false.

"The men in the tower. Make sure of them too," she said, "no survivors. Not a man, not a horse."

Chapter 23.

Dumnoni lands.

The senior priest of the Dumnoni had been without peer for fifteen years or more. The son of a priest who was the son of a priest, who was the son of a priest. Normally he did not talk much to people. Anyone else doing such would be regarded as aloof, a lone wolf, an oddity in the gossip loving community. Instead, he was a listener, a solver of problems and illness, a sounding board for ideas and hopes. Delivering wisdom always just shy of outright judgement-making with a nod or shake of the head. No one would dare to ignore his advice, but he was always open to debate and persuasion, a bit of gift accepting, before he arrived at his prognosis.

He lived alone by the water, gaunt faced and tortured by his calling, an unhappy, morose man, feared by the children though they had no reason.

To the spirits and the gods he was a babbling stream of communication. Unlike some priests he found real truth when the spinning sickness in his head heralded vomiting and foaming and a rigid stricken paralysis that left him drained and thirsty. In those minutes of madness, the gods sat by his writhing, clenching, heaving body and spoke. When it passed, for a fleeting few moments, he saw their faces, visions beyond words, communication without need of lips nor tongue. By asking, by submitting to them in his head, he could reach out and have communion. At other times, to please his people he prayed at their request even when the spirits were not listening.

"Mistletoe and oak. Great binders of men and gods, holly and hawthorn holders of the sacred fields, brothers to the skies above. Hear our prayer. Without blood sacrifice we ask for you to deliver the blood of our enemies to us. We bare our backs to the whips of your vengeance if we do not bring back gifts of heads and weapons. These we promise as tribute. Look kindly on our humble strength and grant us the weight of the ancestors. Grant us their anger and their knowledge. Grant us their undying love for our land and our people. Grant us their skill and their deceiving ways of war. For our women, children; homes and cattle. Grant us victory."

He opened his eyes, wiping his mouth. His face was wet with spittle and saliva. Above him the sky was normal. He could hear blackbirds chattering. Ravens were calling. He sat up and got to his feet, brushing twigs and grass from his tattered robes. The high chiefs were sitting like white faced children on a log set well back from his small, tree shaded chapel at the water's edge. Asuvad was there.

He picked up a wooden bowl, dipping it into the pool. He smelled it and drank, before offering it to each of them to drink from. Asuvad was last to taste the cold sweet liquid. He took back the bowl, drank again and upturned it before holding it up to the sky, with outstretched fingers. Then he dropped it on the grass as if it was no longer important and came and sat crossed legged before his chiefs.

Inhaling, he clawed back his greying long hair. His long brown robe was beginning to fall apart. He would not change it for a new one until it parted at the shoulders and dropped off. He would sit naked and silent, waiting for the tribe to present a new one. There was no asking. Just waiting and counting how long they took to notice. Some of the chief's braver children brought food every morning. A new robe might arrive within hours.

"Well?" they asked, "what are the signs?"

"The signs are calm, like the water. A fool might think the gods had not listened. But I say the gods are happy for the Dumnoni to take war to the sons of the wolf."

"You are certain?"

"Nothing is certain when men ask the gods for favours. Look at the water. Does it move? Is it dark?" he quizzed.

They all stared hard at the small pool.

"No, it is clear to the bottom," Asuvad answered.

"I say the gods are content. They do not oppose you," he affirmed.

"Will we be successful? Will we drive the wolves away?"

"They do not say what will happen. They are content, the water is calm. That is all I can tell you. You must decide for yourselves whether you will be successful," he stated, refusing to be drawn further.

He got up and stalked off into the woods. He could not have been clearer. The chiefs sat digesting the briefness of their audience with him. As ever, the message was open to interpretation. Heruscomani clapped Asuvad on the back and they bearhugged.

"Tomorrow we are going to attack the end of the wall where the sun sinks," Asuvad grinned.

Heruscomani's face shone with anticipation. War was coming and the gods had stepped aside to let it happen.

"Our heralds are out gathering as many of my people as possible for the army," he replied, "attacking tomorrow will leave us a little light on warriors. It's too soon for them all to gather but I think we will have enough to stand with you and surprise the Roman pigs."

"You and me, we will lead them. Together," Asuvad vowed, offering his arm out again in friendship, "you and me will take our tribes and together we will cross the ditches and climb the earth walls. There will be a blood feast for the gods. Every oak in every glade from the lowlands to the mountains will have a Roman head on a branch. We will make sure they never dare to step north of the marshlands again. They will not imprison us."

Heruscomani was silent. He rubbed his face with his hand, pulling at his chin, one of his mannerisms. Asuvad saw his friend taking stock of what they were proposing. He was the older man, a chief in his own right. Asuvad waited for him to speak.

"The priests must want it," he said, "otherwise there can be no support. Without the gods we are weak. The water is calm. The priest has spoken."

"We join together as one army?" Asuvad asked.

His warriors would want to know.

"I agree. We will gather on the hills to the north of the western forts," Heruscomani promised.

Chapter 24.

Hill of the Resting Lion.

Eilaver wasted no time bringing her men off the hill, drawing others to her from the surrounding area. The Roman signalling detachment might have alerted Carumabo, but what would they make of a second signal so soon after the first? They could not think there was trouble, could they? The latest messengers from Dunpeledur met her on the low ground and were singing a new song.

"My lady, you have acted too soon. The priests say the time is not right. We must wait for a clear white moon."

She waved that suggestion away. The moon would not be full for another ten nights. Nothing could wait that long. A sudden premonition of standing alone against the legions made her heart cold.

Drawing herself together she said, "but the king spoke for war? You came here and said I should fight. I took the king's spear and I've driven it in to their flesh. I have Roman bodies in the ashes of my barn. I have done more in a day than the king and his fathers have done in years. The fort on the river is next. It is out of sight of their roads and lines. It must be sacked before they come looking for their patrol. The people will rise, I know them, they want to," she blurted.

She could feel rage beginning to get the better of her self control.

'Perhaps I should drag you up to my stables and my barn and show you the bodies? And then you will act like men and not like cowards, afraid to raise a hand to the wolf.'

The younger of the messengers spoke first.

"He will not lend his men to it my lady. He wants war to avenge your priest but it's the priests my lady, they say it is not the time. My lady, if you fight now, you will fight alone."

He let the threat hang for her to consider.

"Then tell the king I will remember his words and what his actions were. My husband's priest Vusiavi will be avenged. I will fight them alone if I have to. But there will no more tribute for Dunpeledur, no more of my young men to serve the king's side. No silver and cattle. Eilaver of the Votadini will break her allegiance with the king unless he comes now to fight with me. If I have to fight alone then so will he. Tell him that," she shouted.

Indutus sidled over and took his place behind her right shoulder. They knew who he was.

"My lady, you cannot mean that," they said.

She felt the anger welling up.

"I am not some fat old man who brags by the fire at night to his court, full of ale and Roman wine, that's been paid for by slavery."

"No of course not, we honour you as Ferrdigon's rightful queen and his successor, but do you understand what this means? Forgive me my lady, but Ferrdigon would not have said these things, let alone acted the way you have. If you have killed Romans, they will come and bring the sword to your hillside. The blood that runs on the grass will stain it red."

"They have brought the sword before and we are still here," she spat back.

"We have never fought against them since they came north in the times of our forefathers. And why, my lady? Because we are all cowards? No, we have not fought because they are too powerful. They have too many warriors and their machines cannot be broken," the eldest messenger intervened, attempting to put reason back where it belonged.

"Their machines can be burned," she said.

"That is true," said the elder.

She wanted him to say more. Why did that admission feel as though it weakened her argument and not Dunpeledur's?

"The Veniconi, the Taexali, Dumnoni and the northern tribes don't think the sons of the wolf are too powerful," she said.

The elder began to speak and then bit the words off, he changed course.

"My lady, the northern tribes do fight well but they also run to the hills when they are outnumbered. They always have," he said with practised diplomacy.

"A sensible tactic I'd say," she snapped.

"Yes, but they do not stand and defeat the sons of the wolf. No one does. No tribes have ever sent them away completely and returned to their old ways. Not even the mighty Iceni of the south ever completely overwhelmed them. They say she had thousands, hundreds of thousands of warriors in her army by the end. So many warriors a wise man would stop counting and say 'you have enough.' But they were not enough. They were lured and they were trapped. And they were outthought. Women, children, the old and the young, all perished under the swords. She lost, my lady."

He pointed an anger finger to the north.

"Over there are thousands of Roman soldiers. Thousands, my lady. And down there," he pointed south, "are thousands more. How many men do you have?"

"They never took her alive," she reposted.

"What does that matter? They will come here and burn everything, enslave all they don't kill. But think on, my lady, because Dunpeledur will not suffer," he said, his patience wearing away.

He understood her desire to kill Romans. He felt that way about them sometimes too. But he had never taken his sword from the scabbard. Once unsheathed it could not be returned with honour unless it tasted the blood of an enemy.

"Dunpeledur said it would fight," she ranted, refusing to back down.

Indutus eased a little closer. She sensed his famous temper was fraying too. She knew he did not like the way they were talking to her. Whatever his faults, he was faithful. The elder switched his attention to her champion. His face changed into a bleak baleful promise, defying the implicit threat.

"It will, but only when the priests say the gods are ready."

"I cannot wait for Dunpeledur's priests," she said.

The messenger tried once more, putting out his hand to almost touch her elbow but stopping fractions short, as if she was his daughter.

"You must," he breathed, "you know you must my lady Eilaver. Think of your people. You can gather as many warriors as you want to attack the fort, but you know and they know, we all live on the wrong side of the wall. We have nowhere to run to. We are already trapped. Besides, you cannot raise enough men to take the fort."

"I can raise enough to set it on fire," she replied.

He pulled his hand back to his side.

"True, but if the garrison comes out to fight it will be at best two or three to one against you."

Eilaver scowled. But it was an unavoidable fact.

*

The Tungrians were German, and their forebears had stood against the mighty Julius Caesar himself. The senior centurion left Carumabo and trotted up to the signalling station, enjoying the ride. His horse was eager and brimming with energy. She shot up the long slopes. Dawn had come and its clear light made the fields and the view of the sea a pleasant one. The decanus in charge saluted as he dismounted.

He returned the salute, "well? What's happened?" he asked.

"Please follow me sir, it's looking a bit strange if you ask me," the decanus said.

Intrigued, the centurion complied and followed the line of sight indicated by the decanus. Far in the distance the signal station on the 'lion hill' was burning. Was that it flaring up? He knew all about the new station but harboured personal doubts it was the best place to put it. There was a better, unoccupied hill that might have served the purpose.

"So, the signal is burning. What is it saying?" he asked.

The decanus faced about.

"It's not saying anything sir, it's just burning. We had a test signal yesterday. But this is not the same fire. It's a new one that shouldn't be burning, it's not part of a signal sequence because the only agreed signal we can have with them at this distance is for a general warning. And also, it's too big."

"What?" he said.

He had a sudden uneasy feeling.

"You see the way the fire keeps flaming up?" the decanus lectured.

He looked harder, it was not clear to him at all.

It was too far away but he decided to accept the signaller's better eyesight.

"Mmnnn, what are you saying exactly, decanus?"

"It's as if the whole tower is burning," the soldier replied.

He froze halfway through the sentence as the implications hit him.

"What line of signalling do you have from here?"

"None, it's bloody useless, sir."

"Explain a bit more clearly please decanus."

"I have to send a rider over to the nearest station that overlooks the plain if I want to get a signal up to the wall."

"Dis Pater," he breathed, "send a rider now to that station. Tell them to get a signal to Velunia. The signal to read "Enemy. Act. Quick."

The decanus coughed.

"Well say your piece man," he said, not taking his eyes off the distant yellow that more and more, now that it had been pointed out to him, really did look like a major fire.

"Em, no strength numbers, sir?" the decanus ventured to question.

He shook his head,

"It doesn't matter for now. It's trouble and we may need to 'Stand to the Eagle.' The prefect will worry about numbers when we have all men back in the fort and the enemy at the gates. Send the rider and bring your men back to the fort. That next station, how far is it?"

"Just a couple of miles on the high crest over there."

He pointed to a tree clad ridge. The signal tower sat in a cleared area like a bald scalp.

"Can that station defend itself?"

"It's got an eight man detachment sir, wooden tower."

The decanus' implication of legionaries roasting was not lost on him.

"Get them to send the signal and retire to the fort only if they see enemy approaching. From that height they should have enough of a head start to get back. If they can stay and keep receiving signals they should do so for as long as they can, but I want no heroes decanus, make that plain."

"Sir," the man saluted again.

He mounted his horse.

"Send a rider to the prefect at the fort. Tell him what you have told me. Tell him I recommend 'Stand to the Eagle' until we know what is going on. The tower may be on fire, but it could just be a careless accident. I am going to have a closer look. Try to see what in the name of Jupiter is happening."

He kicked his horse and pushed along the track back to the proper road. The lion hill was seven miles off. He realised he would not be able to judge the situation without going up onto the hill itself. As he trotted the horse, he decided signallers typically only brought bad news. They had a penchant for disaster that was happening to someone else or a disaster that was coming your way. A closer view would only be a closer view. Why the fire was burning did not matter if the whole tower was alight. He had not brought a shield. Sucking his teeth in annoyance he decided there was no time to go back for one. In any case he needed intelligence not a fight. If it got to that point, he had all the intelligence he needed.

Ninety minutes later he circled the low incline of the hill from the northwest taking advantage of a thick screen of trees. From a low crest he saw the smoke, drifting in grey pall across the hill top. The flames were visible. The whole tower must be on fire. He pulled his horse to a halt and patted its neck, letting it rest after pushing it to get here. He had never been this close to the hill and its variety and shape was astonishing. It was almost sculpted. A hill of infinite variety. No wonder the local tribe had made a home on it. That was what his people would have done. There were brown buzzards circling high over the red cliffs. It looked too open and spread out to withhold sustained assault by a few cohorts, but defended with sufficient, well-placed archers and plenty of throwing spears, taking it by force could turn out to be a long bloody process. There was a majesty about it though. It was not just another largish hill rising above a plain littered with other largish hills. The shape of the lion was something he had never seen before. An animal spirit must hold sway up in the rocky heights, perhaps? The horse raised its head and shook its mane.

"Good lass," he said.

He nudged her forwards keeping a lookout for hostile warriors. He had not gone far before he found what he was seeking. Tungrian and Votadini, two different tribes from two different lands, fighting on different sides looked at each other. He counted five of them, painted-up for war. He pulled the horse around as they shouted insults and started running towards him, kicking it hard and retreating back the way he had come. Their shouts faded and he kept her galloping until he was sure he was well clear of them. Slowing to trot he pushed the mare more than she was used to, promising her a good rest if she kept going.

When he got to the fort his commander was waiting, looking down at him from the southern gate tower.

"Hail. How does it fare?" the Roman commander enquired, refusing to acknowledge any possible sense of alarm.

"The Votadini are painted for war. I have seen the blue of them and I have ordered a signal to Velunia. The new signal tower on the lion-hill is burning."

He trotted through the gate and dismounted, patting the mare in gratitude and blowing onto her nostrils. The praefectus met him at the bottom of the gateway scratching his head in disbelief.

"So, they are coming to do what? Shout insults and throw stones? What has stirred them up?"

"I don't know sir, but I think we should expect an attack."

"An attack? From the Votadini? Are you serious man? I have ships unloading on the quayside. Waggons ready to be loaded to go up to Velunia. Perhaps I should go and talk to them. Throw a few blankets at them, pat a few children," the praefectus said with his habitual condescending smile.

"I told the signal teams to come back. Have they arrived?" he asked, choosing to ignore the little barb.

"Both squads are back, so now I have no communication at all with Velunia. Very well, we will remain ready, but send a mounted patrol out. Let's see if these Votadini really are stoked up for a fight or is it just a few hotheads."

There was that air of petulance he knew well.

"And the fire on the hill sir? The signal station? Do we just wait?" he asked.

"Very well send a rider to Velunia if you must. Message to the duty officer on watch as follows.

Expecting trouble from Votadini.

Have retired to fort.

Please support.

Perhaps a patrol will chase them back onto their little hill before they get here," the praefectus turned away still talking, feigning the subject had already lost his interest.

'This is not the time for a sham,' the centurion fumed.

He got hold of a decurion and had the message on its way to Velunia before the praefectus changed his mind.

Chapter 25.

The western end of the wall.

In the last moments of the night, as the horizon began to reveal itself, Asuvad and Heruscomani made a final offering to the gods in front of their men. The priests stood back. They had done all they required. Below the hills the unfinished western end of the wall lay open and ripe. The Clota was within touching distance, flowing unseen in the distance.

"Which legion is here?" Asuvad asked.

"Their Second legion. They have not made their defences strong yet."

"We split and attack those two forts," Asuvad said pointing through the gloom to the stockades that from the heights looked close together.

The progress of the ditch seemed to have faltered in the heavy clay. Both it and the rampart trailed off in height on either side of the nearest fort. It stood isolated like an island.

"No, we attack that one first and get around them. And then we attack the second fort, from the sides and the back. All their defences face the north. We will not attack them there. We will use their own lines to help us."

They rose and shook arms, both bare chested for war; blue torsos, iron helmets, spears, shields and swords. Around them warriors gripped arms, slapped chests, punched shoulders, shook weapons. Only the need for stealth prevented shouted challenges and chanting the pre-battle war-songs. The Dumnonii led the way on foot down from the heights making for the first of the forts. They crouched down in tall wet grass and took stock of their target. Heruscomani led the Veniconii off to the right. The morning air was cold and there was patchy mist lying in the hollows. Perfect for hiding their advance.

Asuvad hunched down and assessed the frontage of the fort. There was an initial mound. That was the diggings from the ditch, he surmised.

'Clever, make the ditch seem twice as deep as it really is', he appreciated the trick.

It was surmounted with a scree of rough and broken branches to make it more of an obstacle. A fall from the top of the mound into the bottom of the ditch would take the wind out of any warrior. The far side of the ditch rose up onto a narrow bare corridor under the rampart, designed as a killing zone. Then the rampart proper, topped by the wooden fence, the one patrolled by sentries. It was a sequence of obstacles. From this close distance it was obvious no single part of it was intended to halt an attacker. But the combination of them, would take the steam out of an assault, slowing men down as they navigated each section, exposed them to javelins coming down from above. Behind that, the predatory outline of the legionary fort squatted below the skyline waiting for the morning to bring its trumpets. On both sides of the actual fort the continuing rampart had not risen above waist height.

The slow light picked out sentries moving and talking. He was close enough to see the patterns in the turf stacked in the wall. Once the whole line was fortified and garrisoned with legionaries, he saw how it would be an immense undertaking to storm it from the front. In the sections between the forts and watchtowers where there were no legionaries patrolling it could be more vulnerable.

He crawled forwards on his belly bringing his men with him. The sentries were very close. A cough would betray them. He prayed his men kept silent. They squirmed up the outer face of the upcast mound and saw the bits of branches and rough bushes buried into the mound. With a little pulling he felt one beginning to rock in its foundation. He glanced along the line on either side. His men were doing the same, making gaps to crawl through. He heaved himself and his shield through the space he had made and managed to stop himself falling down the other side. Holding up his arm he tried to warn those around him.

The ditch below was deeper than he expected but the raising up of the rampart parapet, as they had seen from the hills, was only complete at the front edge of the fort. Now that he was within touching distance he saw with delight it fell to waist height in less than a bow-shot on either side. A plan blossomed in his head.

'Get onto those lower sections and we use them to run along and attack the front wall and its gatehouse from the sides.'

He pulled back from the top of the mound and signalled his men down. Hiding in the shelter of the outer mound, he drew them together.

"We must get up onto those low sections of the wall. An attack on the gate will cost us too many men. We will distract them into defending the gate but we are not going to attack it. We must make them think we are. Make our fire here, get the torches well-lit. When you get up onto the lower walls, we will fire the gateway. That will be your signal to attack. Those doorways must burn. When we get onto the wall, we must hold it. From there we can fire into the fort. Make sure everyone understands. The doorways and the wall are all part of the fort. Get ready. I want twenty men with torches here with me. There must be no war cries until we are inside. We must be foxes. The wolves must not know what happening until it's too late."

He paused looking to the west where Heruscomani, Aulercas and the Veniconii should be taking their positions ready to sweep behind the defences. Their task looked easier. The Romans had not begun to consolidate the ground in that direction.

"How long Asuvad?"

"The Veniconi will owl-call when they are in position. Go now and wait for us to throw fire at the gate. Stay quiet 'pride of the Dumnoni', today there is glory for each of us. Look there it is, up there on those walls."

They moved off in two groups leaving Asuvad and his small band. From two small pots, his men took burning embers, blowing them into flames. He steadied them with his palm.

"Not yet men, not yet, wait for the owl," he said.

Minutes passed and he could feel them getting restless. The safe covering of darkness was falling away. The sky in the east was beginning to glow brighter. The owl-call floated in the air.

"Now" he said.

They put the flames to the wood and cloth torches. The sentries were nowhere to be seen. He took a chance and decided not to throw his fire-brand, scrambling instead down into the ditch and fighting his way up the far side. The earth was soft and yielding, he sank ankle deep as he climbed. He stuck his head up half expecting a Roman javelin to hit him. The sentry walk was still empty. Heaving himself up onto the berm he crossed the short space to the wooden gateway, laying his torch up against the base of the gate. There were Roman voices speaking somewhere close at hand. Waving his arm, he brought his men over and they stacked the torches along the door. The gate was sold oak and it dripped with dew.

"What now," hissed a warrior. He made an instant decision.

"Wave one of those torches, let our men know," he said.

He stepped back. There were enough torches to have a sizeable fire, but it was having little impact on the timber. He searched in his head for the Roman word for "fire."

Deep in the fort a trumpet-bugle sounded. They all looked at him. Without defenders the earth rampart was vulnerable and easily scalable. His men understood.

"NOW," he hissed, and they hurled themselves at the rampart, clawing their way up, using knives to gain a grip. He thought he heard an answering roar from the direction of Heruscomani's men. Shouts erupted from the fort's walkways and heads appeared above its north gate. The voices he had heard, of course it was guarded: he should have realised. That was why the trumpet had blown. They had been spotted. At the top of the rampart, he kept his voice low.

"Throw me a torch."

One was passed up to him, he grabbed it, trying to ignore the white heat.

"Bring more," he ordered and then he was over the low wooden palisade and crouching on the inner walkway before he knew what was happening.

Mayhem was breaking out on either side of the north facing gateway as the wings of his attack struck at the corners from the low walls. The noise of trumpets calling was deafening and the shouts of legionaries and warriors were all around. Legionaries came streaming along the walkways, battering warriors down with their broad shields. Some fell into the fort, others back out over the sides. Hails of javelins impaled the Dumnonii. How could they have wakened so fast? It was as though they had been waiting for the attack. Warriors were falling all around him. The whole of the northern and western walls were enveloped in the fight. Bit by bit his warriors were somehow withstanding the javelins and gaining a foothold. More trumpets blared and for a second the defence faltered. He understood why. Heruscomani's Veniconii had struck against the lesser defences of the south gate and its walls.

Down below him perhaps two hundred legionaries stood in a tight knit defensive formation pushing back against his Dumnoni who were pouring over the walls at the front of the fort. Individual warriors were flinging themselves against the Roman shield line which gobbled them up. He flung the torch into their midst. There was an immediate recoiling away from the brand.

"Fire," he screamed to his warriors, "use the fire."

He whirled around, the northern gateway that had failed to ignite was now open and warriors followed his lead hurling fire brands at the legionaries. He leaped down and joined the hand-to-hand fighting as the fire broke the formation open. His warriors rushed in to exploit the confusion. Whistles were blowing and the legionaries began backing in towards the centre of the camp. The struggle for control of the ramparts seemed to be over.

On the far side of the fort he heard the distinctive Veniconi war-cries. They too must have forced an entrance. The dawn light was getting brighter. He saw hacked bodies lying in pieces. Horses were whinnying from an unseen stable. The trumpets kept blowing but he was certain the weight of the two tribes was stifling the outnumbered legionaries. It was working. He felt the surge of elation; a war chief's prize, a successful attack. The Romans were falling in greater numbers. He could not see what caused the defence to crack.

As he got fought his way closer to the south gate to find Heruscomani, he saw legionaries were already escaping through the east gate, heading towards the safety of next fort on the wall. Too many were getting away. He wanted them all dead. The remaining formation splintered, penned in a frenzy of bloodshed. Most of them had no armour. He felt the glow of victory. The surprise had been complete. They had not been waiting for him as he first thought. Without their iron armour they were vulnerable. The wooden barrack blocks became whirling individual fights as soldiers tried to fight their way out into the lanes between the buildings. He saw the fort's signalling platform beyond the fort. The bonfire was fully alight and no one was paying the least attention to it. It was too far gone to be extinguished now. He heard trumpets from further away. He had done enough here, there were still prizes to be taken.

He stood and shouted, "leave them. We must attack the fort over there before they have time to organise."

Heruscomani and Aulercas lay waiting in the drenched grass listening as the fort sounded like it had been hit by a storm. From silence to a solitary morning trumpet and then an eruption of noise.

"Asuvad," Heruscomani grinned, "steady men, we must give him time."

They waited and listened, imagining the carnage unfolding with the fort. Within a short time the east gate of the fort began creaking as it opened.

"Steady," he said, keeping his men hidden.

Around the open gate a group of his men fell to an exiting rush of Romans. Aulercas shouted in frustration. More of the Veniconi were already pursuing, skirmishing along the road, shepherding and driving them east towards his father's ambush.

"They are coming just as you said they would, father."

Heruscomani gripped his son's shoulder, "they have lost the fort to our brothers," he replied.

He pointed with his sword to the legionaries evacuating the fort then turned to the refuge they were running towards.

"Make sure they don't get there," he called out.

The roadway supporting the wall and the forts was more of a broad tamped-down trackway than a Roman metalled road. It followed the contours of the slopes. The retreating Romans were fighting their way into his trap. He waited and waited until he could hear their voices shouting to each other, the clear voice of a leader giving commands. There were no javelins to worry about now. These men were only armed with swords and shields. The leading ones running with their eyes fixed on the distant fort. It was the hindmost who were having to do the fighting.

'Let's change that,' he said to himself.

"Rise up my brave Veniconi, take your swords to the hearts of these dogs," he shouted.

His men stood up, rising out of the ground with the new sun at their backs. Aulercas heard cries of alarm from the Romans. The feathered helmeted leaders did not even pause but came pounding on at a steady jog straight at Heruscomani. They did not look like panicking soldiers to him. If there had been any panic in the killing ground of the small fort it had already evaporated. They were coming on in a determined way. Veniconii were snapping at their heels but there was no doubt their officers had found some control. The gap closed.

"Spears," shouted Heruscomani.

The warriors sent a cloud into the legionary ranks. The Roman shields took most of them. The two sides met with a bone breaking crunch. Heruscomani took the full impact of a centurion's shield and it drove him back. Aulercas came in to help him. Together they hacked at the soldier, but he met their swords with his, their shields with his shield; his own men propelling him into the Veniconi ranks like a human battle ram. The legionary armour giving him momentum that jolted Heruscomani. They grunted as they cut their way step by step. The chasing warriors caught up. This time the rear legionaries turned and fought, stepping backwards, trusting their brothers to defend their backs. The Veniconi line was buckling, and they scented it, getting the upper hand and cutting their way through. Heruscomani called his men to stop.

"We wait for Asuvad's Dumnonii," he shouted.

The Romans pounded off along the road, fending off handfuls of Veniconii intent on taking every life they could. They stripped the few dead and killed the enemy wounded. Asusvad came trotting up bringing his men. Some carried severed heads. Aulercas saw the blood smeared warriors and felt cheated he had missed the better part of the fighting. Then his conscience rebuked him. His duty was with his father.

"We bring gifts for the sons of the wolf, they jeered.

Heruscomani conferred with Asuvad. Now that they were behind defensive line, the south gate of the next fort was the obvious target.

"The signal fires have been lit," Asuvad said, "there is no time to delay, we must strike before they are strengthened with more men."

Litana's Sinistra gate swung open. A large squad of legionaries fanned outside in a defensive arc to shield the refugees from the debacle now burning to the west. A whistle brought the screening party back inside.

"Cibra has been taken, the barbarians are heading this way," panted a legionary as he laid his weapons down to accept a drink of water.

The fort's centurions crowded around listening, frowning and scowling. It was not the responsibility of an ordinary 'mule' to make such a report. Two centurions from Cibra began calling their men to number off in centuries. A mixed bag of optios and tesserarii struggled to reset order and calm in the face of men who had watched their humiliation at the hands of the barbarians. The fort's praefectus ordered the scorpion catapults to open fire on the oncoming warriors.

"Headcount?" demanded the officer of the watch.

"Centurions of Cibra, report your headcount."

It came to one hundred and eighty wounded and able.

The praefectus called the senior centurion, there was no pretence at civility. "You've left three hundred men in Cibra who are now, I assume, all dead. Look over there, you can see it burning. Tell me how Cibra can be taken at the danger time of sunrise and its cohort can be reduced to one third of its strength."

The Cibra officer sheathed his gladius before coming to attention. He did not bother to wipe the sword clean first. His honour was hurting. He had done more than any officer to get these few men across the two miles from Cibra alive.

"I did not see the attack begin," he said with a degree of obvious justification.

"You were not the duty officer?" the praefectus gave a fraction.

The angry centurion left that tiny olive branch on the ground.

"They must have manoeuvred around the ramparts and attacked both the Praetoria and the Decumana gates simultaneously. We retired through the Dextra when I saw that further defence of the fort was not possible."

"And your commanding officer?" asked the praefectus.

They were personal friends.

"I never saw him. I fear the commander is dead," replied the centurion.

He almost apologised.

"Because you left him," snapped the praefectus.

"Sir the enemy are coming on now sir," one of his own officers interrupted.

The praefectus wheeled away barking orders.

The full daylight was revealing the Dumnonii and Veniconii encircling the lesser protected walls. It was the nightmare of every praefectus along the line. The soft stomach of the south.

"Get our signal fire burning and send riders. We have a major incursion on our hands. Tell them Cibra has been taken and I require support immediately," he ordered.

His face changed as he turned about and spoke to the Cibra soldiers.

"You have a chance to avenge your comrades. Make sure you take it. You may have the west wall. Now show me what you are made of."

Heruscomani and Asuvad conferred on their losses. Heruscomani was frustrated by his failed attempt to halt the fleeing garrison. He had sprung his trap, the men had risen up in a line but the Romans had punched their way through. The leading soldier cutting his way, showing an example. He refused to admit, even to himself, that the leader held his nerve and his men. Many of Asuvad's men were still pillaging inside the fort.

Asuvad was jubilant, grinning with joy. He had been tested and he had beaten his enemy hands down. His men were bragging. There would be great songs composed about this. An entire fort put to the torch and the sword. The priest had spoken truly when he said the waters of the pool were calm. The gods supported him. It was a dizzying feeling. He had sought, asked, and they had replied. The first fort had fallen at the first heavy surge. The Romans had buckled and run. Between them, he and Heruscomani still had a sizeable force. Speed was their ally if the second fort was to be taken. But it had to be now. Daylight was here, the alarm beacons were burning. This next one would not be so easy. But, if he could engineer the taking of a second fort, he would be famous forever. His name would not die. He glanced at his Veniconi friend. Heruscomani was still upset. He clapped him on the shoulder.

"Come friend, you will have your feast of glory now. Fill your plate with their wolf bones, your ale-cup with their blood."

He turned and shouted.

"Let the Veniconi have the honour of leading this, as we had there."

Huge roars of approval rang out. Heruscomani smiled.

"Thank you, my friend. You and I will always be brothers in war. Anything I have is yours, except my wife", he laughed.

"VENICONI," he shouted.

"VENICONI!"

"VENICONI!" they answered and began running to within bowshot range of the fort on ground made flat and easy by the legions.

Great iron bolts came hurtling into them. Flights of arrows rose up from the Roman ramparts. They charged on, impelled by rage and Heruscomani's appeals to their prowess. Swarming up to the defences, they shrugged off the storm of javelins, curling in a wave along the ditch, probing at the south, west and east gates where the ditch was passable into the fort. Romans were crowding the defences. Bodies were lying at the gateway wounded by spears, others staggering back, falling and obstructing those at their backs. A monumental spear and javelin exchange was happening in the killing ground as Asuvad had feared. The ditch had men lying in it. The Romans were fighting in near silence whilst Heruscomani's warriors shrieked their battle rage.

Pressure of numbers began to tell as more and more warriors began to assault the ramparts. It became a fight of swords and daggers, shields into faces, helmets ringing with blows, broken teeth and faces punctured through to the brain. The defenders began taking casualties, laid open by the belly height of the palisade fence. The heavy iron bolts were no longer firing.

Asuvad ordered the burning timbers on the signal platform to be pulled apart. The alarm must be passing back along the line of forts, but he wanted to use the fire against the fort again as he had done before. The worry of how long he could keep the attack going before the next fort sent troops and cavalry, uppermost in his mind. Standing back to direct the assault, he sent men to the eastern gate to keep the defenders busy. He scowled. It should have been already under attack. This was not going as well as he had expected. His men were getting cocky. This time they had a real resistance on their hands. From this side there were no low walls to use as attacking platforms. They were committed to breaking down the other gates. But the Romans in their efficient way had given him a gift.

"More fire," he yelled, "get the fire. Haul those logs to the gate, get it burning."

The signal fire was burning like a Cetshamaine celebration. Huge flames were leaping skywards. The heat was ferocious. His men got as close as they could, as though trying to corner an angry bull, using their shields to protect them from the furnace. He joined in, using his spear to prise smaller logs from the sides. The primary timbers in the centre of the beacon were too difficult to handle. More men rushed in to help. With spears they managed to push the beacon over. The burning wood crashed down spreading fire and sparks all around, sending the warriors jumping back. The daylight was now their enemy.

"Hurry, my brothers, hurry," he exhorted them, "we must get the fire to the gates now before it is too late."

"I did not come to die in a Roman fire," a voice snarled.

He ignored it. Pulling out the best of the logs, they managed to get them to the south gate. He turned for a moment and looked towards the first fort. Warriors were hurrying to join the attack.

"At last," he said.

Did they not understand every man counted now? There would be time to gather spoils later. Water buckets were appearing on the gate tower in response to the fire beneath it. A game of chance started as every solder leaning over the gatehouse risked a spear or an arrow.

Heruscomani was at the western gate. He threw a severed Roman head up over the palisade.

"Say hello to your friend, you dogs, you will join him soon," he crowed.

His men had decided it was worth trying to repeat the same ruse of using the north wall. They were starting to get up there, gaining a vantage point to run along the wall and attack the corner watchtowers. Heruscomani joined them looking down into the calm order of the garrison. There was no panic. The glint of armour proved these were still legionary troops, not auxiliary. They were lined up on all four sides inside the fort. A steady stream of men feeding up to support the walls. His heart sank. They were not buckling, and his men were losing impetus. The trumpets in the fort were now cacophonous. There was something else. Whirling around he looked hard in the direction of the next fort.

He stared at the road. There were soldiers and standards on it. A cavalry unit was racing up from the south. It was too far to tell if it was from a regular legion too. He had run out of time. He turned and called to his men.

"Retreat, there are too many and more are coming. We must get back."

He jumped down and ran to find Asuvad. The Dumnonii were still hard at it at the south gate.

"Romans, more Romans are coming," he shouted to Asuvad "they'll be here soon. They will pin us against the ditch. I'm pulling my men back," he cried.

"How many?" Asuvad demanded.

Heruscomani made a rapid decision. Lives were precious. The two tribes could not do it all. And the horsemen changed the balance completely.

"There are too many of them Asuvad. We have done enough for now, pull your men back, we cannot risk being caught here. They will cut us to pieces," he said, poking his sword in the direction of the cavalry and the reinforcing infantry. Aulercas came running up with blood on his face. The fort's defences were cracking. He was sure of it. But the alarm beacons had saved them. Just a little more time and they would have stormed it. Asuvad looked at him.

"We are pulling back. We have too few men to fight any longer. As your father says, those horsemen change everything."

"Pull back," Heruscomani ordered his men, "there is always another day to fight."

Asuvad saw Aulercas' dismay.

"This is only the beginning," he promised.

Chapter 26.

The flames of Cibra burning were a sobering sight. The column halted as the cavalry raced up. The centurion strode forwards to meet the ala commander.

"Sixth legion," said a confidential voice in the ranks, "they'll fuckin' sort them out, short style. Don't take no prisoners those boys. Have heads hangin' off both sides of their saddles before you can say."

"Silence in the ranks you gutter dog," screamed an optio.

"Bloody tellin' you they will," the mule chuntered on.

"I'll flog the next man who speaks."

"Sixth legion they are," the voice repeated, happy in the knowledge that he was safe in the ranks of his mates, not alone with a whole tribe to defeat on his own.

"I won't warn you again."

"Lucius, for Mithras' light, shutup, you'll get us all flogged," hissed another.

"I always wanted to be in the cavalry, they get all the best girls."

"Lucius, I'll do you myself if you don't shut up."

After a short discussion the cavalry swept forwards to the fort then disappeared in a dip beyond. They saw them once more and then the cavalry was gone, leaving the column to pick up the bits left behind by the incursion.

The centurion ordered the trumpets to sound 'advance' and they moved off again. Along the road devastation lay at their feet. The centurion could have detoured around off the road but instead he made them march over it, through it, stepping on bodies of comrades and barbarian alike. Headless men without armour. Pools of blood. Out-stretched arms calling for help that was here too late to save them. Hands that once carried rings lying minus their jewelled fingers. The coppery stink of fresh blood and the farmyard of bowels slashed open. They marched on it and through it. It splashed up on their legs and marked them: cold and wet and vile. Faces that had been resolved and steeled for a rescue action, hardened. It went very quiet. Even Lucius stopped.

'Point made,' the centurion said to himself.

"Eyes front, steady in the ranks, keep moving, no talking," the tesserarii chanted.

Inside the burned Decumana gate dead legionaries were lying everywhere. Dead animals and dead barbarians. Nothing was alive. The smell was appalling and sickening. Burning wood and something worse; flesh. The centurion brought them to a halt. He went to the rampart and checked for himself. That made them pause. A tesserarius moved along the column, looking and checking the men's faces.

"Steady lads, steady," he crooned.

Lucius cleared his throat and spat sideways, "bastards," he voiced.

"I'll have quiet in the ranks, bastards or no bastards," called out an optio, his tone gentle as if he was speaking to a skittish horse.

"They'll be dying on our spears long before they get back to their stinking huts if I know the cavalry," he added.

The centurion returned. The barbarians were already well beyond range with the cavalry pursuing, heading back over the low ground towards the hills. The tribes had shown their hand. He put his shield down at his side.

"Sentries to the walls. Immediate report on damage to the ramparts and gates. Get all fires put out. Find and tend to any survivors," he said.

He walked towards the burning principia wondering whether the signifer had taken the cohort standard out to rally the men. The building had been ransacked but it was defying the flames that were going to reduce the grain store, the workshops and the barrack blocks to ashes. Paperwork was scattered on the stone floor. It was a small fort and the entrance led through to the holy room at the back next to the commander's office and his clerks' rooms. The aedes room was empty, the standard was missing. He sighed a mixture of frustration and grief, stepped back and went to the principia entrance

"Find the standard," he called out.

A dozen different men turned to the order. Back inside, the camp commander's room was still occupied by the camp praefectus. Or most of him. His bloody remains slumped over his desk dressed in what had been his off-duty short toga. His head and hands had been removed, most likely for trophies and for the rings and bracelets he probably wore. The desk was a puddle of his gore. The few pieces of furniture he had lay smashed in pieces. The correspondence chest was open but untouched. Whatever he had been doing had died with him. The centurion decided he could not salute a headless man, took a last look and walked out.

*

Velio and Gallus Tiomarus were working along the line with a century from a Second legion cohort. Attempting to show the Second how the Twentieth did it. The drill today was javelin work. Co-ordination and timing of the volley. Throw at the optimal distance and only on direct command of the officer, no mavericks acting alone. Standard issue was two javelins per man and Velio was hammering it home.

"Two javelins means two dead barbarians. And acting in a concerted fashion increases the chances of that result."

It should be bread and olives to trained legionaries in his opinion and so it was proving. The Second legion knew its stuff.

It was turning now into 'can we push the range five paces more? Can we push it ten paces more?'

A physical workout. He heard the beginnings of a hubbub in the distance but carried on, looking sideways along the row of legionaries. Out in front were a series of painted posts set at twenty pace intervals out to one hundred paces. Gallus was standing well to the side of the hundred pace mark out of misdirected throwing range, letting him run the drill.

"Speed of attack is what you have to think about," he bawled so they could all hear him.

"The enemy charging at you. He's not going to stop running. You know this and you all know what you have to do to stop him. A man running at you from one hundred paces will be past the 'sixty pace' marker and getting close to the 'forty paces' marker in a matter of seconds. Two javelins must go out from each man before he makes contact," he emphasised, pausing to wipe his mouth.

"Those two volleys have to count. If you don't hit your target both times and if your javelin is not twisted one of them is going to pick it up and give it back to you, and you probably won't enjoy that much."

They laughed.

"I want a volunteer," he called.

"Sir," an enthusiastic legionary stepped forward.

Gallus began moving back in closer to the 'hundred pace' line.

"You. Go out there and stand in line where the instructor is. When I shout, you run in towards the line. You lot, keep your javelins down, I don't want a casualty here. Just watch count how fast he covers the ground. Put down your javelin lad, you won't need it. When you get out there draw your sword, wait for the command and attack us as if you meant it. Got it? And stop when I tell you."

"Sir," he replied.

But he didn't get the chance. 'Stand to the Eagle' started blowing. Gallus gave him a quizzical look as he jogged back. Velio shrugged. The century came to the attention at the first notes of the call.

"Perhaps best to get them back in sir?" he said to their centurion.

The centurion took the suggestion without demur.

"Optio take them back," he ordered.

The optio had a voice like a bull,

"Century at the ready,

Form column,

Face right,

Retire to barracks.

March."

Gallus turned to Velio, "Sounds like trouble."

The centurion of the Second legion bit his upper lip with his bottom teeth.

"It's been coming for a while."

He rattled his vine stick against his greave. Velio and Gallus waited.

"Right, I want you two to report back to your unit at Bergessia. There's a waggon that'll take you. Get your kit and get moving."

They left the marker sticks in the ground, picked up their helmets and swords and fell in at the rear of the century. Inside the fort the other five centuries of the garrison were drawn up and waiting. The ramparts growing busier as the men took position.

The centurion pointed to a waggon driver, "tell him to take you back now."

Chapter 27.

Bergessia.

Velio climbed down off the waggon, waiting for Gallus to pass him their shields and javelins. They waved to the waggon driver and walked the short distance up the road to the Decumana, saluting the sentries as they went. Bergessia was already on alert but there were no signs of an attack coming.

"All clear?" Velio called up to the gate tower sentry.

"Nothing sir," shrugged the sentry, his face concerned, "false alarm, sir?"

Velio tried to quash that with a definite shake of his head.

"Well keep your eyes open. There is something happening to the west. Signal fires don't burn for no reason," he replied.

"Perhaps they've sorted it sir," the man answered, venturing a conversation.

Like most of the instructors, Velio was one of the more approachable tesserarii in the cohort and a lot more so than most of the optio and centurions. Velio could see the sentry was unsettled. Whatever needed sorting, might be coming this way.

"We'll soon see," he said.

He sat down on the grass outside their billet with Gallus. Their own centurion put in an appearance, accepting a piece of their bread, pinching a few olives, talked of the alarm and went on his way to the headquarters for an update. They carried on eating.

"You think they'll keep us here until all the forts are built Gallus?" he asked, "I mean until the whole thing's finished?"

"Carumabo's already got its auxiliary garrison, so it's happening Velio, it's happening," Gallus said, chewing on for a moment, "usually they'd hand over to the auxiliary as soon as the fort is ready and shift us back to base."

"That's what I mean, why are we still here?" he said.

"You not enjoying the scenery, Velio?" Gallus teased.

"We've just about done our bit. The masons are carving the dedications for the wall sections, so I hear. That must mean we'll be heading south soon. Don't you think?"

"Velio, have you got a girl I don't know about? Is that what this is? Worried some cavalry-boy with a bigger weapon than yours is going to have his wicked way while you are busy defending the frontier?" Gallus winked, laughing.

He shook his head in good humour, patting his gladius, pretending to misunderstand with a mock innocent look.

Gallus nodded his head, "is that the one Gaius made for you? To replace the one you left, up there? You've not let me see it yet."

He waved his hand in the direction of 'the north.' Velio drew the sword and laid it on the grass where they sat. Gallus chewed on, looking down at the new sword, inspecting it.

"Gaius is making a bloody fortune out of me," Velio muttered.

"Very nice," Gallus opined, "looks just the job for slicing up barbarians intent on causing a bit of mayhem on the Ides of each month. Good balance?" he said, knowing Velio would not have accepted anything but the best from the blacksmith.

He picked it up, twirled it with ease and laid it down on the grass again. Velio knew a true master when he saw one.

Gallus cleared his throat.

"Pity about the other one, but you did the right thing Velio. A proper soldier's sacrifice that was. Giving the blade back. You made yourself a lot of friends in the cohort when the word got round about what you did," he paused, reflecting, "it might have belonged to one of them officers up there Velio. Did you think of that?" he whispered, wary of upsetting the shades of dead comrades.

Velio blushed under his tan. Gallus did not normally talk too much about personal things. He liked to keep his world business-like. This was new ground between them.

"I didn't think too much about it Gallus. I was standing in front of the pyre before I realised it. It was a horrible place Gallus. A terrible place for it all to end, you know?" he said in a rush.

The fear he had been keeping bottled up was out before he could stop it. He half expected Gallus to say something cruel, but the senior instructor made the stiff-finger sign and murmured, "give me old age and kind women or a quick death in battle that I don't see coming."

He raised his cup of water and they toasted.

"Now, enough of this," Gallus went on, "if the barbarians don't attack today or tonight then I reckon the flap is over. You, best go and check on the men of the Fourth century, Fourth cohort, of Rome's finest before the optio does, the little tyrant. Make sure they're all at post and not skiving. Lazy bastards."

*

Epeius brought Servius food and watered wine and kept his mouth shut. Servius looked at the wine.

"Help yourself," he said.

The tribune's face said everything that needed to be said. No doubt he would be wondering when to lift a pen to update Governor Urbicus. Epeius poured himself a cup as ordered to keep on Servius' right side and sat down behind his desk.

The hours dawdled away, and he kept himself busy with the tribune's correspondence, putting only the most urgent documents in front of him. Servius sat staring at the map spread open on his table as though he could make it speak, if only he concentrated hard enough. Epeius wished with all his heart he could go fetch a sword and shield and stand up on the wall out of harm's way.

The guards at the front of the headquarters changed over and still no word came. Twenty five miles, that was all it was, the ancient greeks could run the distance. Why in Hades had a rider not come? It was not his place to vex the tribune any further. So, he sat and kept his pen moving. Towards the end of the day, Servius went out to stretch his legs and talk to the men. He sat back easing his shoulders, trying to massage the daylong tension out of them. Servius returned with a question and a fraught expression.

"Have you seen tribune Paterculus today?"

He shook his head. Servius went back outside. He did not come back for several hours until a despatch rider arrived, and he had found Glaccus.

*

"How many men sir?" said Hanno Glaccus.

"I'm told half a cohort's gone from Cibra Hanno, lost. Perhaps a century from Litana too. Hanno, I think I'm going to redeploy the line. Put the Twentieth with the Sixth in the east. Send the whole of the Second to fully engage in getting the western defences up to speed." Servius said.

"It's a pity the legate of the Second is lying in an infirmary bed. It would be a comfort to have him leading his legion. They do not know me Hanno. I must trust their discipline. They have to build the paces set for them every day without fail. I can't let the barbarians do this whenever they want. This must be the last time we get caught sitting in the latrine. Once the defences are complete it will be a different matter, but for now we must get that section finished. The Second must work faster. Flog a few if you must. And tell them I want Cibra fully repaired and rebuilt in one week. The next news I receive from them had better be the laying of their distance slabs."

Glaccus nodded and kept nodding as Servius rumbled on.

"Do you want me to act as your liaison officer with their tribunes and senior centurions, sir?" he said.

Servius stopped, scratched his forehead and gazed down while he thought it through. Glaccus was in no position to tell tribunes of the Second legion to pull their fingers out. He smiled a wry admission of defeat.

"Thank you, Hanno, let me think a bit more about it. If there is any sniff of a suggestion that I can't rely on them then I will certainly use you but forget most of what I just said. I will send an order to my opposite in the Second. I know him very well. He won't thank me for it, so I'll have to be diplomatic. There goes my legion Hanno. But the ditch and the wall must go quicker over there. It just must."

"Was there anything else, sir?" Glaccus asked, keeping a tight lip.

"Tribune Paterculus seems not to have returned with his patrol from his visit to inspect the new signal tower. He's late. Unless he has gone on to visit Carumabo he should have returned by now," Servius replied.

He looked a little weary.

"Coincidence?" Glaccus offered.

A look of real anxiety crossed Servius' face. He ceased shuffling manpower in his head. His problems just kept multiplying.

"Jupiter, Thou Best and Greatest, I hope so Hanno."

He paused, "Hanno, if they were to give me a legion, you'd come with me, wouldn't you?"

There was an uncertain tone in his voice that Hanno did not like. Servius was always direct, precise and clear in his commands. Now was not the time for him to have doubts.

"Of course I would sir," he replied.

"Thank you, Hanno carry on," Servius said and turned away, striding back to the principia taking salutes as he went.

Hanno decided it was a glimpse of the man's inner demons. He went out to the berm above the ditch to find peace away from the noise. If Paterculus and his patrol was missing it was likely part of what was beginning to look like a general uprising. A turma of cavalry was not a lot of protection if things got sticky. He had called it a coincidence but from Servius' reaction neither of them believed the chances of that were high.

But if Paterculus really was dead, it relieved him of an unpleasant burden. Servius favoured Pinneius, thought him perhaps exceptional for his exploits in finding the Ninth. In any event he had thought him worth promoting long before then, so the feats up north on the first patrol had been not much short of miraculous. The young soldier had not put a foot wrong and Servius no doubt patted himself on the back for impeccable judgement in raising an otherwise ordinary soldier.

Whereas Tribune Paterculus hated Pinneius. He was fixated with getting vengeance because of a stupid cut inflicted because of his own overbearing stupidity. Practising with combat weapons never ended well. Without fail someone got a nasty cut. Pinneius cut his arm. That was not really Pinneius' fault. Then he had allowed himself to be personally coerced into securing an assassin for Paterculus to kill Pinneius. He blamed himself for that mistake. He really should have stood up to the tribune at that point. What had he been thinking? But legion politics in barracks was never easy and it was less so on this frontier.

To put a red feathered crest on it all there was the oaf Carruso; a man who was too stupid to see the elephant trap full of spikes waiting in front of him. Why in the sober light of day had Titus Rebilis ever recommended him? And now Titus was dead, Tribune Paterculus was late returning from a simple mission and the tribes had risen in the west.

'Holy Mothers of the Parade Ground,' let it be true he is dead. Protect me from an order I was forced to obey. Velio Pinneius is a better man, a better soldier than the tribune. Holy Mothers, protect the honest soldiers who pray to you.*'*

And Brutus Carruso? What to do about him if the young tribune was dead? Just pay him off to keep his silence?

'Ah, go slow Hanno. Find out what has happened to Tribune Paterculus. Servius is reordering the whole line. So, cohorts and vexillations are going to be shuffled. The main danger is in the west. Paterculus is missing in the east.'

He began to breathe a little more as the germ of a solution grew. Servius would help him out of this mire without realising.

'All I have to do is let the re-ordering happen,' he told himself.

The Sixth and Twentieth legions were vexillations, the Second had most of its full strength, five thousand men plus supporting auxiliary. If Servius was going to send the whole of the Second to complete the western end of the line and reposition the Sixth and Twentieth to the east and centre, he might be able to get Pinneius in a place where Carruso might try his luck. Pinneius would send him to his ancestors without much fanfare and he would be liberated from bad promises and the evil intentions of jumped up tribunes.

He surveyed the landscape in front of the ditch. A dead tribune meant someone was going to get a promotion. And it did not always have to be sanctioned by the emperor. The governor might do it. Though if Tribune Paterculus still lived, the game was still to be played out. Pinneius would have to take his chances, but a man who has given his own sword as a sacrifice to the memories of a long dead legion, a man who in his own small way conferred honour on their graves, was not to be fried on the skillet of a tribune's ego. He cursed his own weakness, he had made a bad mistake. He should have stood up to the tribune.

'Fledgling warrior, huh.'

Paterculus, if he still lived, could be yearning for the boat to Gaul and the horse that would take him down the road from there to Rome. He straightened his lorica, took off his helmet to comb his fingers through the horsehair plume, patted the pommel of his gladius and walked back through the gate, stopping to inspect the sentries, told the duty optio to get a grip of his men, they were slovenly beyond redemption, were they going to fight the barbarians looking little better than savages themselves? And went on his way to the century barracks to put them on their toes as well. Thirty minutes later a sweaty messenger from Carumabo stood in front of him. It was a bit more useful than the first signal he had received. This time the man could stand in front of him and report.

Expecting trouble from Votadini.

Have retired to fort.

Please support.

"Mmmnn,' he thought,' a job for the boys of the Twentieth legion I think.'

He raised his fist in thanks. The Holy Mothers had heard and answered his prayer. He went striding to his own room in the barracks to make a small offering on his private altar.

*

Eilaver gazed at Carumabo signal tower sitting abandoned and empty and decided to leave it untouched in case burning it betrayed their location. She led her warriors down a long slope to the great river. Its islands lay close in to the shore, the air smelled clean and fresh, the distant hills on the far side of the estuary offered green and safe refuges. But she knew it was a lie. The land over there was within easy reach of the Romans though they had stepped back from it for now.

The closer they drew to Carumabo itself the cooler her men were becoming about attacking it. The Romans had made one of their roads from the fort link up with other routes heading south. Staying on it seemed an easy way to give their position away. She let Indutus scout through the woods bringing them unobserved to the edge of the fort's open ground. All the trees had been cleared down to knee height for the archers to fire their maximum range. It was a difficult zone they would have to cross.

Indutus halted, surveying what lay before him with an expression of concern. She knew he would lead a charge if she ordered him to. His pride would not let him refuse her order. He moved along the edge of the covered ground viewing the sides of the small fort as best he could.

It was Ferrdigon who had been so keen to offer the camp commander the gift of a male wolf. A simple ruse to find out what troops would garrison the fort once the regular legionaries departed. At the time, she had smirked at the open-handed deception; a gift of a wolf, some easy conversation, and vital information gained in return.

Tungrians, a tribal levy from Germania, long time servants to 'the wolf.' They were not as well armoured as regular Roman troops, but they would fight with a ferocity to match her men.

Indutus was fixated by the turf walls of the fort and the sentries patrolling the palisade fencing. Now that she could see it for herself it was bigger than she had thought. Ferrdigon had been dismissive of it as just another Roman fortress but, clearly, taking it by force would not be easy.

"We could take this, but we do not have enough men here, Eilaver. To attack today, as we are, would be to join the fathers who went before us," Indutus growled.

"Then I will get more men," she said.

"From where?" he asked with a bluntness that surprised her.

This was not the way he spoke to her. His eyes bored back at her, expecting an answer. Out here, beyond the limits of her hall and the fortress, she realised his knowledge of war was superior to hers.

His words were a test, and her warriors were listening to him so she explained.

"I must get the king out of his hall in Dunpeledur. He speaks for avenging the priest. The clear white moon he wants is coming. In a few days it will be here. He cannot keep saying the priests will not permit it. Now we can gift him the opportunity," she said.

Some nodded at her. Others kept their expressions sober.

"Then we must wait until the moon pleases the king's priests and he brings his men to your side," Indutus came back at her, "but until then, what do we do? We cannot hold the Romans at bay on the hill if they come. And afterwards, what then?"

She saw with a jolt that killing the Roman patrol was not a single act. Nor was it the spark to burn this fort to the ground the way she had hoped.

"If we rise, the Veniconi and the Dumnoni will rise, the Selgovae too. It can happen here. It can begin here. But first I need the king to support us," she replied, keeping her voice calm.

Ferrdigon had never brought the men so far down this path before. She understood their nervousness.

"So, we are not going to attack today?" he pushed.

"No. We need to find the weak spots here and then we go back. I know it's hard, but we will go back to the hill. Knowing where the weak spots are will make our arguments to the king stronger. I was going to burn their towers. Now I think I will leave them. We need to hide the bodies on the hill. The Romans will come looking for their men and the tribune."

The warriors nodded as if to say, *'yes remember the bodies on the hill.'*

*

Servius saluted the men in person with the trumpets playing 'Farewell Brother.' Glaccus was on horseback with the vexillation and cohort standards at his back and his kit in the company waggon. Velio and Gallus marched along in full kit. Behind them Brutus Carruso tramped along.

The weather looked set fair, the road was dry. Perfect marching weather. It was like a holiday from the boredom. Glaccus took the road south with nearly two full cohorts of the Twentieth legion at his back, the Fourth and the Fifth. Servius insisted the Sixth must keep digging. There was no point in taking too many. It would just slow progress on the wall and if he was going to get his legion that would not do.

Glaccus was glad to be soldiering again, away from the same old view over the flats, wondering if he would ever get another chance to go into battle. This wall could be the end of all of it, up here at least. The loss of Cibra could be viewed as a reflection of the rate of constructing the fortifications. If the Second had kept up to schedule the Veniconii and Dumnonii would not have had the nerve to launch such an attack. Thus, he would argue, the Second had, more or less, brought it on themselves. No, the wall did not need Hanno Drusus Glaccus Ticinus for much longer.

Down south, the Brigantes could always be relied on to run amok. Other than that, Britannia was of no interest if the tribes were penned up. Let the auxiliary sit around and babysit them. Perhaps Germania beckoned? Perhaps he needed to look after his career a bit more instead of tagging along on Servius' cloak-tail? He could request a transfer to a different legion on that frontier, maybe? But then Servius would be disappointed and a rise up the centurial ranks would not be so certain. Get another promotion under Servius and then put in for a move? It was something to think about.

He turned his attention to the new matter in hand. Tribune Paterculus was now three days overdue. Plus, no further riders had come from Carumabo so, he had to presume, the Tungrian praefectus had recovered his courage and did not require rescuing any longer. A message sent in haste was often a message regretted. Guarding a harbour was about all these auxiliaries were good for, apart from when they were doing their duty by dying to preserve the legionary ranks.

Three days was an uncomfortable time for a patrol on a simple errand to be absent with a high ranker like the tribune leading it.

He intended to cover the distance with the two cohorts today. So how was it that mounted troop could not send a report back thirty miles to update Paterculus' whereabouts? The cavalry should have been suggesting he send despatch riders to Servius. Was he just being bloody minded and ignoring the advice? It would be poor soldiering if that was what this was all about. Had he taken the troop on an unplanned training exercise? Even so, Servius would tear shreds off him for that. It was only thirty short miles at most.

He pushed the column hard. The cavalry escort forging ahead trying to scout ground they already knew well. Better to be safe though. He sent a rider to alert Carumabo he was operating in the area.

The Hill of the Resting Lion was the obvious place to search. And if the tribune was not there? He pursed his mouth. Then it might be time to take this

Votadini woman aside and explain a few truths to her. He scanned the faces of passing Votadini as they travelled along the road, driving animals, carts; smoke rising in the soft landscape from small farms and villages. It all felt far too normal. It bothered him more than anything had bothered him since the wall began rising out the ground. He halted the column twice for short rests. He had no personal knowledge of what the fortifications were like on the hill. He had never been there. But the intelligence reports said it was a strange place with two deep valleys, sheer cliffs and only a single open side to access.

The column arrived at the low slopes late in the day. He cantered around on his horse gauging how much time the remaining light would give him. He gathered in the two cohort commanders and pointed this fact out to them.

"Camp tonight, rise at first light, catch them early?" he offered the thought before making it a decision-order.

"That will give them time to run," the Fourth's commander observed with a neutral tone.

Glaccus liked him. Neither of them was bothered by the thought of natives fleeing out of their way. The commander of the Fifth was looking at the strange hill.

"Damn funny place if you ask me," he said, "think they'll fight?"

"They're Votadinii, what will they do? Throw pots, weave baskets?"

"Let's find water and make camp," said Glaccus, "if they run overnight then I have my answer and Tribune Paterculus may no longer walk among us."

"Dis-Pater," swore the Fourth's commander.

The next morning he assigned troops to guard the exit points, knowing full well this was flag waving at its best. There would not be a soul up there who feared them or felt they had anything to hide.

'So be it,' he thought.

With the Fifth cohort deployed he marched all four hundred and eighty seven men of the Fourth up onto the hill.

Velio grinned at Gallus, "let the games begin," he chirped.

Gallus gave him a father's kind of look in return. Then a voice began chanting a filthy ditty about the ladies of Herculaneum. Even the centurions took it up. The chanting brought the Votadinii out of their fortress to watch as the cohort drew closer and closer until it halted beside the pool. They stood outside their gates, waiting. Hanno Glaccus was delighted. It was just the sort of reaction he wanted. He got off his horse. There was a woman at their forefront whom he guessed was Ferrdigon's widow, Eilaver, surrounded by a strong retinue of personal warriors. There were a few spears visible, no shields, no helmets, no particular signs of defiance and no sign of the tribune or his men. He handed the reins to a legionary and straightened his helmet. The commander of the Fourth came and stood by his side.

"Bring the standards forward," he said.

The commander gestured to the three signifers to advance.

*

"What should we do?" Indutus urged.

"We go down, we keep them away from the village, it's the best chance to make them leave," she replied, "we stay calm, no provoking them. Do you hear? Only I will speak. Indutus, bring my spear."

"My lady," answered her champion.

She led them down the slope, taking care to walk with dignity befitting her status. As the ground levelled, by the pool, she kept her arms folded judging where to stop approaching and force him to move to her.

Glaccus took a few steps and halted as well. His standard bearers and the cohort commander came with him. Indutus responded, taking position on her right. He grounded the end of her spear into the ground and held it just below the spearhead.

"Greetings. I am Eilaver of the Votadini. What brings you to my hill centurion with so many soldiers? Have I done something wrong? Have you come to take more of my young men for your armies over in Gaul? I hoped the time for that passed with Ferrdigon."

He shook his head.

"Greetings from Emperor Antoninus Pius and the people of Rome," he announced.

He decided to get to the point.

"I cannot say if you have done anything wrong. Only you know if that is true."

"Then I say we have done nothing wrong. Please take your men away. You make my people afraid," she replied.

He almost laughed, he had never seen a less afraid group of Votadinii men in these parts, but they did look troubled.

"I am looking for one of our tribunes, a high-ranking officer, a young officer. He came to visit you to see the new beacon working," he carried on.

Eilaver began shaking her head, her arms tighter about her.

"He left here four days ago. His beacon worked. Your fort on the river lit its fire. He was happy and he left."

"He stayed with you, a little?" he probed.

She shook her head again.

"I had him and his men fed. He decided not to stay. It was getting dark. The marshes down there, you understand, are dangerous and deep," she said pointing to the low grounds below.

"Ah, I see. He left in darkness rather than stay in your halls until the next day. He risked the marshes. Did he get lost?" he said, playing advocate.

"How can I know? He left. He could have stayed. You say he is lost. Perhaps he rode home, Roman," she crowed a little jibe.

Not a full insult, just a little prod.

"We have been in this land for nearly a hundred years Eilaver. Where do you think our 'Home' is?" he parried, and her expression darkened.

"It's not here," she answered.

"I did not say he was lost, only that I am looking for him," he said again, trying not to get irritated with her.

"You think he is lost. Well, if he is, it was not because of me or my people. I have done nothing wrong," she repeated.

He could see her warriors spreading out in a protective arc. They were getting tense. Apart from those few spears and swords they were only armed with daggers on their hips. Eilaver touched a slender leather sheath hanging below her throat. He paused to let her sweat a little. Silence could work wonders when applied at the apposite time. Did she not understand he could have them slaughtered in minutes?

"So, he is not here, but he was here, he left four days ago. You do not mind if I send a few of my men up to check?" he summed up.

She turned and gestured to the hill fort with complete insouciance.

"When you have finished, you will eat with me? We are not enemies, Roman."

"Please, I am Centurion Hanno Glaccus."

He touched his chest in goodwill.

"But I cannot feed all your men. You have too many," she complained.

He inclined his head.

"Centurion, take a squad up there and look for signs of the tribune and the patrol."

The centurion turned and called out, "first sixteen with me."

Velio glanced at Gallus. Gallus raised his eyebrow. More work to do. Brutus Carruso looked at the back of Velio's head as they followed the centurion past the Votadini and up the steep path to the gates of the little citadel. As they climbed the short slope, Velio could feel his breathing quickening. It was steeper than it looked. More of the Votadini came out, lining the path as it reached the gates. They did not quite block it but managed to make clear their feelings about the inspection. Velio could feel sweat easing out of his face and forehead.

"Spread out, check everywhere. Go gently."

The centurion stood at the gate and sent them in.

The smell of burnt wood and flesh was everywhere. Velio sniffed it. He had not noticed it until he got through the gate.

'The wind must be in a good direction', he thought.

Brutus Carruso got sent to the top end of the compound with three other legionaries. The centurion directed the other mules' search. Velio walked over to the burned out remains of a largish hall. The smell must be horseflesh. Awful. There was not much of the barn left. Just a couple of upright poles. The heaped ashes in the centre were white. And cold. And they had been well stirred up, which caught his eye, but there were no horse bones, and no horse skulls so they must have pulled those out and stirred up the burnt remains of the timbers and turfs. Horses or cattle; goats even. They were roasted now, that was for sure. He put his hand on his gladius and drew it. Behind him Gallus did the same.

'One on the alert; all on the alert.'

He kicked the ashes, prodded a few remaining timbers, the outline of what were either horse stalls or animal pens in the circle of what had been the barn. A few bits of iron harness were lying in the debris.

"No bones Gallus," he said.

Gallus gave a brief nod.

"Perhaps they ate the evidence," he said, "perhaps they don't like bread."

How could Gallus joke at a time like this?

"Would you eat your own horse if you had just seen it burned? What man would eat his horse if this was an accident? And what started this? They would have had the horses out before it was too late, surely?" he asked.

"Night-time fire, everyone asleep, a spark from a torch, who knows Velio?"

"Why the stink if they got the animals safely away?"

Gallus licked his lips, bumping the edge of his shield against one of the few remaining timbers. It fell over at the touch.

"Good question Velio," he replied.

Over at the far side of the compound a ruckus broke out, the centurion looked over at Gallus to go and sort it out. He went striding up. Carruso had a Votadini by the throat up against the wall of his own house, his gladius was drawn, and his wrist cocked ready to wield it. The shield was on the ground. Gallus picked it up and rested it against his legs.

"Legionary Carruso, what passes here?" he ordered.

Carruso spoke through a tight expression, "the little Britunculi here has got something he wants to show you, sir."

Gallus knew enough of Carruso to back him to the hilt.

"Show me," he ordered.

The man wriggled under Carruso's bear-claw grip. He was late teens, early twenties perhaps, a fine youthful moustache adorned an intelligent looking face.

He was not very tall and Carruso had him at his mercy. The youth had one hand on Carruso's wrist trying to lessen the vice on his throat. The other hand was hidden behind his back. Carruso shook him like a recalcitrant pup. The youth's head wobbled. His eyes glaring at Carruso without fear. Gallus considered that an unwise tempt to a legionary.

"Show him you little runt," Carruso shouted in the Votadini's face.

Like an animal testing the wind for predators, the lad's hand appeared from behind his back.

"Show him," Carruso repeated, his voice almost a kind persuasion this time.

The hand opened. The richly ornate, personal pugio dagger of an imperial tribune rested in his palm.

'*Shit,*' thought Gallus.

"Bring him," he ordered, "Centurion," he called out across the compound.

Heads turned and with a speed that Velio found hard to credit, the compound turned into a sea of armed Votadini. He was still raking around the ruins of the stable when Gallus called out. The fort's gate swung shut. He, Gallus, the centurion, Brutus Carruso and thirteen others were cut off and out of sight of Centurion Glaccus and the rest of the Fourth down at the pond.

Three Votadini began closing in between him and Gallus. They came together stalking him back towards the ashes and rubble of the stable-barn. He felt slippery ashes through his boots and stopped retreating. He was not going to fight on slippery ground if he could avoid it and he raised his shield taking the guard stance, flexing the gladius in a circular swirl as he worked out which one would come at him first. Their eyes flicked between his and his sword. None of them had a spear. That was good. Nothing long range. All close in and bloody. Everything he practised.

Two had found iron rimmed shields that were narrower and longer than his legionary issue. They must have had them hidden and he had sleepwalked past them. The shield-less one was snarling in Votadini but was not coming on. He kept his sword swirling letting them think about the sharp point he wafted like a toy. The words meant nothing to him. Just snarls of men working themselves up into a lather. He stepped forwards forcing them to act. His gladius a steely silver blur cutting sounds in the air. He saw legionary casualties mounting in the compound. The Votadini must be three or four times their number and they were working together. The centurion was fighting to get the gates re-opened. Gallus was nowhere to be seen. Carruso was pulling his gladius out of a youth's belly. The rest were in small knots trying to cover each other's back. All this and his three opponents had not summonsed up courage to attack. So, he did.

The warrior on his right blocked his sword and tried to sweep his legs under the rim of his shield. He blocked that and pushed, slashing beyond the man's neck and pulling the blade back in the standard slicing move below the chin. It caught him out and blood spouted from the artery in his neck, the shield arm fell away and he followed up with a fast, short poke, three inches into the belly. The Votadini collapsed. The second shield warrior caught a blow to the metal lorica straps on Velio's shoulder and the blade slid down like a grater, cutting his elbow. He butted his shield rim into the face, bursting the nose. He couldn't feel any pain, but his sword arm seemed to drain strength like wine leaking onto the floor. He went in with the hammer-blow sequence he spent most of his time teaching to others, the man retreated. Velio felt his arm weakening, jabbed at the man's throat and caught a lucky hit. Two down.

The third grabbed the falling man's shield and butted it into Velio. He tripped and fell backwards, sending a cloud of choking ashes up into his face, his shield arm flung aside, sword arm unable to cover his belly. The Votadini stepped in bending over to spike Velio with his sword. He dragged his shield across to dislodge the weapon from the Votadini's grip. His assailant's face froze. All his movement halted. A gladius blade protruded out of his middle. Blood dribbled from his mouth. He looked down at Velio with a stunned, confused expression. His mouth worked like a trout, a hand jerked at his collar and the gladius point was worked around before he was flung aside.

Brutus Carruso towered over Velio in wet and bloody armour, the glint of battle in his eyes. He breathed out a deep breath of relief and was about to thank him when Carruso pinned his sword arm into the ashes with his boot.

"Not quite, tesserarius sir. The tribune ordered this. And we must all obey our orders, shouldn't we sir?" Carruso snarled.

It was the same look he had given when Velio ripped his defence apart in front of his comrades.

Carruso knelt over him, putting his gladius flat on the ground, out of sight, with the point touching just below the bottom limit of his armour, ready to slip it sideways through his lower stomach; it would be an unsurvivable wound. No flashy downward stroke to betray murder. He looked up at the leaden footed legionary who had asked him for sword lessons. The one whom he had told was a little on the slow side but otherwise competent. Carruso had his other hand on Velio's shield holding him down on that side too. He smiled up at him. Carruso frowned. The tesserarius was not supposed to smile when he died. It was an insult to Tribune Paterculus. His sword tip touched the skin. He really wanted to twist it a bit, but a quick push would be much safer. It would be all over, those bastard Votadini would have killed another good man. He felt a coldness on his neck, just under the neck-guard of his helmet. Only one thing in the army had that touch.

"Farewell Brutus Carruso," Velio murmured.

Gallus thrust once and hard through the legionary's neck. Carruso rolled sideways off Velio, as dead as Marcus Hirtius.

There was a huge roar. They both looked. The gates were opening in a wide arc as reinforcements poured through. The Votadini retreated to the upper part of the compound. He noticed the lack of women and children amongst them. He should have spotted it before. Apart from the woman Eilaver, the only Votadini were men of fighting age. The trap had had been short and bloody. There were a lot of dead or wounded legionaries.

"I never trusted him Velio," Gallus said, bending over and pulling his pugio out of Carruso, "we won't say anything about this to the centurion. We'll chalk it up to the fight."

Velio sat up and looked for the first time at the wound on his forearm.

"Needs stitching that does, Velio, but a cloth'll have to do for now," Gallus frowned, "bind it up tight."

He pulled Velio up out of the ashes.

"What set all that off Gallus?" he asked.

"Your friend Carruso here was going his job for once. Found one of them with the tribune's dagger. It all just broke out when they knew the game was up."

"Doing his job? Then why this?"

Velio took the crude piece of cloth Gallus was offering him and wrapped it around his arm, tying it off with one hand and his teeth.

"Here, let me tie that," Gallus said fixing the knot, "I told you before, Carruso didn't like you, didn't I?"

"But he killed the Votadini," he protested.

"And then he was going to kill you. The Votadini would have taken the blame. Who would have been any the wiser?" Gallus said.

"But why?"

"Ssshh, trouble."

Their optio came striding over, "are you two hurt? What happened to him?" the optio's focus, quick and precise.

Carruso was in the ashes weeping blood into the churned earth.

"That Votadini bastard got him sir. The tesserarius chopped him, them two as well," Gallus lied straight faced.

"Can you fight with that arm Pinneius?"

"It's just a cut sir," he grinned.

"It'll need seen to sir," Gallus corrected.

The optio looked around, "well done lads. They wanted a fight, they're going to pay for it."

Chapter 28.

Hill of the Resting Lion.

Glaccus stood very still as he watched the bodies of his men being brought out of the gates. The wounded managed to salute him as he sent them down to the pool to rejoin the cohort and he returned every one of them. The commander of the Fourth put his hand on Glaccus arm.

"Now is not the right time to take revenge Glaccus. We came for Tribune Paterculus."

He nodded back, "indeed we did. First, Cibra fort and now this. Have we been sleeping my friend?"

He shook his head in disbelief.

"This was madness, she must have known she could not stand up to a cohort. It's insane, completely insane. These people know no reason."

He flicked a glance toward Eilaver being dragged up the hill.

"Tie her up and check the signal tower," he ordered.

"There's no women or children sir," Velio's centurion advised him.

"Give me the dagger," he demanded.

The centurion handed over the weapon that had unleashed the bloodshed. He looked at it for a moment and felt a mixture of emotions surging through him. It looked like Tribune Paterculus' dagger. Which meant he was most probably dead. And if he was dead so were the cavalry troop escort.

"Horses," he said, "I want the horses found and the women and children."

"What about them sir?" the centurion jerked his thumb towards the Votadini warriors.

Glaccus looked at the faces of the warriors. Slaves or corpses? What should it be? The Fourth's commander was shaking his head at him.

'Mercy for now.'

"Tell them we are going to take all their women and children as slaves."

He paused and watched Eilaver's expression for the least sign of change, weakening, tears, or any attempt to plead with him. She stared back at him with uncompromising ferocity. Her warriors shouted to her. His men edged closer, pushing them further and further back against the natural slope of the fortress.

"Tell me what happened to the tribune," he said keeping his voice steady, holding back his anger.

She smiled a curling lip like a female wolf and stood defiant.

"Do they know what's going to happen to their women and children?" he checked.

"They do now sir."

Death would be an easy way out for them he decided. So, let them spend the rest of their miserable lives working for the greater glory of Rome; in a mine or somewhere where there would be ample time to repent.

"Very well. Take them prisoner, execute any who resist."

He turned through three hundred and sixty degrees. Pointing around him he said loudly, "and I want all this torn down, burned, erased for ever. I want no sign left that the Votadini ever lived here or dared to raise spears against the men of the Boar legion."

Chapter 29.

Velunia fort of the wall.

Servius came to the ramparts as soon as heard the first trumpet signal incoming soldiers,

"The Twentieth vexillation, sir," reported the duty optio.

"They have not wasted any time, have they," he replied.

The optio chuckled.

They stood waiting together, commander and junior officer as Glaccus' column drew ever nearer.

"They have hostages, I'd say, sir," said the optio.

"It looks that way. Ask the centurion to join me when he has had a chance to wash up," replied Servius.

He sat in his quarters late into the night. Glaccus long since departed for his bed. His story of Ferrdigon's widow troubled him. The cavalry was still out searching for the women and children, hoping to recover thirty horses into the bargain. The woman must have set a trap for Paterculus and his men, and he had walked straight into it, or he had done something stupid and provoked her. Unbelievable. Ferrdigon would have been hard pressed to provoke a dormouse, but in the short time since he had died, she had lit a fire under her people. Well, she was under lock and key tonight. The Falernian wine jug he had shared with Hanno Glaccus was still heavy.

The guards swapped over outside with muffled exchanges. Their voices were low. He filled his favourite drinking cup and for the first time in his command worried about what he was going to say to Quintus Urbicus.

"I've lost Cornelius Vatinus Paterculus. I think the Votadini have taken his head but as yet I have no proof? And Glaccus has taken the nearest Votadini chief and her warriors as slaves."

Things would have to be tidied up a great deal more before he could report anything.

The battered helmet on the table kept staring back at him and he wondered, not for the first time, why he was still keeping it. It radiated no comfort. And at this precise time of the night the reason that took the Ninth so far north from its base was as unknown as the fate of Paterculus. He allowed himself to speculate. The solitary undisputable fact was their base, Eburacum lay in the territory of those unrepentant savages, the Brigantes. Beyond that the question descended into difficulty. A campaign of retribution on them should have had no need to reach so far north as where he now sat. Unless, unless they had been lured.

Lured by whom? The Novantae or Selgovae were the next warlike tribes close enough to possibly be implicated. But that would have pulled the Ninth further and further away from their supply lines? A legion on the march needed feeding. The wall of Hadrian was still an emperor's dream destined for the future at the time the Ninth marched. There would have been no major forts close enough to support them once they left Brigantes territory. If they had allowed that to happen then a coalescing of hostile tribes around them might have prevented a march south again. That was possible.

So, was it pitched battle that did for them? He pinched the bridge of his nose and tried to think like a commander whose line of retreat was severed and whose opponent either refused to stand and fight, or perhaps kept nipping at his units until he was committed to the wholesale destruction of his enemy, come what may, whatever the price

But Pinneius and Titus Rebilis had found pieces of the Ninth even further away to the north. Was the legion vexillated into sub-units in the field to take separate actions? Had the enemy been clever enough to engineer the division of the legion into chasing different targets? It had to be that. And then they had picked off the smaller commands? A miliaria of one thousand men was a different beast from a whole legion, even a weak one. A thousand men is a big command. A thousand trained legionaries could look most enemies in the eyes and not worry about casualties. But splintered off from the legion, the confidence men absorbed from their comrades lessened. Only one vexillation could have the legate as their commander. He would have kept the talismanic eagle standard with his command and the rest would have felt naked without it.

The spread wings of the eagle were not simply a sculpture; he appreciated the power and the protection, they conveyed Rome.

Had the legate lost control on the bleak endless wildernesses of the northern moors? Was that it? A sad end of a legion mistakenly divided into chasing shadows, out-thought and out-manoeuvred? No great battle to mark the end but a steady winnowing of men and morale too far from support? Until the commands were too weak to resist and collapsed? Like a latter-day expedition of Varus but with no dark German forest playing the part?

Was it Titus or Paterculus who had suggested to him, there might have been men taken as slaves living within touching distance of rescue if only the other legions had known? He drank at the thought of that unholy shade. And in the end, when the game was up, in this corrie he had not seen, did the legate turn to his officers once last time to give his one and only, "sorry, men" before they died?

Nothing had ever been found in Brigantes held land, or the area south of the Clota-Bodotria line. He was at a loss to make sense of it. He picked up the helmet with one hand and sipped again, contemplating.

"If only you could speak truth to me," he said.

Titus Rebilis was dead but not before he had cremated what he could gather of the legion's officer corps. Pinneius had stated Titus said a prayer of some sorts over them and made a promise for further prayers. But further prayers over a helmet were not really the same thing as prayers for the dead. There were no human remains to pray over. There were no shades of the dead lurking in the fort tonight, aghast their bones had never been honoured. Titus' few words had laid them all to rest. And Pinneius had sacrificed his gladius to appease their soldiers' spirits. A prayer of sorts and sacrifice. There was only one thing more that needed doing.

"May the earth lie gently on you, brothers," he muttered, "the men you left behind lived on. Your legion never really died with you, they took it with them wherever they served."

He shivered, checking the shadowed corners of the room. Titus Rebilis and Cornelius Paterculus were both in their own way, victims of the Ninth legion. Were they sitting now, two comrades in the Elysian Fields, blaming him for their fates? He could not have saved Rebilis from his soldier's death, but he might have taken a kinder view of the zealous young tribune. He swallowed. The room was empty and through the new glass windows the night was evil and dark.

He picked up the helmet and filled a small flask with the good Falernian. With his cloak covering the evidence he went outside past the sentries who snapped to attention as he passed. He raised his hand in acknowledgement and wrapped the cloak around himself.

Walking around the side of the building out of their sight he dropped the helmet and the wine flask in the headquarters refuse pit, carrying on and arriving back at his own door where the surprised sentries came back to the attention again. Back inside he sat at his table and drank more wine. He bit his lip. The duty clerks and household servants would be up early in the morning. By this time tomorrow the helmet would be forever buried under fresh rubbish. Titus Rebilis had not lived to file a report of the patrol or his actions. Ergo, the helmet never existed; his actions had never occurred, and what the auxiliaries thought of it was of no consequence.

After a few moments he picked up a pen and began the usual greetings to Governor Urbicus. The problem of the Ninth was effectively resolved. What, if anything, Urbicus chose to tell the emperor was up to him. As for Paterculus, perhaps he should send young Pinneius to do the impossible again? He swilled the Falernian around in his cup while he thought about it. If Pinneius found Paterculus' body he would put him straight up to centurion. He could be Rebilis' replacement. The optios would be vociferous but there was not much they could do about it.

"Centurion Velio Pinneius." He smiled. It had a ring to it.

The End.

Historical note.

Construction of the Antonine Wall began between AD140-142 approximately.

The Antonine defences may have been temporarily abandoned for a period during the AD150s and it is unclear whether this is because it was over-run, always a tempting thought for a writer - or whether because its manpower was required elsewhere in the province; a consequence of shuffling troops around as necessary.

In terms of the assault that forms the climax of the story I posit that it is not unreasonable to assume its building generated a fair degree of negative reaction from the tribes, even during the period of construction. In fact it seems quite unlikely that the hostile tribes to the north of the Forth/Clyde line sat back and did nothing to hinder or prevent its construction.

What is known is that the earlier 'turf and timber' phase was consolidated at some point by a phase where the forts were rebuilt in stone even although the rampart remained turf.

Was this a sign of later re-occupation after a period of abandonment?

It was finally abandoned around AD 162 (probably on the order of Emperor Marcus Aurelius) when the legions effectively retrenched to Hadrian's Wall, so it had a short life span. Estimates of the time required to build it vary from three years to twelve.

The Votadini tribe are recorded as peaceful a tribe to the Romans, co-operating with the Roman army of occupation. A bit of a brief generalisation for a tribe that covered a significant tract of territory that may have covered the Forth down to the Tyne

This does not prevent the possibility of renegade elements arising. Equally what "peaceful/co-operative" in the ancient world translates to in modern terms might be simply "not overtly hostile." Nor does it mean they were always so. They were simply not classed as insurgents like the Brigantes. Did they have a hill fort on Arthur's Seat hill? The most recent evidence emerging suggests they most probably did and its construction may have been more robust than an earth-work and palisade.

The names used for some of the forts come from Cosmographia of the Ravenna Geographer, circa 7th century, cited in George Macdonald's 1911 work "The Roman wall in Scotland." In it he states this is the only source of actual names used that has come down to us. A pity, it would have been interesting to know more. Similarly, the name used for the ruins of the great legionary fort on the banks of the river Tay in Perthshire, Inchtuthil -'Pinnata Castra' -is not verifiable. So, the attachment (and spellings) of these names to forts is entirely mine.

Carumabo fort sits at the mouth of the Almond, where it joins the Firth of Forth. The modern, heavily silted, Almond can bear only a little resemblance to what it once looked like two thousand years ago. Given the prevailing westerly winds and the limitations of Roman sailing ships, I think it most likely to have been the site of a small supply port.

As for the fate of the Ninth legion, historians are split into those who think they died in Britannia and those who are convinced they were withdrawn at some time after AD108 to fight in the eastern front of the empire and later destroyed. That might be true, but I have always wondered if the legion was withdrawn from Britannia and destroyed years later, out of sight and knowledge of the British tribes and its Roman garrison, why do we have such a strong cultural tradition they died here? The fact is no one knows what happened to them.

You can contact the author by email at. info@lochardfiction.co.uk

The further adventures of Velio Pineius and his comrades feature in Sword of The Boar, Centurion of The Boar, and Wine of The Bioar
Available on Amazon.

Printed in Great Britain
by Amazon